THE
LIGHTKEEPERS

THE
LIGHTKEEPERS

a novel

ABBY GENI

COUNTERPOINT
BERKELEY

Library of Congress Cataloging-in-Publication Data Is Available

Cover design by Elena Giavaldi
Interior design by Megan Jones Design

ISBN 978-1-64009-000-2

COUNTERPOINT
2560 Ninth Street, Suite 318
Berkeley, CA 94710
www.counterpointpress.com

Printed in the United States of America
Distributed by Publishers Group West

10 9 8 7 6 5 4 3 2 1

For Scott

PROLOGUE

THE BIRDS ARE making their battle cry. Miranda can see a group of gulls wheeling in her direction. White feathers. Glinting beaks. Mad eyes. She has enough experience with their capacity for violence to recognize their intent. They are moving into attack formation, circling her like bomber jets homing in on a target.

Miranda is on her way to meet the ferry. She picks up the pace, striding up the hill, her backpack swinging on her shoulders. The boat is late, which is no surprise. The ferry is always late. It is one of the few constants of the islands.

The lap of waves fills the air. The archipelago is shrouded in mist today. In the summer months, the fog is often present. There are no balmy, golden afternoons here, no sunbathing. The horizon is obscured, the sun a damp pinwheel. Miranda slips and skids on a crumbling patch of stone. Despite her eagerness to be gone, she must step carefully, consciously. Her progress is impeded by nests and baby chicks. The gulls have covered the ground like snowfall, making use of every inch of grass and granite. In their midst, Miranda is incongruous, a lone pine tree in a field of white.

The birds are not a silent presence. Their wings rustle. The chicks squawk to be fed. The parents shriek back indignantly.

Every now and then, there will be an explosion, a dispute over territory—feathers flapping, a spatter of blood. Miranda herself is not immune to their possessive, fanatical angst. A few gulls have been tracking her progress since she left the safety of the house. Any minute now, they will strike. Their wings are splayed, eyes glittering. Closer and closer.

But Miranda has come prepared. She is wearing thick leather gloves, exposing less flesh for the gulls to bite. Around each ankle, she sports a flea collar to keep the bird lice from crawling onto her skin. She wears a mask over her mouth to deal with the powerful stench of ammonia from the guano. A hard hat sits awkwardly on her head, and beneath it she wears a stocking cap, an additional measure of cushioning. Miranda is swaddled in a poncho, too, already streaked with slimy droppings, which the gulls have aimed and flung like weapons. When the ferry comes, she will shed all these items. She will remove her gear like a spy changing out of a costume, peeling off her wig and false teeth, unstrapping her gun, and fleeing the scene—becoming, in a moment, unexceptional, a face in the crowd.

Her knapsack is packed, such as it is. She does not have many possessions left. A collection of shells. A lucky puffin feather. A shark tooth, small and serrated. It is strange, after all this time, to make her exit from this place carrying nothing more than a backpack. But things do not endure here. The jeans Miranda brought with her so long ago have been reduced to rags. Her books have succumbed to mildew. Her ergonomic pillow is full of mouse droppings. The only items she has retained—at considerable effort, requiring the use of watertight containers and all her cleverness and vigilance—are three digital cameras, one large-format instrument, and several cartons of undeveloped film. These are her treasures. She has photographed the islands in all their moods, from the crystalline sunshine of winter to the wild autumn storms. There are more than a dozen isles. Miranda has recorded each one. Chocolate Chip Islet silhouetted against the glitter of the ocean. Sugarloaf, a puffy mound. The Drunk Uncle's Islets poking their bald heads out of the surf. And the people here. The few who are left. She has photos of them, too.

The impact comes without warning. A gull slams against Miranda's temple, knocking her off balance. She cries out, her hard hat tilting across her eyes. Wings thunder around her shoulders. The gull does not escape unscathed either; it crumples to the ground, visibly disoriented. Miranda does not stop. Shaken and disheveled, she continues toward the water. She knows better than to pause out here, in the open. She mounts the cliff, breathing hard, finally reaching the crest.

Forty feet from shore, there is a solid wall of fog. The ocean is coated with coils of mist like smoking embers. Miranda readjusts her hard hat. The birds are keeping their distance now, regrouping, reconsidering. They shriek threats and warnings. They swivel and dive in her peripheral vision, menacing shadows.

Then the rumble of an engine echoes across the water. It is barely audible over the clamor of the gulls. As Miranda watches, the prow of the ferry noses through the band of fog. There is something audacious about its appearance, like an act in a magic show.

The boat seems to force itself into existence, appearing out of nothing, out of mist, out of dreams. Almost against her will, Miranda raises both arms over her head, waving desperately. The craft is still too far away for her to tell whether Captain Joe has waved back. She watches as the boat trolls through the surf. The gulls whirl around her, screaming. They have not given up. They will maintain their malevolence until the bitter end. Miranda knows what they would do to her if they could. She knows how dangerous the islands can be. She knows this better than anyone else.

Half an hour later, she is on board the ferry. Never famous for her sea legs, she leans against the railing, feeling her gut heave in concert with the lurching deck. She is ready to depart, to leave the islands for the first time in a year. She stands twenty feet and a world away from the coast. Captain Joe hustles around the boat, doing mysterious sailor things: unwinding a rope, tugging a lever, testing the strength of a latch. As the ferry grinds away from the shore, the ocean pivots, rotating on its axis. Everything about the landscape looks different from this perspective—the islands small, the mist a soft curtain, the birds as delicate and ineffectual as paper cranes. Miranda holds her breath, unaccustomed to the sensation of safety.

She has removed her flea collars, poncho, hard hat, and mask. Still, she is unhappily aware that her clothes—steel-toed work boots, a stocking cap, and a man's jacket she swiped as a keepsake—are not exactly normal. Her attire would be inappropriate for any place other than the Farallon Islands. Once she reaches California, she will probably be mistaken for a homeless person. Passersby may pity her and offer her their spare change. If they only knew.

The ferry cleaves through the water. Its wake sketches a path back to shore. Miranda plans to watch the islands recede into the distance until the fog devours them. The archipelago is a collection of miniature islets, a tiny formation, a speck on the map. Southeast Farallon is the only one of the bunch that is even fit for human habitation. It has a shelf of greenery, on which the cabin sits, along with the lighthouse, the boats, and two small trees that stand proudly in the wind, their canopies overlapping for company. Scattered around this central island are sculptures of bare rock so insignificant that they can't support plant life, beaten as they are by the surf and patterned with barnacles. As the boat steams away from the shore, Miranda bites her lip. She half hopes to catch a final glimpse of another human being—poised on the cliff's edge, lingering there to see her off, to wave goodbye. But after all that has happened, she should know better. No one is standing there. The islands appear deserted. The lighthouse is black and solid against a bank of clouds. The cabin is barely visible, hidden by the hillside.

The waves grow larger, swelling beneath the hull. Saddle Rock swings into view, teeming with sea lions, some dozing in a pile, some bounding comically over the beach. Soon the ferry reaches the fog. From inside the deckhouse, Captain Joe is singing—a cheery tune carried on the breeze. As Miranda watches, the islands become ethereal and vague. A haze removes their sharp edges, blurring the outlines. She squints through the shroud, taking one last look at the coast. For a moment, she feels like a boat herself, tugging at her anchor chain. During the past twelve months, a length of iron links has tied her to the archipelago. She has been altered over her time in this place like a vessel moored in a harbor—eroded by the tide, beaten by the waves, holes punched in the hull, dirtied and battered beyond recognition. Now she feels the chain beginning to distend. It aches as it stretches beyond its limits. Finally, with a wrench, it snaps in two. When that tether gives way, Miranda almost faints.

For the last year, she has spent every morning listening to Galen spit elaborately into the sink. She has stood at the oven range with Charlene, giggling as the two of them doused a pan full of scrambled murre eggs with every spice in the larder, all in a futile effort to make their breakfast taste a little less fishy. Miranda has taken numerous walks with Mick, orbiting the coast. She has waited by the front door, watching Forest carefully lacing up his boots, taking ten minutes longer than everyone else, as though the fate of the world might depend on each precise knot. Miranda knows all their quirks. She knows the way Galen laughs, his eyes crinkling shut, his mouth so wide that you can see every filling. She knows the way Lucy hums in her sleep, hour after hour, clearly audible in the quiet cabin. She knows the smell of Andrew's sweat, earthy and sharp. She knows the exact span of Mick's white hands.

She will never see any of these people again. In a way, she is glad.

On the long boat ride, she removes her cap and does her best to brush her matted hair. She grapples with the scary marine toilet. She examines her photographic equipment. Some people name their cars—beloved objects, imbued with personality. Miranda is in the habit of naming her cameras. The best of her brood is Jewel. It is large-format, and it has enough dials to bamboozle both Galen and Forest, who were prone to picking it up and playing with it whenever Miranda's back was turned. This is the monster that has, like an overactive queen bee, spawned a hundred cases of film, as yet undeveloped, waiting to hatch in the darkroom. The second camera is Charles, a period piece. Charles is at its best in the morning and the evening, when the sky is golden, the air thick with light. Charles imposes its own take on the world. And the remaining two (Gremlin and Fish Face) are digital SLR cameras: simple, flashy, wildly expensive. Miranda cares for each of them tenderly, a benevolent mother. She remembers their birthdays, the important date when she purchased each one.

Two of her babies have been lost over the past year. Casualties of the islands. Their names were Tomcat and Evildoer. Gone forever.

Now Miranda makes her way into the shelter of the deckhouse. She settles on a bench. Outside the window, the fog is undiminished, encasing the boat like a roll of cotton. The world beyond the hull is reduced to auditory impressions: a foghorn, the plash of waves, a gull crying. Distant now. A musical sound.

She reaches into her bag and removes a manila envelope. It is a bulky thing, swollen and rustling. She upends it into her lap, releasing a blizzard of paper. There are lined pages torn from notebooks. There is printer paper, covered front and back in Miranda's own handwriting. There is graph paper, and tissue paper, and wax paper stolen from the kitchen. On every surface, Miranda's cursive is unusually cramped, like ants marching in line. Paper in any form was scarce on the islands. She had to make the most of each piece. During the spare winter months, she ripped pages out of magazines and filled in the margins. She made do with old receipts, the original printing faded, the surface now marked with her script. She even wrote on toilet paper. The contents of the manila envelope represent a full year's work.

Moving cautiously, Miranda spreads the papers across her lap. There is order here, of a kind, though it would not be discernible to anyone but herself. Some might see the scribbling of a madwoman. Or the poetry of this place. She finds a note from a sunny afternoon in September. That long, frantic letter in autumn, the handwriting almost too desperate to be legible. The pages from the wet week of Thanksgiving still bear the rumpled memory of the damp air. There are notes from December, March, the spring, the summer.

Maybe she will find no answer here. Maybe there will never be an explanation for everything that has happened to her. But this is her last chance to understand. The ferry's engine thrums. A faraway gull keens like an infant in distress. Miranda sits for a moment with her head bowed. Then she begins to read.

SHARK SEASON

1

I WILL NEVER FORGET the first moments of my arrival. The Farallon Islands were not what I had been expecting. They were both smaller and stranger than I had pictured. A tiny, aquatic mountain range. It looked as though a single, powerful wave could wash the whole thing away. I stood on board the deck of the ferry. Waves smacked the hull while Captain Joe dropped anchor. The dizzy horizon danced as the boat swayed. I shaded my eyes with a hand, staring up at my new home.

Long ago, this place had been called the Islands of the Dead. Now I could see why. Southeast Farallon was less than one square mile across. The other islets were bare, bald, and broken. There were no sandy beaches. The shores were streaked with seaweed, the peaks fragmented and craggy. The islands were arranged by height, like wedding guests in a snapshot. There was a crudeness about their contours. God might have made the world, but he seemed to have deputized his underage stepson to fashion the Farallon Islands out of some lesser brand of clay.

At my side, Captain Joe was shouting into a walkie-talkie. A crackling voice responded. I had spent the past five hours on board the ferry. I was disoriented, in desperate need of a shower. The boat slid up one side of a wave and down the other. I squinted against the sunlight. We were moored alongside a sharp cliff. Rock against clouds. Something was descending over the edge.

It looked like a deflated birdcage. There was a heavy iron disc at the bottom. Ropes and netting swung against the sky. This, I knew, was the Billy Pugh. (The origin of the name is unknown. I asked and got no answer.) Captain Joe was giving instructions. Someone on the other end of the walkie-talkie replied, the voice garbled by static. The ocean was inky, capped with slimy bubbles.

I would be transported to shore by crane. There was no dock on the Farallon Islands. No marina. No semblance of normalcy. The ferry was twenty feet from the cliffs and could come no closer without being broken open on the reefs below the surface. The Billy Pugh landed on deck with a clatter. Without ceremony, Captain Joe guided me inside the network of ropes. He arranged my feet on the base: a metal circle, scratched and scarred. Above my head, the mesh was gathered and synched around a hook. Above that, a steel cable snaked upward. Somewhere at the top of the mechanism was a crane. A shadow against the clouds.

I turned to Captain Joe.

"This is safe, isn't it?"

"I'll send your luggage up after," he said.

The ground lurched under me. I gasped, knotting my hands into the ropes. The Billy Pugh did not look secure enough to hold me. I was moving fast, rocketing upward. Ten feet. Fifteen feet. I could hear the whine of the steel cable. The disc shifted beneath my feet. I tried to keep my balance as the Billy Pugh swung like a pendulum. The ocean fell away, the ferry distorted, Captain Joe reduced to a foreshortened cartoon. I thought I saw a dorsal fin in the distance. I thought I saw three of them, moving in unison. I thought I would throw up.

There was a bang. The Billy Pugh had landed. I pushed my way through the gap in the ropes and collapsed onto the Farallon Islands.

What followed was a blur. I lay on my back. Proud that I'd passed my first test. Waiting for the nausea to subside. The granite was cold on my skin, uneven beneath my spine. I could see the crane better now—a rusted spar that lunged over the water. The Billy Pugh was descending again. Someone close by must be operating the thing. I did not know who had transported me to the islands, who was on the other end of Captain Joe's walkie-talkie. There were six permanent residents here. Six biologists lived in isolation and wildness on the Islands of the Dead.

The crane's mechanism was perched on top of a nearby hill. Someone was inside, but from this distance I could not make out any distinguishing features. All I could see was a human silhouette. The winch rotated, the cable unspooling. The Billy Pugh dropped out of sight. I watched a seabird pass. I inhaled the odor of mildew and guano. The islands were pungent enough to singe my lungs.

My luggage followed me on the same perilous trip. By the time I got to my feet, the Billy Pugh was sitting beside me again, stacked with my suitcases. The ferry was already leaving. The prow was pointed to California, the wake a churn of gray sludge. I could not see Captain Joe. He had descended into the deckhouse without so much as a goodbye tip of the hat. It did not do to linger in these waters.

I looked around for my unknown assistant. But the silhouette in the crane's window was gone too. Whoever had been there, operating the machine, had not seen fit to introduce himself, to help me with my bags, to welcome me to the islands. There was a lump in my throat. For now, I was on my own.

It took me a while to make my way to the cabin. Dragging my suitcases. Panting and sweating. It was early afternoon, cold and clear. A seabird winged by in the distance, braying its harsh cry. The ocean boomed. White spray rose above the cliffs. The lighthouse stood sentinel against a hazy sky.

On the porch, I felt like the victim of a shipwreck. The cabin appeared abandoned. There were cracks in the windowpanes. The boards sagged beneath my weight. There was no doorbell. I was still winded from the labor of my walk. My luggage was strewn around my feet. I remember steeling myself to knock. I remember arranging my face into a pleasant, oh-how-nice-to-meet-you expression.

But before I could move—before I could blink—the door was yanked open from within. I stepped back, startled. Two men lunged into the doorway.

One was old, the other young. Perhaps it was the influence of my sea-addled gut, but they both struck me, in that moment, as otherworldly. The elderly one could have been cast in a movie as Poseidon—a thatch of silver hair, a weather-beaten face, an air of gravitas. The younger man was as slim as a sapling. He had calloused, muscular hands. A minor deity, perhaps. A sprite with limited but surprising powers.

Now, of course, I know their names: Galen (old) and Forest (young). At the time, however, I had no idea. I took a deep breath and grinned.

"Hello," I said.

"Get your tail in gear, or we're going to miss the whole show," Forest said. It took me a moment to realize that, although he was facing in my direction, he was addressing the man behind him. I just happened to be in between his interested gaze and the sea.

"Fine, fine," Galen grumbled, cramming a hat over his white bangs.

"Hi," I said, louder. "I got off the ferry a few minutes ago. I'm—"

Forest pivoted, smiting himself on the brow. "I forgot the damn camera. Can you believe it? I *forgot* the damn—"

"Too late," Galen said. "We'll have to make do without it."

They barged onto the porch, and if I had not moved aside, Forest would have collided with me. He was zipping up his coat. Galen scanned the shoreline with a pair of binoculars. I opened my mouth and closed it again. My nerve failed me. I could not attempt to announce my presence to them a third time. I watched mutely as they stepped over my suitcases and darted down the stairs.

For a moment, I actually wondered if I might be dreaming. It did seem a bit like an anxiety nightmare: the dreadful boat ride, the massive waves, a horrible mesh cage, a soupy ocean, distant dorsal fins, mysterious figures on the landscape, no greeting, no assistance with my suitcases, no surety, no safety.

Both men trotted off down the path. I watched their figures receding. They had almost reached the crest of the hill when Forest finally turned.

"Oh, of course. You must be Melissa," he yelled. "Welcome! We'd stay and chat, but—"

Galen took over the sentence, finishing the other man's thought.

"—there's a feeding frenzy in the West End Cove," he shouted. "Get into the house. Don't go outside. This place is tricky."

I could not bring myself to bellow back that they had my name wrong. They were already out of sight, dashing away like kids after the ice cream truck.

2

T HIS LETTER, LIKE all the others, will never be mailed. In the past, I have found all kinds of creative solutions for the letters I write to you. I've burned them. I have buried them in the ground. I have shredded them into confetti. While hiking in the mountains, I have folded my messages into origami flowers, hanging them in the trees. When I took a rafting trip down the Mississippi during a long summer, I would fashion the pages into boats, which I set on the current, watching them drift like water lilies, darkening slowly, sinking when my back was turned.

I have been writing to you for almost twenty years. But none of these missives have ever reached you. None of them have ever been read. After all, I wrote my first letter to you the week you died.

THIS IS WHAT I remember:

Your exit from the world was sudden. You kissed Dad on the cheek, went to work, never came home. I was at school when the accident happened. I heard the sirens. An ambulance went haring past the windows of my eighth-grade history class, drowning out a lecture on trade routes in Europe. A little while later, the intercom buzzed into life, a crackling hiss that filled every classroom in the building with the aural equivalent of sand. There were a few thumps as the principal grappled with the microphone. I remember the look of annoyance on my teacher's face. Then my name was spoken. My name was spoken again. I got to my feet, feeling all eyes on me, and began shoving books into my bag. I was not apprehensive. At the time, I did not connect those two things—the ambulance and my name.

It turned out that your car had stalled. The morning was cold, as only D.C. winters can be cold, the air so damp and heavy that it lay over the world like cheesecloth. You had no knowledge of mechanics—that was my father's job—but you went through the motions anyway: cursing, opening the hood, staring in bafflement at the labyrinth of cogs. Finally you abandoned the vehicle where it was, at the corner of 13th and G, and strode up the hill toward the nearest garage. The sidewalks were wet and slick. Handfuls of blue salt, strewn over the pavement by landlords and store owners, coped imperfectly with the pockets of ice. I imagine you, a slim figure in brown, your face muffled up to the eyes by one of your own hand-knitted scarves. You paused at a crosswalk. You waited for the green. In the middle of the street, you observed too late that a dump truck had begun to skid on a patch of black ice.

The police would later refer to this as a No Fault Accident. You were correct to be in the crosswalk just then. The driver had seen the light changing and attempted to stop, but the slippery pavement, combined with the inertia of his cargo—thirteen tons of gravel—had prevented him. Everybody had followed the law. Somehow this bothered me. I would have preferred an accident in which somebody was at fault. It was difficult to grasp that there was no one to blame for the loss of my mother—not even you yourself.

What I recall most clearly about that day is sitting outside the principal's office kicking my feet on the carpet and wondering whether I'd brushed my teeth earlier. The only reason I could come up with for having been dragged out of class was that you, in your well-intentioned but over-scheduled way, had once again forgotten to pick me up for a dentist appointment. You were notorious among the staff at Dr. Greenberg's. I imagined that someone had called with a friendly reminder, and you had gone flying out of work, coffee on your sleeve, your purse dispensing bits of Kleenex down the road from an unzipped pocket. That was the drill. Any minute now, I was sure that you would appear in the hallway, breathless and bewildered.

When the door opened, however, it was not you at all. Aunt Kim stood there, her face ghastly. Her demeanor was enough to bring me to my feet. Aunt Kim was usually as imperturbable as a slab of granite. Even now, she was not exactly in tears. She was just pale, and her coat was buttoned wrong. At the sight of me, she flinched. Then she approached the receptionist. The two of them held a whispered conversation, glancing my way. I was alarmed to see the receptionist's expression change, her habitual bored glaze giving way to a sympathetic grimace.

There were three sisters in your family. You were the oldest and best. Kim and Janine, the twins, were as identical as peas. They enhanced this quality by dressing in gray, keeping their hair short, favoring wispy scarves, and sporting brown lipstick. Each twin, on her own, was conservative and unremarkable. But whenever I saw them together, they were downright eerie, like walking mirror images, like an optical illusion. Same gestures, same sidelong glance, same vocal tone. When the three of you were in company, this impression grew stronger. You shared their build: slim, small, and birdlike. You were a little taller, a little bolder. Your laugh rang out a little louder. But there was so much you three shared— that swing of the hips, that tilt of the head, that rough, throaty murmur. Echoes and parallels and mystery.

When it came to temperament, however, you were unique. You lived on your nerves, exhaling emotion like breath. A beautiful sunset could stop you in your tracks. A friendly debate at a dinner party could whip you into a table-pounding frenzy. Kim and Janine lacked your sparkle. They were stoic and calm—women who viewed any display of emotion as a sign of weakness.

Now Aunt Kim took my arm and led me outside. Her mouth was a thin line.

In the car, Aunt Janine was waiting. At the sight of her, the alarm bells in my mind began to jangle. The twins were serious about their respective jobs. They never took sick days. Their holidays were always constrained. The sight of them in the mid-afternoon, away from their desks, still dressed in their work clothes, their mouths tight, their hands trembling—I did not understand it. I did not like it one bit. Aunt Janine offered no explanations. She motioned me into the back seat.

Aunt Kim drove. Her hands were so tight on the wheel that her knuckles blanched. I was still hoping that all this had something to do with my teeth. The windshield was decorated with coils of frost. Through the glass, I saw the sleepy gleam of the Potomac River between the buildings. Aunt Kim's cell phone rang. She did not answer it while driving; she was not that sort. She pulled to the side of the road first. I recognized my uncle's voice on the line, though his words were indistinguishable.

"Oh yes," Aunt Kim said brightly. "Right here. Mm-hm."

I rolled my eyes. Clearly I was being discussed.

"Which?" she asked. "The one in Bethesda? Oh, I see."

I kept my gaze on the river.

"Be right there," Aunt Kim said, still in the same brittle, cheery tone.

Without a word to me, she turned the car around. She and Aunt Janine exchanged a glance, communicating through twin telepathy. One narrowed her eyes, the other nodded, and they both looked away. We passed my school again. In the intervening minutes, that stone building had been diminished somehow. Through the window the place appeared curiously distant, as though viewed through the wrong end of a telescope. The traffic was bad that morning. D.C. traffic is always bad. We drove in a silence that seemed intensified by the chilly air. Several times, I saw Aunt Kim reach automatically for the radio. It was the rule of law in her car that NPR must always be blaring. Each time, however, her fingers drew back as though burned.

Her cell phone rang again. Once more, she pulled to the curb, earning herself a barrage of honking from the cab behind us. My uncle's voice sounded down the line, though I still couldn't catch any words.

"Nearly there," Aunt Kim said.

But then her face went blank. All the expression was erased, like a wet cloth on a chalkboard. There were just two eyes, a nose, and a mouth, slightly open. In that moment, she looked so much like you.

My uncle was speaking, a muffled stream.

"I understand," she said.

Once more, she turned the car around. I saw my school approaching in the distance. Apparently we were going to spend all day passing back and forth in front of it. I cleared my throat, but Aunt Kim did not look at me. Beside her, Aunt Janine folded up one hand and pressed it unsteadily to her mouth. They still had not exchanged a word. They did not need to.

"Where are we going?" I asked.

It was Aunt Janine who answered.

"We're taking you home," she said.

FOR A FEW days afterward, my memory is empty. Somebody else dressed in black and attended the funeral. Somebody else handled the cloying embraces. All I have are brief, watery flashes. The icy air of winter pervading the house. My father's red, swollen eyes. The wake was a blur of soft carpeting and muted lights. Every adult in the known universe seemed compelled to approach me and say something about God working in mysterious ways. "I'm sorry for your loss," each of them said, as though they had all received the same script. A single moment does stand out plainly for me: one of my little cousins tugging at Aunt Kim's sleeve. I was standing nearby, awkward in my somber dress. In her bell-clear voice, my cousin asked about you. She wanted to know whether you would be there soon, whether you would sit by her.

I was fourteen years old. At the front of the room, there was a gleaming mound, half-obscured by flowers—your coffin. I knew what was in that coffin. I knew the answer to my little cousin's question. But I still found myself pausing, heart in my throat, waiting for Aunt Kim's reply.

"Don't be silly," she snapped. "Get yourself a cookie and be quiet."

I blinked. Time passed. I was standing outside, on the pavement, in the clean wind. This kind of thing happened often, for a while. Blink, and an hour would elapse. Blink again, and a whole afternoon might go by. It was as though someone were slicing at my internal calendar with a pair of scissors, removing time.

A few nights later, I came to myself again. I was sitting in my bedroom. My father was downstairs; he too had gone into a kind of walking coma, subsisting on televised football and cups of black coffee. He would have been glad of my company, no doubt, but I was avoiding him. I was avoiding everyone. Aunt Kim had urged me to call her anytime. Aunt Janine had independently said the exact same thing in the exact same tone. One of my classmates had dropped off that week's homework, which was piled on my desk, awaiting my attention. There were a thousand things I could have been doing. But the world had turned upside down, and no one else seemed to have noticed. It was astonishing that my school continued to function, that I would be back there on Monday. It was incredible that cars still rolled down the street outside. Curled on my mattress, I practiced saying the word *dead*. Dead to rights. Dead sure. Drop-dead gorgeous. Now that I thought about it, the word was everywhere. It cropped up in everyday conversations, in moments where it had no right to be, like a warning note, something I had been foolish enough not to pay attention to before.

Then I remembered the Dead Letter Office. A few weeks ago—or a decade, it seemed—my class had gone on a field trip to the local post office. It had been dull, in the particular way that forced visits to government institutions are always dull. Rooms filled with filing cabinets. A sweaty tour guide in a blue uniform, armed with cue cards and a litany of groan-worthy puns. Long hallways. No break for snacks. The Dead Letter Office was where the mail ended up if it could not be delivered. Our tour guide had shown us around proudly. The place was special, he said. The large, grand Dead Letter Office in New York City had even been featured in a Christmas movie once, since all the wish lists that were addressed to *Santa, North Pole* amassed there during the holidays, heaped like an indoor snowdrift.

Alone in my bedroom, I hurried to my desk. I grabbed up a pen—with a spray of feathers in place of an eraser, as I recall—and a sheaf of paper. Then I wrote for ten pages, front and back, without stopping. *Aunt Kim's necklace at the funeral would have made you laugh—she has no taste—Aunt Janine wore flats because of her bunions—it was so strange to see them there without you—two instead of three—everyone was chatting and having coffee, the whole family wandering all over and giving each other hugs—but the twins kept stopping and looking around—like they were waiting for you—* I was barely conscious. My hand moved across the page, and words followed. *They made you wear an awful dress at the funeral—I thought you should have your jeans on, but Aunt Kim said No Way—I put a package of gum in the coffin—I don't believe in heaven, but you sure do—maybe the gum will help your ears pop on the way up—*

Finally it was over. The letter was done, folded into an envelope. I crept downstairs. Moving quietly so as not to rouse my father, I collected a stamp. On the envelope, I wrote just one word: MOM. Then I threw on a coat and hurried down the street to the mailbox.

THERE ARE ENVELOPES for you in every state I have ever visited. For nearly two decades, I have written to you. Perhaps it is strange that I still have so much to say. I often find myself turning to you, reflexively, a question on my lips; I still engage in imaginary quarrels with you. I store up the memories I have left—the ones that have not fallen by the wayside—and run them through my hands, examining them. The raucous cackle of your laugh. The honey-and-lavender odor of your hair. Your habit of humming on long car trips. Your penchant for linen skirts. I still experience that surge of bottomless sorrow. Even now, this can only be alleviated by a few minutes spent at my desk, scribbling away, head bent over the page.

The whole matter has been complicated, of course, by my continuous traveling. For my work, I have circumnavigated the globe.

As a rule, a nature photographer never stays anywhere too long. Straight out of college, I took a job capturing images of desert animals, rambling across the horn of Africa over a period of weeks. In my father's words, I "caught the travel bug." Since then, I have hiked up mountainsides and gone spelunking through caves. I have broiled red in tropical climates and slept in makeshift igloos. I have set foot on every continent. I have swum in nearly every ocean.

I once spent a grueling month in Kenya—always breathless from the altitude, always hot, right down to my bones. I once spent a week photographing the blind dolphins of the Indus River. (Centuries of living in such murky water had rendered their eyes moot.) I once flew to Australia for a three-week photographic bonanza, snapping every inch and angle of the baobab trees, their improbable silhouettes, as fat and waxy as candles.

In many of these places, there has been no Dead Letter Office. There has sometimes been no postal system at all. I could not turn to the guide who had steered me out into the glimmering stream of the Indus River, pass him an envelope—addressed simply MOM— and tell him, "Take care of this for me, would you?" I could not toss my letters into the recycling bin or the gutter, either. I would never degrade them to that extent.

Instead, I have tucked them under boulders and tree roots. I have crammed them into the chinks of brick walls. I have stapled them to telephone poles alongside posters for missing dogs and ads for music lessons. I have pinned them to the clotheslines of strangers. I have made kites out of them, letting them soar on gusty days, then releasing my hold, watching the wind carry them away.

3

YOU WOULD HATE the Farallon Islands. I can tell you this in
no uncertain terms. Of all the places I have traveled, this one
is the wildest, the most remote. There is no respite from the
howl of the wind and the pounding of the waves. Mick—the nice
one—has assured me that I will become inured to the noise, but it
seems more likely that I will go off the deep end first. I am chilly
all the time. I go around buried beneath so many layers of clothing
that I have taken on the shape of a snowman. I arrived a week ago,
but time moves strangely here. It is easy to lose track of it, to lose
track of oneself. I already feel as though I have been on the islands
forever.

In other places I have visited, I have been able to photograph
everything I needed in a month or so. But this archipelago is something else. The islets are the central stars in a galaxy of marine
life. The birds and seals are the inner constellations—permanent
residents who eat, mate, and raise their young on the rough-hewn
granite. There are great white sharks, periodic visitors, pulled out
of their mysterious orbits to linger offshore. Whales, like far-flung
comets, pass by in search of krill. There are tufted puffins. Sea
otters. Comb jellies. I am slated to be on the islands for a full year.
I will need all that time to capture this end-of-the-world spot.

At any hour of the day, I can watch seals on the shore. I can watch birds wafting across the sky. I can watch a bank of clouds looming in the west like a new continent in the process of forming. The occasional airplane—glinting silver in the distance, an emissary from the civilized world—strikes an incongruous note.

Then there is the cabin. The kitchen sink broke on my very first night, and to my great amazement, I found myself on my knees beneath the counter, wrench in hand, following directions as Mick shone a flashlight in my eyes. The toilet cannot be flushed very often. The television has a screen so infused with static that it is basically a large, boxy radio, offering audio only. The cabin is the sort of structure in which every single board creaks audibly whenever someone passes up or down the stairs. Food, photographic equipment, and clothes have to be stored in plastic tubs to keep out the rodents, the bird lice, and the damp.

The past week has been a bit like going back in time. There is no cell tower on the islands, no Internet, no landline. There is just a radiophone, clearly marked: *For emergencies only. Mick, this means you!!!* To communicate with anyone on the mainland, I will have to write a letter. I will have to write it by hand, since the computer is iffy at best, and the printer, old and battered, is in a perpetual state of low ink, paper jams, or some sort of complex wiring dysfunction due to the damp. Once my letter has been stamped and addressed, I will have to wait for the ferry. Days will pass without any sign of it, during which everything I have written will gradually become obsolete. When Captain Joe finally turns up, he will transport my envelope to the continent, slipping it into a mailbox for me. Apparently it can take a month or more to send a message and receive a response.

While I am on the Farallon Islands, I will have to hang on to my letters to you. I cannot in good conscience give them to Captain Joe, asking him to transport them over miles of ocean and mail them, at the cost of considerable time and effort, to no one. I can't even bury or burn them; we do not taint the environment by putting anything into the earth, and fires are a waste of precious wood and paper. I will have to stash my letters to you under my mattress, like porn.

Most visitors choose to leave this place immediately. The ferry stops by every other week—depending on the weather—and the new arrivals usually flee like bats out of hell at the boat's earliest reappearance. At the moment, there are six permanent residents, not including me. All of them—spearheaded by a woman called Lucy—have made a bet about how long I will last. I overheard them snickering about it. Nobody believes that I will make it a month, let alone the full year.

IT IS AUGUST, a season of wind, clouds, and great white sharks. The stretch of ocean around the Farallon Islands is called the Red Triangle. Every year, there are more shark attacks here than everywhere else on earth combined. Yesterday I went out with my camera for the first time. I brought Evildoer, my lightest and most portable instrument. I was hoping to catch one of the sharks on film.

As I walked, the shoreline shifted and broke away beneath my boots. I had been told to be careful on the grounds. I had been told this over and over. The granite was eighty-nine million years old and rotten—if stone can be said to rot. The islands are deceptively fragile, made of rock that is not solid. There are hollow areas, crumbling patches. I crossed the stream, a filthy yellow trickle. It looked poisonous. It was poisonous. There was a system of concrete pads, funnels, and filtration hubs to collect and purify the rainwater that falls on the archipelago. Only a crazy person would drink from that brook.

In addition, there were mice everywhere. Southeast Farallon is the most rodent-dense place in the world. They are an invasive species, carried here decades ago on ships. The creatures have been flourishing ever since. They lack natural predators. The seabirds ignore them. The seals have no interest. The sharks can't get near them. I knew the numbers before coming to the islands, but I had not really understood their full import until I stood on the gray slope and saw motion everywhere. Tiny shapes dodged and darted in my peripheral vision. The mice were rock-colored, too small and quick to track. The overall impression was of living, moving stone.

I stopped to take a picture. I was using Dutch angles in my photographs—canting the horizon, adding inclines where there were none in real life. The islands had menace in spades, but there was no harm in adding a little more. I wanted my pictures to capture the full effect: craggy stone, black water, the smell of salt, the possibility of sharks. I remembered a professor of mine, back in college, explaining the Dutch angle to me for the first time. Used for dramatic effect. A tilt that leaves the viewer off-balance. It can convey disorientation, unease, intoxication, even madness.

I knelt, trying to frame a shot of Saddle Rock. This was a thin slice of island far offshore, jutting against the sky like a weapon. I felt a lurch underfoot. I lost my balance, reached out wildly, and turned over a rock. It was a good-sized thing, a boulder. I began to fall. The boulder began to fall with me.

People say that time slows down in moments of extreme stress. I have done a little research on the subject, and what actually happens is that memory becomes incredibly retentive. Usually the mind only holds on to images and events that are important. We remember the big things and forget the little ones. In moments of stress, however, the mind grabs on to everything. Time itself moves the way it always does, but afterward, looking back, the impression is one of photographic recall. In retrospect, we feel as though the second hand must have slowed down, as though we were able to see the surrounding world in fantastic, specific detail.

The rock flipped over. Behind it was a waterfall of brown. Mud, I thought. But no—it was mice. Dozens of them, tumbling over one another, squeaking. Their little feet groping. Whiskers quivering. A plague of rodents.

Something made contact with my elbow. I had begun the process of landing on the ground. The blow knocked the wind out of me. There was a tearing sensation. The flesh of my torso was ripping. A sharp stone. Splattered with blood. My side had been gashed open.

I could not tell how deep the cut might be. It hurt to breathe. The boulder was still rolling toward me. It struck my thigh.

Then the mice came, falling like rain. Their cold feet on my belly. A paw in my mouth. A nose in my eye. Tails slithering all over my skin.

They kept coming. Dozens, maybe hundreds. I could only imagine that I had opened the front door to some network of their tunnels and unleashed an avalanche. I could do nothing but succumb to the onslaught—scratching my skin, covering me with their filth, leaving droppings in my hair.

At last they were gone. I held still a while longer, curled tight, my hands over my head. Then I opened my eyes.

In front of me was a horrid sight. My camera lay on the ground. Dented and smashed. Shattered glass everywhere. I cried out. This hurt more than the wound in my side. Evildoer was broken beyond repair.

MICK STITCHED ME up in the kitchen. It was evening, the sky darkening, the wind roaring. The others were all around me. Making dinner. Chatting about their day. Six people, slightly out of focus. They seemed unmoved by my predicament. I had lost one of my dear cameras. My thigh was purple where the boulder had struck me. I had scrapes and bruises all over. Mick was working a needle through the flesh of my torso. But the biologists seemed to take the whole thing in stride. They did not offer me sympathy. They merely handed Mick the first aid kit and went about their business, as though blood and mouse attacks were a part of normal life.

He had given me a shot of some numbing agent. Still, I did not look down as he shoved the needle into my skin. Mick had clearly done this before. The first aid kit on the islands was as well-stocked as an emergency room. Cuts, sprains, and dislocations could be dealt with right here. No fuss, no muss. If anyone suffered a serious wound—a broken bone, a head trauma—it would, of course, require a response from outside the islands. Captain Joe. A helicopter. Nobody wanted that. It was expensive. It was time-consuming. My injury was not worthy of such extreme measures.

Mick took up a pair of tiny scissors. With a flourish, he cut the thread.

"That should heal fine," he said.

"What if I get an infection and die?"

He smiled. He had a pair of reading glasses perched on his nose, at odds with his rugged bone structure and shock of unruly hair.

"You'll have a scar," he said. "But we've all got them here."

"Really?" I said.

"I slashed my thigh open a few years ago. All the way open. Knee to hip. And Lucy nearly took her ear off when she fell down Lighthouse Hill. Galen and Forest have got too many to count. You should see them naked." He whistled between his teeth. "Marks everywhere. Like a road map."

I glanced down and realized my hands were shaking.

"Why do you all live here?" I said. "Why the hell did you come to this place?"

There was a silence. A feeling of tension. Lucy paused on her way to the kitchen. Galen, seated at the table, froze. But I persisted.

"I'm really asking," I said. "Why did you all come here? I want to know."

The silence intensified. Galen stood up, unnaturally tall, his head nearly brushing the ceiling. No one was looking at him. Or at me.

He turned and left the room. Mick reached into the first aid kit and removed a pad of gauze. He began taping it over my side. Then he gave me a wink.

THE NEXT DAY, I went out and dug a grave for my camera. I found a shovel in an old shed. I cut right into the granite, the stone giving way before my blade. I laid Evildoer in the hole. It was terrible to see—the LCD cracked, the lens gone, the mode dial chipped, the casing fractured. I covered the poor thing with earth. I knew better than to make a headstone. It would not last, not here.

A mouse flitted past me down the hill. At once, I lifted the shovel and swung it. I wanted to smash the creature to a pulp. I aimed for the furry spine, but it was too quick for me. I made contact with the granite instead, sending a ringing jolt up both arms.

4

THE FARALLON ISLANDS have their own ghost story. I heard it for the first time today when Mick steered me outside for a walk. I did not want to go; my leg was cramping, a residual soreness from my fall, a deep ache. My side had not yet fully healed and was giving off twinges of pain. I had been overdoing it on the slick, rocky terrain, unaccustomed to this new topography. Still, I couldn't say no. In the weeks that I'd been here, Mick had become my favorite.

I imagine you flashing that wry, maternal smirk—and I won't say that you're wrong. Mick is not quite handsome. He has a rough-hewn frame and a lantern jaw, and it seems that he was manufactured on too large a scale. He gestures while he talks, his burly arms sweeping through the air. He is kind. There is an easy, generous sweetness about him, a characteristic I have not found in any of the others here—a trait I would like to possess myself.

Today he showed me the coast guard house. I have been curious about this structure since my arrival. It stands perhaps a hundred feet from the cabin, and from the outside, the two buildings are as alike as twins. They share a geometric symmetry; both were clearly constructed for longevity and sturdiness rather than beauty. They have gray, drab walls, cloudy windows, and black roofs—all the

color beaten away by the wind and rain. Mick and I circled the
coast guard house several times. Until today, I had not understood
why it was uninhabited. It seemed wasteful to cram seven of us into
one tiny cabin while another option sat right next door, empty.

Once I got a closer look at the coast guard house, however, I
began to understand. Its walls had an uncertain aspect, like soldiers
who no longer felt the need to stand at attention. Every window was
cracked. The door sagged on its hinges. The porch was rotten. The
only inhabitants appeared to be bats. Their droppings were splattered across the walls and windowsills, curdling the air with the
stench of ammonia. I found myself standing at a distance, as though
the whole thing might suddenly collapse. Mick shaded his eyes with
a hand, looking up at the dingy walls with something like fondness.
He explained that the coast guard house was a relic from another
age; it had been constructed over a hundred years ago. Our cabin
was equipped with modern comforts like heat and electricity, but the
coast guard house never entertained such luxuries. It sat untouched
and ignored by the current population, like the ruins scattered around
the city of Rome. A dying place on the Islands of the Dead.

As the afternoon wore on, Mick and I wandered. You might not
believe that anyone could walk so far on such a small island, but
we roamed for hours. Mick led me across Blowhole Peninsula and
Cormorant Blind Hill. We passed the helipad, a slab of pavement,
crisp and out of place on the plateau. (Its presence there always irks
me. Only an emergency of the direst sort could summon a helicopter from the mainland. A medical crisis. Life or death. The helipad
is a constant reminder of menace.) Mick and I passed Sea Pigeon

Gulch, where birds floated serenely on the tide. He was able to identify them for me—an auklet, an oystercatcher, a puffin. It was a bright, cloudless afternoon, the sky an almost painful shade of blue. The ocean was so flat that my depth perception disappeared from certain angles. It looked as though the water had been pinned up like a blanket from a clothesline, a vertical fall of cloth.

I have yet to make sense of the islands' layout. There is a map tacked to the living room wall, and I have often examined it—an image that gives the impression that a chunk of granite has been dropped from a great height, shattering and strewing islets every which way. The oddest names are printed on that map. Garbage Gulch. Funky Arch. Emperor's Bathtub. Some of the landmarks have more prosaic, shape-oriented titles: Tower Point, Low Arch, the Tit. The rest are named after the creatures you might find there. Sea Lion Cove. Mussel Flat. Great Murre Cave. I have studied that map often enough to memorize it, yet I can never seem to get my bearings when I am out on the grounds. In fact, I am half-convinced that the islands are not rooted at all, but move around whenever my back is turned, taking up brand-new positions elsewhere.

Finally Mick and I scaled Lighthouse Hill. I was leery. This is the highest peak on the island. The climb took longer than I had expected. Mick walked directly behind me, in case of accidents. Soon I was sweating through my layers, peeling off my jacket and looping it around my waist. The ground receded beneath me. I saw Lucy and Forest heading toward the cabin together, miniature figures, paper dolls. At last, out of breath, I reached a flight of steps carved into the stone.

As I stepped into the lighthouse, I wrinkled up my nose. The walls were so smeared with guano that they resembled a Jackson Pollack painting. Lichens and moss curled in the corners. The view, however, was something to behold. In every direction, I could see for miles—not quite to California, but across the whole of the archipelago. For the first time, I got a good look at what lay to the north. A huge hand seemed to be lunging up from the bottom of the ocean, a crescent of granite spires. Eagerly I read- ied my camera. Mick was saying something, but I wasn't listen- ing. Among the northern islets, the rules of gravity seemed altered. The light was bizarre, a patchwork of shadows strewn across the waves. One rocky promontory would be outlined in gold, the next as black and empty as the night sky. There was an arch with spines like a stegosaurus. Through my telephoto lens, I saw bodies in the water. The sea lions were frolicking where no ship could ever have ventured.

"—likes your room best," Mick was saying. "She really seems to prefer it there. Forest says he wouldn't take that room for love or money."

"Ah," I said, adjusting the focus.

"I don't mean to scare you. Just giving you fair warning. Forest hasn't seen her personally, of course. Not like me."

"Hm."

"Are you even listening to me, mouse girl?"

I smiled. This sobriquet had been bestowed on me by Lucy, in a spiteful way, as though my unsettling encounter with the islands' signature rodents had marked me for life. When Mick said it, however, it had a different sound. It felt like an inside joke between the two of us.

Names have power. I have always believed this. I've never known an Anne who wasn't docile and mild. A Karen is usually sensible, trustworthy—whereas a Shane is bad news. And a woman named Melissa is always a little crazy.

Evidently, I am doomed to be a crazy woman here. The others still call me Melissa. I have not yet found the right moment to fix the misunderstanding. At first it seemed impolite, and when a few more days had passed, I felt as though I'd waited too long, and now it would be hard to admit that for two weeks I have been responding to a name that isn't mine. Mick usually calls me *Mel*, which I rather like. Lucy calls me *mouse girl*. Galen calls me *you*. Forest calls me nothing. Andrew calls me *Melissa*, with a sibilant hiss, the way a snake might say it.

An interesting virtue of all the traveling I have done is the possibility of adopting new identities among new people. This has happened without fail in each location. During my time in the rainforest—always wet, always hot, crouching in a blind for days in an attempt to get a decent shot of the elusive birds of paradise—I pretended to be hardy and easygoing. During my time in the arctic—always cold, always lonely, photographing the northern lights in a kind of hallucinatory daze, treating the moon like an old friend—I pretended to be solitary and serene. On the islands, it seems I have taken this process one step further.

"I'm talking about the ghost," Mick said. "Pay attention. This is important."

Meekly, I obeyed. We leaned together against the railing, the wind tugging my collar open and fingering my hair.

"People have died on the islands before," Mick said. "Lots of people."

I swallowed hard. "I know. The Islands of the Dead."

"A long time ago, the place wasn't like it is now. It wasn't a marine sanctuary. There were no biologists."

"I know that too," I said. I had, after all, done my research.

Mick went on: "Back then, everyone wanted to see what value they could find here. Fur traders hunted the animals. Sailors set up base camp. Gold miners dug up the ground." His expression darkened. "It went on for decades. Pirates. Eggers. Russians. Nobody cared about the sharks or the seals. They just wanted to make some dough."

I tried to visualize the scene. Staring down at the grassy plateau, I imagined it filled with figures. It was hard to grasp the idea of the islands overrun by strangers. Even I, a nature photographer, armed with nothing more harmful than a camera, had almost been denied access. These days, the place was well protected. It sat under the umbrella of government authority. The land, the sea, and especially the animals were treated as precious, finite resources. Hunting was unheard-of. Littering was not to be considered. Intruders could be thrown in jail. Even the whale-watching tours that motored in from California were required to maintain a considerable distance. It was an ecosystem left on its own—sheltered, unrefined, and unchanged.

The wind picked up, scouring my skin. I shivered, but Mick seemed unperturbed.

"Nobody stayed for long," he said. "The islands were just too dangerous. People broke bones, got hypothermia, drowned. People were eaten by sharks. No one could stick it out." He shook his head. "One group would hightail it out of here, running for their lives. And then some other group would move in. Set up camp. Hunt some animals. Act like idiots. Always the same. The storms would blow in soon enough. People would start dying. A few months later, they'd bolt, too."

In short, I thought with a surge of vicarious pride, the islands had defeated them, one and all. The marauding hordes had been driven back to their native lands, tails between their legs. I lifted my gaze to the horizon. It was a clean line between blue and deeper blue, like a fold in a sheet of paper.

Mick sighed. "Pretty soon, the murre population was hanging by a thread. The fur seals had almost been hunted into extinction."

I shifted restlessly, and he nudged me.

"Don't fidget," he said. "I'm getting there. All this is background." He paused. "You see, these people left something behind."

I glanced up at him.

"A body," Mick said, his voice dropping an octave. "A woman's skeleton. They found her in a cave."

"A cave," I repeated.

"She might have been a pirate's wife or daughter. Or maybe an Aleut slave. Nobody has ever been able to discover her name. Even her nationality is up for debate. She might have been lying in that cave for a year, or a decade, or a century." Mick elbowed me in the ribs, nearly knocking me over. "The corpse was taken away. They

gave her a decent burial someplace. But"—he held up a finger—
"her spirit is still here on Southeast Farallon."

"This is starting to sound like a campfire story," I said dubiously.

Mick ignored me. "The ghost has been seen lots of times. She
wanders around the cabin at night, wearing a white dress. People
have heard her footsteps. She makes the place feel cold on warm
evenings." His gestures grew more animated, and I took a hasty
step back. "The ghost moves stuff around in empty rooms. She'll
knock a plate off a table or tilt a picture on the wall. She whispers
in people's ears when they're sleeping." He took a deep breath and
concluded triumphantly, "I've seen her myself."

"No way," I said.

Mick paused, and I watched him, my eyebrows knotted.

"One night," he said, "I was walking toward the cabin. This
was last spring, maybe." He paused again. "It had been a long day.
One of the seal pups had died, and the mother was mourning. I
couldn't seem to let go of it. My brain was overloaded. I didn't feel
like myself. Then I looked up, and I saw somebody in your room."

"*My* room?"

"The ghost likes your room," he said, flashing a mischievous
grin. "Didn't I mention that? A thin person, very pale. Just standing
at the window and staring out. I didn't think much of it at the time.
But when I got to the cabin, nobody was home. Nobody had been
there all afternoon."

In spite of myself, I felt a chill track down my spine.

I am aware that throughout history, photography has had a
strong connection to the dead. Or perhaps the undead. Ghosts are

often said to turn up on film—invisible in the moment to the human eye, appearing only afterward in the darkroom. I have seen some of these images myself. Floaty, pale shapes. Figures that cannot be explained by aperture or exposure. Blurred silhouettes at the back of an empty room.

"I believe you," I said. "I believe in ghosts."

Mick threw me a glance I couldn't interpret. I lifted my camera and pointed it down the hill at the cabin. I took a picture.

5

To my surprise, it has already happened. In fact, it happened this morning: I woke at dawn, and the islands felt familiar to me.

I have had this experience on my travels before, but it never palls. In the desert it took me a while to adjust to the bone-dry air. In the tropics it took me some time to grow accustomed to the overpowering odor of the trees, the blinding showers of hot rain. I once lived in a cave, snapping photos of bats for a week. Even then I did finally adapt to the odor of guano, the *plink* of water, the way the darkness seemed to crawl toward me along the walls. The process of habituation is always the same. What was alien becomes familiar—what was strange becomes ordinary—the glimmering viscera of the world are pulled inside out.

Yet it has rarely happened as rapidly as it has here. I opened my eyes this morning and was glad to be where I am.

Then, however, I heard grunting and moaning from downstairs. At once, I threw on my jeans and dashed into the hallway. Lucy and Andrew live directly beneath me. They are the cabin's resident couple.

I know this will intrigue you. You always used to begin your perusal of the *New York Times* with the marriage announcements. I remember it well. You believed that you could predict with great accuracy whether each pair of newlyweds would go the distance. You included an immense variety of factors in your analysis. Whether either of them had been married before. Whether either was significantly older, better-looking, or richer than the other. Whether their body language signaled ease or awkwardness in the snapshot. I was a logic-minded child, and I did point out that you had no way to verify your guesses. You could speculate all you wanted, but we would never know for sure. Still, your faith in your prognostications remained unshaken.

I will therefore share what I have gleaned about the lovebirds of the Farallon Islands, and you can decide for yourself whether they will succeed as a twosome. Lucy and Andrew are the same age—midtwenties, almost a decade younger than me. They are oddly matched. She is the sort of woman who would seem perfectly at home in pioneer garb, churning butter. She has a round, expansive, comfortable frame, her face as pink and wholesome as an apple. She is almost beautiful. In certain lights, from the right angle, she attains a fleeting loveliness. Most of the time, however, she is sturdy, warm, and homey.

Andrew, on the other hand, is a human glacier. He is pale all over, practically an albino, from his flaxen hair to his white-blue eyes. His disposition, too, is icy. During the past month, I have yet to see him express any emotion except a kind of ironic, adolescent disdain. He always wears a crimson stocking cap with a gold phoenix emblem. He keeps the cap tugged low over his ears at all times, which adds to the impression of jaded youth. His notes in the daily log are humorous but cutting. *Important research now shows that the ocean is evil*, he wrote one morning. And another day: *Rescue ship still hasn't gotten my signal. Mustn't give up hope. Which cabin mate will I eat first?* And then, just yesterday: *I know which one I will eat first.*

Lucy and Andrew came to the islands together. They began dating in college. Yet their personalities, like their physiques, could not be more dissimilar. Lucy is a human dynamo, a boundless spring of energy. Every morning, she is up before dawn, on the grounds, binoculars in hand. Rain and wind do not deter her. She is the bird girl, and her knowledge is encyclopedic. Whenever a feathery shape flits across the sky, she can, without even sparing it a second glance, identify it as auklet, cormorant, gull, or puffin. She rarely sits down. Her meals are eaten as she stands at the bookcase, flipping through a reference tome or gazing out the window, her expression wistful, like a house cat wishing to be let into the garden. Still chewing, she will throw on her jacket and hurry toward Sea Pigeon Gulch.

In the evenings, we all tend to drop off early. (It is remarkable how the internal clock aligns with the circadian rhythm—if there's absolutely nothing to do after dark.) But Lucy does not doze. She cleans. I can hear you spluttering that *of course* the woman is the one doing the mopping and sweeping. And yet, in Lucy's case, it's more than that. Nobody can venture outside safely at night, on the slippery shore, on the uneven slope. It is tricky in broad daylight, impossible in darkness. I learned this the hard way during my first week in this place. Trapped indoors, Lucy must do something else with her excess vitality. As she wipes down the countertops and scrubs the pots, her eyes shine with purpose.

Andrew, on the other hand, is bone-lazy. He can't be bothered to rise before ten a.m. Out here, that is an eternity of time wasted, the entire morning gone. He is a bird specialist too—he and Lucy met in a biology seminar—but he does not walk the grounds with her. He stays inside where it's warm, writing notes for a research paper that never seems to reach completion.

A few other details that might interest you:

1. Andrew and Lucy have sex every day. *Every* day, without fail, rain or shine. I sleep directly above them, and each sigh and moan passes right through my floorboards.

2. I don't think I have ever seen a woman adore her man more. Her sun rises and sets on him. That kind of devotion is unsettling.

3. I do not like Andrew. I don't like him at all. There is something about him that I do not understand or trust. A deadness behind the eyes.

THROUGHOUT THE MORNING, I wandered the grounds. I cannot explain the joy I was feeling. Everything about the islands seemed exquisite to me. The salt-infused air. The crash of the surf. The shimmy of the mice darting across my peripheral vision. The granite that crackled and fragmented away beneath my boots.

I wanted a picture of the light on the water, broken up by islets. I had learned from my fall and injury. My camera now hung on a secure strap around my neck. I knew to stop in my tracks, plant my feet, and check my surroundings before I succumbed to the beauty of an image. I was in the process of framing the shot—settling myself like a tripod—when I looked down and gasped.

The islands had given me a present. There, between my feet, lay a seal stone. These were rare and precious things, left on the shore by the elusive fur seals. Gastroliths, they were called. Mick had described them to me, but I had not expected to find one myself. I had not thought I was worthy of such a miracle.

I knelt down and picked it up. It felt wonderful in my hand. Perfectly round. Smooth and dense. It looked as though it had been inside a polisher. It was made of something darker and more compact than the flaky granite of the islands. The fur seals ate these stones, maybe for ballast, maybe for digestion. No one knew why. Up to ten pounds of rocks in the gut. Grinning, I turned it over in my palms.

I slipped it into the pocket of my coat. There was something reassuring about its weight, its heft. Its perfect sphericality. Its wildness. It had been carried in the belly of a seal until it was rendered flawless.

There was a noise behind me. I whirled around and saw Andrew. Crimson hat. Hands in pockets. Smirking face. He was a little too close. I hadn't heard him until he was almost on top of me. I stood up quickly, dusting off my hands.

"You want to be careful," he said.

"What do you mean?"

His eyes were so blue. They looked like windows, as though I were seeing through him to the sky behind.

"You don't want to get hurt again," he said. "A little thing like you."

I was gripping my camera like a shield. Andrew smiled and sloped off, shoulders hunched, heading for the cabin. I watched him go with relief.

Then a hint of motion caught my eye. There was someone else outside—a shape on Lighthouse Hill. I thought it was Lucy. But the figure was gone so fast that I could have been mistaken. It could have been a trick of the light.

6

W E ARE DEEP into Shark Season. I came to the islands in late summer, and my arrival coincided with a vast influx of white sharks. (The *great*, I have learned, is only used by ignorant nonbiologists.) On my travels, I have encountered dreadful creatures before—leeches with a penchant for armpits, crocodiles masquerading as logs, irate lions. For nearly five months, I once lived in the rainforest; I slept in a hut and bathed with a bucket. The rules of my visits were strict: no littering, no hiking except on the designated trails, and, whatever the provocation, no destruction of any living thing. This included venomous tarantulas and foot-long centipedes. I loved that place as a photographic object, but by the end I was dying for a cup of real coffee, a change of clothes, and the feel of a stiff breeze on my skin. I found that, of all things, I missed the look of straight lines. There were none in that eruption of greenery.

But the white sharks have a lethal charm all their own.

Galen and Forest are our shark specialists. In the past month, I have learned a bit more about these two, but my initial impression of them has not changed all that much. Galen is white-haired, venerable, and never in a particularly good mood. He still strikes me as being an elderly god of the sea—possibly omnipotent, probably omniscient. He knows everything that happens here. He watches the tides. He organizes repairs on the cabin, the boats. He can recite the history of the Farallon Islands with the scholarly air of a college professor. He has a thousand animal facts at his fingertips. Though his raison d'être is the sharks, I have seen him sitting on the porch beside Lucy, helping her to dissect the wing of a dead cormorant like a trained veterinarian. He can read the coming weather at a glance.

Forest, on the other hand, is an enigma. A dark-haired, cold-blooded naiad. Galen's right hand. Forest eats, sleeps, and breathes work. I have yet to hold a conversation with him that has not centered on something to do with biology: the anatomy of harbor seals, the local varieties of comb jellies, or the weather patterns as related to bird migrations. The one time I dared to ask him where he'd grown up, he shot me a withering look, like a Victorian butler reprimanding an impertinent housemaid. Like the others here, he seems to have no past, or a distinct unwillingness to discuss it. Once, long ago, I read that all nuns who joined a convent were forbidden from speaking about their lives before. The Farallon Islands seem to be a religious order in their own right, with a similar vow of silence.

Galen and Forest catalog and track the population of white sharks. Throughout the autumn, the two men rise at four-thirty in the morning to start the watch. During every hour of daylight, one of them is in position in the lighthouse, keeping an eye out for blood on the water. Against every basic human instinct, they hurry toward a feeding frenzy. They board one of the boats and head out to sea, armed with video cameras, tagging equipment, and the "dummy," a surfboard painted like a seal to lure the sharks in closer. The two of them live to make contact with these creatures. Galen and Forest are lunatics, to put it frankly. Galen has mentioned that he dreams about the white sharks every single night. Forest sketches a shark's silhouette—lean, rough, and spiked with fins—on any nearby surface. He does this unconsciously, doodling on the table, on a book I once left open on the couch.

At this time of year, there can be two or three kills a day. The sharks eat the seals and sea lions. There is enough prey here to sustain a massive host of predators. The birds will mark the spot like an X on a map. Watching from the lighthouse, Forest or Galen will spy a collection of gulls diving over a patch of sea. The cry will go up. Boots are thrown on—coats flung over shirts—a thunder of feet on the stairs. Forest uses a child's scooter with streamers on the handlebars to make his downhill run from the lighthouse that much faster. One of these days he will break his neck.

There is no pier on the Farallon Islands. The tides have seen to that. Any attempts at building a dock have invariably been washed away. There is a powerful undertow. There are riptides that come and go without warning or rhythm. There are reefs and shoals. The islands are home to two small boats, both of which must be lowered into the sea by crane. They are too large to ride in the Billy Pugh, of course. Instead, they must be hooked directly to the steel cable itself.

The first is a rowboat (called the *Lunchbox*, I am sad to say, since its crew tends to feel like a tasty snack when moored next to a white shark). Then there is the *Janus*, a seventeen-foot Boston

Whaler. This is a sturdier thing, with benches and a deckhouse, as well as a railing that, to my untrained eye, appears to be for decorative purposes only. The *Janus* is equipped with a motor, which makes this boat the preferred method of transport. Both boats spend their free time resting on a mattress of rubber tires at East Landing, a thirty-foot cliff. I have seen them being lowered into the water, swinging merrily on the end of the chain, plummeting into black waves larger than themselves.

I have not yet been brave enough to venture out on Shark Watch. I have stayed safely on land. It is unnerving to think that those monsters are always out there, patrolling the dark surf. Waiting. For the most part, the white sharks remain hidden, tucked inside a wave, buried in the deep currents. Once or twice, however, I have glimpsed a dorsal fin cresting the water, as menacing as the periscope of an enemy submarine.

MY LOVE AFFAIR with the islands has continued. At times I feel drugged, wandering the shoreline with a stupid grin on my face, camera aloft. Each snapshot seems like a benediction. We may never know what another person is thinking—never truly get into anyone else's head—but photography brings us as close as anything can. When the members of an audience at an art gallery look at a picture, they can step for a moment inside the mind of the artist. Like telepathy. Like time travel. At some future date, when people gaze at my photographs of the islands, they will see what I saw. They will stand where I stood, on this granite, surrounded by this ocean. Perhaps they will even feel some of the elation I have experienced here.

Earlier today, I found myself at North Landing, where a dozen California sea lions were lolling in the light. They maneuvered around like canine mermaids. Their bodies seemed split in two; the upper half was alert and upright—pert little ears, sharp eyes, and a snout bristling with whiskers—whereas the back half was weighted down with fat and fins, slithering across the flagstones. They toasted themselves like marshmallows, plunging into the frothy shallows to cool off.

Soon I realized that one of the creatures was injured. It did not romp and play with the others, diving and hunting fish. Instead it lay on the shore, one flipper cradled against its chest. Through my telephoto lens, I could see a deep, fresh wound. The flipper had nearly been severed from the torso. The gash was new enough that it had not yet begun to scab. Instinctively I put a hand to my rib cage, where my own flesh had been cut open a few weeks before. Probably the animal had survived a run-in with a white shark. This was surprisingly common. What the sea lions lacked in mass, they made up for in gymnastic agility. I could imagine the shark lunging forward as the sea lion pirouetted and somersaulted away. But it was clearly in bad shape now. It was weak and dazed-looking.

I knew, however, that there was nothing I could do. There would be no point in going to fetch Mick or Galen. The biologists were on the islands to observe and document. Nothing more. Noninterference was the core of their belief system. They would never intervene in the life—or death—of one of their charges. I had received a stern lecture on this very subject from Galen a few days back. An injured animal was a specimen to be studied. Its demise was an event to be recorded for posterity. The food chain was paramount. Sympathy and affection were beside the point.

I turned away. Bending down, I took a few close-ups of shark teeth. The grounds are speckled with them; they dot the landscape like flowers in a prairie. Delicate reminders of danger. People used to believe shark teeth fell from the sky during lunar eclipses. Honestly, I am not sure myself how they travel so far inland.

After a while, I moved off to get a few candid snapshots of my human companions. They had proven to be as camera-shy as the animals. I had learned to be crafty. Crouching behind a boulder, telephoto lens in place, I saw Lucy sitting cross-legged on the shore, engaging in a debate with a puffin. She could imitate most birds' cries well enough to cause confusion in their little minds. This one clearly thought she was another puffin encroaching on its turf. Presently another shape intruded into the frame. I adjusted the focus and saw red hair, a too-big windbreaker—Charlene.

I have not mentioned Charlene yet, since I haven't been sure what to say. To begin with, she is young, even younger than Andrew and Lucy. Charlene is still in college. A mop of unruly red hair. Pale skin strewn with constellations of freckles. She is an intern, not a biologist. (For the record, Charlene is the only intern who has ever lasted more than a fortnight on the islands. She has been here three months already.) Her identity is effaced by her subordinate position, by the eagerness she displays whenever she is asked to help with the simplest task, from hosing down the *Janus* to itemizing the contents of the cupboards to making coffee. I have yet to get any sense of her personality.

Now, through my lens, I watched both women get to work. They were too far away for me to catch any of their conversation. It appeared that Lucy was teaching Charlene how to tag the birds. Lucy is a master at this tricky process: capturing a feathery body, holding it firmly but gently in both hands so it cannot peck her or injure itself, and attaching the orange band. Charlene was obviously nervous, her brow furrowed with concentration. Lucy spoke soothingly, patiently, as Charlene fumbled and frowned, letting bird after bird slip through her grasp. Suddenly, both women burst into laughter. I got it on film: Charlene's head thrown back, her hair a crimson halo, and Lucy doubled over, clutching her stomach. Their mirth scared the remaining birds into flight. The flock swirled upward, a waterfall of wings.

I found myself distracted. The problem of Lucy has occupied my mind lately. I cannot figure it out. She is the belle of the Farallon Islands, the darling of the group. I have seen her giving Charlene a neck rub or offering to do the dishes when it's Forest's turn because he looks tired. I have observed her sitting on the couch with Galen and delighting over a ludicrous error they have stumbled upon in a reference book—the kind of thing that would only be discernible to a pair of biologists. Lucy laughs easily and loudly. She is open, cheerful, kind.

But not with me. It has taken me a while to catch on to the reality of the situation. To be frank, I was fooled at the start by her appearance. Plump and pink, she looks like the sort of woman who ought to be wearing an apron or kneeling in a garden, her hands deep in the earth. In her interactions with me, however, she has been odd from the beginning. Every so often, she will throw out a backhanded comment. ("Wow! That shirt is *interesting*." "You must have great teeth, mouse girl. I can hear you chewing all over the cabin.") Lucy will snicker when I trip on a loose floorboard or drop my spoon at the table. Withering looks. Covert eye rolls. I cannot read the riddle.

My roommates and I have the dynamic of a family, minus any semblance of warmth. We share a home. We see one another all day, every day. I must do my best with them, whether or not we get along. There is no privacy. If Mick is constipated, if Charlene has her period, if Andrew is feeling lustful, everyone knows about it. We each have our own roles. Galen: the stoic parent, ruling through benign neglect. Forest: the brainy son, forever at his books. Me: the shy stepchild, still finding her place in the pecking order. Within this group, Lucy might be the mean sister whose behavior is not obvious to her elders—who deals out punishment in pinches and slaps and then looks up innocently, saying, "Who, me?" She presents one face, hiding another, a double identity I am just beginning to perceive.

7

YESTERDAY CAPTAIN JOE made his first appearance since my arrival. Normally he comes twice a month, but he has been hindered by engine repairs. It has been almost seven weeks now. I was in my room when the boat appeared on the horizon. It might have been dropped there by magic. My heart turned over. I have come to understand why people in olden days imagined that the world ended at the horizon line. It is sometimes hard to believe that anything can exist beyond that cold edge.

Through the window, I saw that Galen and Forest were on alert. Dressed in their typical, ludicrous gear—waterproof pants, bright orange jackets, hats with earflaps—they were heading toward East Landing. I knew the drill. Captain Joe would approach as close as he dared. One wrong turn, and the ferry would find itself torn apart on the jagged cliffs. Galen and Forest would lower the Billy Pugh. Captain Joe would load it up with our groceries, toilet paper, and toothpaste. Galen and Forest would respond by sending back our outgoing mail. In truth, the whole thing reminded me a bit of space travel. Captain Joe would blast off from his native soil, his cargo hold stocked with supplies for the crew at the space station. The journey from California could take as long as six hours each way. Galen and Forest would meet him at the boundary line, where the crane would bridge the empty air. At any moment, something could go wrong. Someone could be injured, or worse.

Captain Joe is not the first ferryman to service the islands. I have recently discovered that there were others before him—many others. Most of them quit the moment they found easier work. A few fled after being hurt on the job; broken bones and concussions were common. One drowned. Five years back.

Our oceanic view is the most dangerous stretch of water on the Pacific coast. In places, the sea is only fifty feet deep. The tides sweep in and out at a quick, breathless eight knots. Powerful currents wind through the ocean with their own internal logic, like rivers carving banks into water, rather than earth. There are monstrous waves. Boats slosh and tumble like marshmallows in cocoa stirred by a spoon.

Soon Captain Joe was on his way home. Galen and Forest headed back toward the cabin, loaded down with boxes of groceries, tampons, batteries, and all the mail that had been piling up for us in the post office in San Francisco. The ferry motored smoothly away from the shore. I watched it go with a sense of desolation. The emotion passed quickly, but for a moment I felt like an abandoned child. Watching a parent retreat into the distance. Alone in a hostile and unfamiliar place.

On board that ferry was a postcard for my father. I had been on the islands for nearly two months, and during that time, I had prepared only one piece of mail to send to the mainland. On it I had written, *Proof of life.*

This has become a running joke between Dad and me—the cryptic postcard. (He doesn't know about the letters I save for you, of course.) My postcards to my father tend to be as brief as telegrams. I will amuse myself by communicating my meaning in as few words as possible. *110° in the shade*, I wrote during my month-long stint in the Sahara. From Paris, where I was sent to photograph the piles of skulls in the catacombs beneath the city, I wrote, *Beaucoup de dead people*. And when I was living in the arctic circle, throughout the eerie summer months, when the sun neither set nor rose—when it skimmed the horizon in bewildering revolutions, drifting higher and lower like a balloon caught in the breeze—I wrote simply, *Bright*.

Dad has gotten into the spirit himself, omitting unnecessary verbs and articles. It is a game we play, trying to top each other. *Office a madhouse*, he will write. *Overworked. Printer ink dangerously low.*

I am aware that my relationship with my father is unusual. Home has been a constant point on the compass since my childhood. For my work, I have bounced around the globe, rootless and unmoored. A month in Costa Rica. Three weeks in Taiwan. Half a year in Australia. Sleeping on couches and bare floors. Letting my stomach tie itself in knots over the local cuisine. Photographing birds and geckos, shacks and trees, people and gravestones. Photographing everything.

And then, like a swallow to Capistrano, I have returned to my father's sprawling two-story house. He has never had the chance to transform my old bedroom into a study or a storage area. I have continued to use it, sleeping on that narrow mattress beneath the mobile of the solar system I built back in middle school. I have kept my own books on the shelves, my own clothes in the drawers. My father and I have transitioned into companionable roommates.

The whole thing is both logical and odd. Most of my old friends from school have mortgages of their own by now, not to mention husbands and kids. But I have never lived anywhere long enough to justify paying rent, let alone buying furniture. Besides, I like my father's house. I help him with the garden. I do most of the cooking. I know the surrounding neighborhood like the back of my hand. Dad and I have our own rhythms and routines, built over years, honed and perfected. His book club. My soap opera addiction. His morning run. My evening walk. His workbench in the basement, strewn with sawdust and tools. My darkroom in the attic, foul-smelling and secret, baths of chemicals shimmering in the gloom. The photos of us on the wall.

That house is where I remember you best. I remember your thin shape curled on the couch, book in hand. I remember your voice raised in song, echoing down the hall from the shower. Each room is a treasure trove of unexpected recollections. Any little thing—an object, an odor, a sound—might trigger a memory, jolting me into the past. A laundry basket might remind me of your hands, working deftly to fold the clothes. The squeal of a cabinet opening might bring back a chance conversation you and I once had while sitting in the kitchen. The sky on a stormy afternoon, clouds mounting outside, might call up an image of you dashing around the house, closing all the windows in anticipation of a hard rain.

There was a postcard for me on board the ferry, by the way. *Miss you*, my father had written. Two words only.

THE NEXT DAY, I found myself on the roof. There was a good reason for this: a leak had appeared in the cabin. At noon, a storm struck without warning. It rained wildly, desperately, as though the sky had something to prove. The gutters overflowed. The air was filled with so much moisture that when the wind blew, it rippled like the sea. Lunch was spoiled by a miniature waterfall. Though Charlene and I knew nothing about carpentry, we were the two who could be spared to tackle the problem. Lucy had disappeared on Bird Watch as soon as the storm blew over. Mick wanted to check on an injured sea lion and document its progress—to record whether it would survive or perish. Forest had finally solved a glitch in the video camera and was hoping to catch a few sharks on film. Andrew was probably asleep. Galen handed me the necessary items: tar paper, tiles, a hammer, and a sad collection of bent, mismatched nails. He explained where to find the ladder. As an afterthought, he reminded me not to fall.

To be honest, I didn't mind being up there. In fact, I wished I could have brought one of my cameras. Any new perspective on an established landscape can shake loose inspiration. The sea, the seals, the coast guard house—they all looked diminished now, unreal. The pictures would have been striking. But I could not risk dropping my camera from such a height. It would never survive the fall, and I did not think I would be able to tolerate the death of another of my precious instruments.

Charlene and I crawled around, crablike, hammering down anything that seemed loose. She had brought a caulking gun, which she squirted at the slightest provocation. The shingles were rough to the touch. We found a few chinks that required maintenance. We got into a confused debate about which rooms were beneath us at any given time. We discovered a chimney. Then we relaxed for a while, gazing across the sea.

As always, I was slightly baffled by the fact that I could not see California. I could see nothing beyond the ocean's edge. There is nowhere more alone than the Farallon Islands. The rest of the world might disappear—the human race wiped out by a pandemic, a meteor strike, a zombie uprising—and we would be the last to know anything about it. We would be the only ones spared. The day was fine, despite a cold, breathy breeze. October had crept in without my notice. The grass was yellowing at the corners like mildew on cloth. The mice were spending more time underground now, their scuffle and scamper less constant. The two trees near us were wilting, no longer embracing. Maroon leaves tumbled across the stones.

For the first time, Charlene opened up to me. In the manner of the very young, she chattered on about herself, never realizing that she hadn't asked me any questions. This was not exactly narcissism. She was at the age in which her own personality fascinated her so much that it eclipsed everything else. Her own capacity for creativity. Her own brand of intelligence. She did not seem to heed the unspoken rule that talk of the past was verboten here. I heard about her family's farm in Minnesota. Without guile, she mentioned something about an aunt who had disappeared for a time and returned with a new name, claiming to have suffered amnesia. Before I could process the oddness of this—particularly when described in Charlene's upbeat cadence, as though it were not odd at all—she had already moved on. She was free-associating, leaping from idea to idea. She told me about her college roommate at Berkeley. She told me about the sweet-tempered boyfriend she had left behind, perhaps permanently, perhaps not.

This seemed like a good opportunity. When she paused for breath, I broke in. With every semblance of nonchalance, I asked if she had any idea whether Mick might be single.

"I don't think so," she said.

"Really?"

"Really." Charlene shot me a worried look. "In fact, I'm sure he isn't."

"Ah."

"Why do you ask?"

"Oh," I said. "No reason. Still learning about everyone."

There was a pause. Charlene was playing with her bangs. Her hair was the sort of fiery red that always made me do a double take. Day by day, I felt the need to check the pallor of her skin, the profusion of her freckles, trying to verify whether such a shade could possibly be real. I did that a lot here generally. The islands were a place that seemed to exist in fantasy, ever-changing and harsh.

Suddenly Charlene stiffened. A look of horror crossed her face. Gazing past my shoulder, she murmured, "Oh no."

"What?"

She pointed behind me. I pivoted with some care, trying not to dislodge any shingles. My feet scrabbled for purchase on the slanted roof.

In the distance, I glimpsed a boat on the water. The *Lunchbox* was bobbing in the calm surf near Mirounga Bay. There was only one passenger. To my surprise, I saw that it was Lucy. Evidently she had rowed out alone.

"I hate it when she does this," Charlene said. "I just hate it."

I peered at the rowboat's faraway contours. Lucy's work—observing, tagging, and cataloging the birds—did not necessitate travel on the water. Galen and Forest, the shark boys, could often be found on the briny blue, but in Lucy's case, a pair of binoculars would suffice. Still, her inquisitiveness might have gotten the better of her. Maybe she had decided to row to the Drunk Uncle's Islets. Maybe she wanted to visit Arch Rock, which was shaped like a gigantic lock with an old-fashioned keyhole. From there, she would be able to see the burrowing owls and cormorants right under her nose.

And yet, as I looked closer, I saw that Lucy was wearing a neoprene wetsuit. Her body seemed different, wrapped in rubber. Usually she obscured her curves beneath layers of clothing, but now I could see the fleshy arc of her hips, the full measure of her generous bosom. She held a snorkeling mask up to her eyes, adjusting the strap. Beside her on the deck was a bulky breathing apparatus, a snaky hose coiling among the benches. Lucy lifted the end of this tube and stuck it between her teeth. Then she sat down and tugged on a pair of bright blue flippers.

"Is she doing what I think she's doing?" I asked.

Charlene sighed. "It's her hobby, believe it or not. She's a diver. She goes down there and looks for anemones. She collects sea urchins and shells. She likes to see them up close."

With a splash, Lucy plunged into the water. For a moment she was visible in the surf, pushing her mask into a better position. A swell washed over her, and she disappeared.

"But the sharks," I said.

The rowboat, abandoned, slid back and forth on the waves. I could hear the smack of the surf on the hull. Lucy's breathing hose was unrolling slowly, spooling over the side.

"We've all tried to talk her out of it," Charlene said. "Especially Galen. He put his foot down. Big arguments in the kitchen. Lucy was polite, but she wouldn't budge. She asked us to show her in writing where it said she wasn't allowed to do it. And we couldn't. There aren't any rules for this. Nobody thought to make a rule about recreational diving."

"It's crazy," I said.

Charlene bit her lip. "She doesn't do it that much. Only a few times since I came. I did ask her about it once. She said it was something she had to do."

The sea was opaque. Slippery waves. Drifting shadows. A clamor of sunlight glinting off the surface. The water did not allow me to pick out a human shape.

THAT EVENING, THERE was tension in the air. Lucy had not returned. I found it difficult to settle to anything. A cat on a hot tin roof. I was amazed that Galen and Forest could sit with their heads together, poring over a tidal chart. I was amazed that Charlene could focus on her book, pencil at the ready, occasionally underscoring an important word with two precise lines.

In my travels, I have learned that biologists are a strange breed. A certain kind of individual is drawn to this work. I have grown accustomed to the type. In Texas, I met a herpetologist who caught wild rattlesnakes with his bare hands for fun. In northern California, there was a botanist who enjoyed free-climbing the giant redwoods, scaling those massive trunks with no ropes or harnesses. In Greenland, I encountered an ichthyologist who imitated Jesus, walking on water. Born and bred in that climate, he was able to determine the density of the ice by sight. I often watched him, heart in my throat, as he strode over the surface of the ocean, sending out ripples in the layer of standing water above the deeper core of dark, porous frost.

In short, Lucy's behavior was not that far beyond the pale. Still, as the evening passed, the clock ticking, the breeze brushing the windows, I was worried. The sea was rough and cloudy. Visibility was limited. It was starting to get dark. Lucy was down there alone, armed with nothing but a wire basket in which she liked to collect interesting shells. In my mind, the water teemed with white sharks, thrashing against one another in the rush to get to her exposed figure first.

In recent weeks, I had learned a lot about these wily predators. White sharks did not typically hunt humans—but it was common knowledge that a diver looked a lot like a seal from the right angle.

Same color, same size. The sharks were inquisitive by nature, too. One might swipe Lucy with its tail, bump her with its nose, even give her what Galen called a "love bite" to investigate her presence. She could be killed, not out of malice or hunger, but from idle curiosity.

I was frankly astonished that there was diving equipment on the islands at all. It was perilous enough to travel around by boat without venturing below the surface. Probably, like the helipad, the diving kit had been purchased for emergencies—a man overboard, a discovery of sunken treasure. Surely it had never been intended to be used for fun.

Each time the door banged in the wind, I glanced up hopefully. Mick was out there, I knew, working the crane to bring Lucy home. At a prearranged hour, he had headed off to meet her. It seemed as though he had been gone a long while. Too long. Charlene set her book aside and began scribbling down notes. Galen and Forest continued their discussion in low, insistent voices. Forest was looking even thinner than usual, as willowy as a ballet dancer, with cavernous cheekbones.

He and Galen were arguing about the white sharks. I was getting better at following their jargon. The Rat Pack was the group of males responsible for most of the attacks on seals and sea lions. A strip of ocean by Indian Head was their hunting ground. The Rat Pack lingered to the south of the archipelago like a clique of teenagers at the mall. Galen and Forest had come to know them well. Some were curious, easily lured to the surface. Some were aggressive, thudding into the *Janus*'s side or trying to bite the motor. They were usually named for their wounds: Bite Head, No Fin, One-Eyed Jack.

The Sisters, however, were something else. The puny males were dwarfed by the female sharks, which could be as long as limousines, twenty feet from snout to tail. These ladies were nobility. They did not demean themselves to hunt with the Rat Pack but maintained their own turf, staying to the east, patrolling from Sugarloaf to Jewel Cave. I had yet to see a Sister myself (though any day now, I was sure that I would find the courage to go out on Shark Watch). They cruised the waters with a lazy grace, and the Rat Pack, those lesser peons, treated them with unswerving respect. The Sisters had so much gravitas that Galen and Forest claimed to be able to sense them underwater even before they surfaced.

There were three in particular who ruled the islands. Galen had named them after the witches in *Macbeth*. They swam together, hunted together. Their dorsal fins sliced through the surf like ships in a fleet. The leader of the trio—Hecate—was the largest shark that had ever been seen on the islands. Twenty-four feet at least. If she were ever hooked and measured, she would break every record in the book, Forest had said. But she would never be caught. Not here. Her two companions were smaller, though still massive enough to merit awe. Nineteen feet, maybe. They were called the Twins, since they bore similar markings.

Now Galen and Forest began to debate the sharks' feeding habits. Live prey. Styrofoam dummies. Better ways to dupe the Sisters into approaching the *Janus* on the water. They threw ideas back and forth like jugglers tossing silk scarves in the air. The fact that

Lucy, their friend and colleague, might be at the mercy of these same creatures at that very moment did not dampen their enthusiasm.

Andrew, however, was the worst of everyone. In the early evening, he was cloistered in the room he shared with Lucy, doing whatever he usually did in there—napping, leafing through reference books, masturbating. Then a creaking of floorboards indicated that he had finished his work. He strolled into the kitchen in his languid way, yawning a little. He wore his usual uniform: slouchy jeans and his crimson knit cap with the phoenix emblem. He did not speak to any of us. I gritted my teeth. It would have been natural—it would have been *human*—for him to stop at the window and glance out for any sign of Lucy, to pace the floor as he awaited her return. Instead, he gave a cry of delight. At the back of the cupboard, he had discovered a supply of tinned peaches, his favorite. For the next few minutes, I had to watch him eating his way through three syrupy cans.

By the time the dinner hour rolled around, my nerves were shot. Charlene was cooking—macaroni and cheese, with tuna mixed in for protein. (This, sadly, is a staple of our diet.) The occasional "Oops" or "Oh *no*" wafted out of the kitchen, indicating that she was having her usual trouble managing the cantankerous cast-iron range. Galen was now dozing in an armchair, his head sagging comically to the side. Andrew had settled next to me on the couch to read, though I could feel his gaze shift to me, heavy and thick. I resisted the urge to wipe his attention off me like oil. When the door slammed again, I did not even look up.

"Sorry," Lucy said in her clear voice. "I hope we're not late for dinner."

She brought the smell of the sea into the room. One hand held a bucket, the other a wire basket that shimmered with shells. She was still wearing her wetsuit, now with a man's jacket draped over her shoulders. Mick's jacket. He eased through the door behind her, kicking off his boots and spattering the floor with mud.

For an instant, I saw that the others were relieved too. As Lucy hung up Mick's coat, Galen shot her a look that swept from her feet to her brow, verifying that she still had all her limbs. Forest beamed, showing his teeth—something I had only seen him do once or twice before. Usually, any gleam of humor from him was just that: a gleam. A crinkle at the corner of the mouth, a bit of frivolity near the eyebrows. This wide-open grin sat oddly on his angular face. Mick collapsed onto the couch with a groaning of springs. His hair had been blown into a ragged bird's nest by the breeze.

Swishing in her wetsuit, Lucy marched over to Andrew and gave him a kiss. He patted her shoulder gently, though I noticed that he kept one finger planted in his book to mark his page.

"How was it?" Forest called from the table.

"Fine." Lucy straightened up. "No problems. I saw the most wonderful bed of sea urchins. They were marching around in extreme slow motion. Inch by inch. The spines waving everywhere. I found an enormous clam, too. One of the biggest I've ever seen. I could probably fit inside it." As she spoke, her hands flitted through the air, miming the shapes of anemones. "It was beautiful. Cold, but beautiful. You can't blink without seeing a stingray or a rockfish."

"Any sharks?" Forest asked.

Lucy considered. "Not really. The only guys who got close to me were a couple harbor seals and a huge sea lion. He nosed me a little. Wanted to bite my air hose. I had to whack him with my basket." She pursed her lips. "Well, I did see some of the Rat Pack at a distance. They were over by Mussel Flat, circling around and acting weird. They didn't bother me."

"No Sisters?" Galen asked.

"None."

Then, to my surprise, Lucy turned to me.

"Come here, mouse girl," she said.

She snapped her fingers impatiently, as though summoning a recalcitrant pet. Gritting my teeth, I got to my feet. Lucy pointed into her bucket, yellow and plastic, filled almost to the brim.

I approached it cautiously. At the bottom of the pool, there was a lump of clay. I bent over, peering into it. Then the object twitched. I let out a gasp as it changed shape, like a flower opening its petals or a fist uncurling. A few brown tendrils snaked across the bucket's floor. A gauzy sac ballooned upward—a wealth of tentacles.

I stepped back instinctively. Lucy laughed. She reached into the water and picked the tiny octopus up. Before my eyes, it changed color, its skin roughening, suffused with deep red. Its skinny arms braided themselves around her wrist in a death grip. The pouch of its body dangled like a bizarre ornament on a charm bracelet. Yellow eyes pivoted on stalks. Droplets rained onto the floor.

"Isn't he *beautiful*?" Lucy said.

8

I T IS OCTOBER, and most of the white sharks are gone. Like sightseers in Venice, they avoid the colder months. Galen and Forest have been tagging them for years, attaching an electric device to each creature. Stuck below the dorsal fin, these machines have relayed back the precise coordinates of the sharks' winter breeding and hunting grounds. The animals travel south to balmier seas; they head west to harass the surfers in Hawaii. I thought I had missed my chance at an encounter.

Then, a week ago, Forest crashed into my room at six in the morning. Dawn was near, the eastern sky aglow.

"Get up," he shouted. "There's a big kill off Sugarloaf!" He kicked the edge of the bed. "And don't forget your camera."

I climbed wearily to my feet. I had not slept well. There was an octopus in the cabin now, and it was occupying my mind. Lucy had kept the tiny creature she had pulled out of the sea. Oliver the octopus—she had named him with cartoonish assonance. She had dug an old aquarium out of some closet, God knows where, and filled it with salt water, a lumpy rock, and a spray of seaweed rising from the pebbled floor like a column of steam. She had made a home for the animal on her bureau. The octopus lived in her bedroom now, directly below mine.

Somehow this made it difficult to sleep. Last night I had lain awake for hours, aware of that monster lurking in the darkness. Its alien intelligence. Its bizarre, oblong eyes. I had been having nightmares. Imagining I heard the octopus slithering in the hallway. The wiggle of his tentacles. The kiss of his suckers.

Twenty minutes later, I was on board the *Janus* for the first time. The sun had not yet risen as we skimmed across the water. A smoky layer of fog obscured the eastern horizon, rendering the light diffuse. The sea itself was as black as tar. We were heading north. The islets there were prehistoric—the sort of rugged, primal peaks that might have appeared behind a group of dinosaurs in a documentary. Even the mist seemed uncanny. Each island wore a belt of gauzy white.

I swear that I smelled the blood before I saw it. Tangy, oily. A group of seagulls was wheeling beside Sugarloaf—a bulbous promontory, aptly named. The birds were screaming. I watched three of them get into a swordfight of flashing beaks. Then a patch of mist moved aside, curtains parting at the theater, and the blood appeared. It was phosphorescent, spilled across the surface of the sea. It glowed against a landscape of gray. (I have since learned that a seal's blood is so highly oxygenated that it just about fluoresces when exposed to open air.) The torn carcass was still visible, bobbing on the waves. The seal was human-sized. Purple strips of flesh. A tail as broad as a catcher's mitt. It had no head. Whatever killed it had decapitated it cleanly. Blood was still fountaining from the raw wound where its neck had been. I leaned over the side of the boat, wondering if I was about to throw up.

I have learned too much about white sharks lately. I know that, as a species, they predate the existence of trees. I know that they have survived four global mass extinctions. I know that they are born live, not hatched out of eggs like most fish. The pups emerge fully formed, about four feet long, with their predatory instincts already buzzing. White sharks have their own sixth sense, used for detecting prey: they can pick up the electrical impulses generated by muscles in motion. They can also smell blood in the water from a mile away. Their odd manner of swimming, the snout swinging side to side like a pendulum, helps them to track exactly where the scent is coming from. To me, it seems reminiscent of the way human beings tilt their heads to locate the source of a distant sound.

I know that white sharks are warm-blooded. Unlike other members of their species, they do not start out each day sluggish and chilled, waiting for their nervous systems to fire up, gradually accumulating enough energy for the hunt. White sharks are always ready to hunt. They are unique in other ways, special and bizarre. They sometimes breach like whales, leaping clear of the sea. Nobody is sure exactly why they do this—to scope out the nearby surroundings, to shake off clinging remoras. Maybe they do it for fun. They have even been known to land on boats. Indeed, a few registered victims of shark attacks were killed outside the water, the accidental casualties of a two-ton fish leaping jubilantly but carelessly, unaware that its bulk was heading not for the open sea but for a hapless ship in the line of fire.

This morning, Forest was at the helm of the *Janus*. Galen had his binoculars in hand. The seagulls were busy, a mass of wings above the iridescent slick. I snapped photo after photo: mist-soaked islands, bloodthirsty birds, and a splotch of crimson burning like a bonfire.

Then Forest cut the engine, pointing into the ocean.

"Look there," he said.

"What?" I said, stepping forward cautiously.

The surface of the water did seem strange. A bulge had appeared, different from the choppy waves. Moments later, a fin broke the surface. The shark was moving fast. I barely had time to take in the massive torso, the slick skin, before it had plunged again, disappearing from view. I gasped as another one skimmed past. It was difficult at first to pick out their silhouettes in the dark sea. Two sharks. Three sharks. None of them bothered to break the surface again. With my untrained eye, I wondered if they could all have been the Sisters.

Forest, however, shook his head. "It's just the Rat Pack," he said. "The ones who haven't left for warmer water."

"Males, males, males," Galen agreed. "Nothing special, I'm afraid."

I nodded, gripping my camera. The white sharks were black. I had not been expecting this. Not only were they black, but Galen began to explain that they tanned in the sunlight until they glittered like coal. Only their bellies lived up to their name. From beneath, they were as pale as icebergs. This configuration of coloring was common in the aquatic world, where light was everything. Seen from above, the fish hoped to blend into the rocky bottom. Seen from beneath, they wanted to be mistaken for the sky.

"There," Forest cried. "Right there!"

Galen almost knocked me overboard as he dashed across the boat. The *Janus* rocked under his feet. I gave an indignant, terrified cry, but nobody was paying the slightest bit of attention to me.

The Sister rose up like a submarine. She moored herself alongside our craft. Her dorsal fin was a black flag. I felt the threat of her. I felt it all the way down my spine. A bulb went on in some part of my brain that had hitherto lain unused. In my daily life, I did not typically keep an eye out for predators. Now I was acutely aware of my place on the food chain. The Sister was twenty feet of menace in a tight, scaly skin.

Forest nudged me. "Take pictures, dummy."

I snapped the greedy mouth and shimmering hide. I could not cope with the size of her. Her length was less startling than her girth. At eight feet across, she was broader than the boat. I could have lain down widthwise on her back. I understood now what all the fuss was about. The Rat Pack was interesting, to be sure. But a Sister was royalty. Certain cultures had worshiped sharks as gods. Seeing one now made it easy to understand why.

Her tail swished. The *Janus* swayed a little; the Sister had moved the entire boat. My hand was beginning to cramp up, curled around the camera. I saw an eye, dark and inscrutable. A row of teeth appeared. The Sister mouthed her prey like a dog deciding whether to accept a treat from its master. Then she swallowed the dead seal. She took it down whole. The gulls, I noticed, were gone. The presence of the Sister had scattered them like leaves in strong wind. The scene was eerily quiet.

"She's on her own for once," Forest said. "I wonder where the Twins are?"

"When shall we three meet again?" Galen said.

For half an hour, we watched her. Galen retrieved the dummy, a Styrofoam surfboard, from beneath a bench. He pushed it over the side. The Sister seemed uninterested, though. She continued to nose through the slick of blood, verifying that she had devoured every last morsel of meat. Her dorsal fin was peppered with holes; it looked as though she had taken a round of buckshot. Galen shook the surfboard temptingly so it quivered like a seal. But the Sister was not fooled. Having finished her snack, she lounged on the surface. She did not hold still—without motion, her gills would cease to function and she would suffocate—but she swam forward in the smallest possible increments, inch by inch. Basking in the sun, she appeared to be taking the shark version of a catnap.

Forest gunned the engine. The *Janus* trolled toward the Sister's retreating frame. I shivered as we pulled up alongside her again. She was big enough to take her place as an islet in the archipelago.

"Pet her," Forest told me.

Galen stretched out a hand and laid it on the shark's back. Cringing, I waited for her to react. One swipe of her tail could have shattered our hull. If she was in the wrong mood, she could swamp the boat and devour us all in a matter of minutes. Galen kept his fingers planted on the patchwork of scales. There was no discernible response to his touch. He patted softly, his eyes wild. After a moment, I reached out too. The shark's flesh was cold, rough to the touch. I stroked her rib cage, a gentle, caressing movement, then drew my hand away with a cry of pain.

My fingertips were bleeding. It looked as though I had used a cheese grater on them. Behind me, I heard Forest chortle. Everything in this place, even the shark's skin, was dangerous.

WHALE SEASON

9

THEY COME IN the late autumn, passing the islands in droves. I have seen them sliding through the sea like nightmares. Despite their size, the whales have an elusive quality. They camouflage themselves as waves, as clouds, as islets, as reflections of light. Blue whales. Gray whales. More than once I have found myself staring at what appears to be an empty ocean, only to observe a column of mist rising against the sky—a gasping exhalation—and realize the sea is full of bodies.

Mick is our whale expert. It is his job to count and catalog the animals' numbers, to keep track of the males, females, and juveniles. They are heading north in search of krill. Baleen whales, the largest animals on earth, survive by eating some of the smallest. They are traveling to the ice caps, where there are fields of krill so dense they make the water opaque. Mick has been there. He has seen gray whales swimming blindly in a bath of food, singing to one another in apparent joy.

The humpbacks are his favorite. They move in family groupings, forming intense bonds. Nomadic by nature, they lack any notion of permanence or home. They are the opera singers of the aquatic world, yet most of their music falls into the subsonic or supersonic range, beyond human hearing. Our ears are paltry, tiny things. My whole body could fit into a humpback's lung.

Before people filled the ocean with noise—boats churning, oil rigs thrumming, undersea cables vibrating—whales were able to sing across the entire planet. Mick told me this. I was struck by the image, not of the animal, but of the music itself. A single, throbbing note. I imagined the vibration passing through forests of kelp, setting jellyfish to movement, tricking shellfish with its resemblance to thunder so they cowered in their homespun caves. One strong note over sandy, wave-swept terrain—the oceanic equivalent of deserts—where nothing could grow and no fish lingered. One strong note over coral reefs and canyons, teasing dolphins into an answering chatter, bothering the seabirds where they rested between sea and sky. Finally this music would find its audience: another whale, clear on the other side of the world.

The presence of these animals has unsettled me. They are not predators, and they are not prey. They exist outside the food chain. In some ways, they exist outside normal space and time. They live in a realm of large, slow things—tides, storms, and magnetic currents. They often plunge into the inky depths of the ocean, down where the sunlight fails. They inhabit a blue world, away from land, dipping from water to air and back again, sliding between darkness and glow. It is rare for them to come close enough to the coast to be seen by human eyes. The Farallon Islands are unusual in this way, as in so many others. Autumn in this place is Whale Season.

It is November. Early November, I think, though I can't be sure. I haven't looked at the calendar in quite some time.

Thus far, I have failed to photograph the whales. I have tried, but they have defeated me. They are always too far away to succumb to my telephoto lens. They are too big to fit into the frame. There is something inartistic about their bodies, too. Some quality is lost in translation. Their ears and eyes vanish among their barnacles and scars. Their mouths are oddly shaped. Their blowholes are grotesque orifices, falling somewhere in appearance between a volcano and a rectum. Even the babies aren't photogenic. Gray whales are fifteen feet long when they're born, clocking in at two thousand pounds.

Undaunted, I continue to work. I have climbed Lighthouse Hill and sat on the slope for hours, looking to the west, where the whales pass by at irregular, unpredictable intervals. They are mysterious. They have been cropping up in my dreams, swimming through the moonless oceans of my mind, swishing their tails, displacing gallons of water, singing loudly enough to wake me.

The other day, I saw a blue whale. I was high on the hill, trying to plant my tripod on the crumbling granite. The creature rose up without warning. The noise caught my attention first—the whistling gasp of its breath. Fifty feet from shore. A rare thing. A marvel. It was bigger than a building, bigger than a dinosaur. I knew the numbers—the amount of school buses that would balance out its body on a scale, the quantity of football fields that would constitute its spine.

But I could not capture this girth on film. I got a snapshot of its nose. Its maw, mottled with algae. A gigantic flipper flinging droplets like throwing stars. The tail, off-kilter. It reminded me of the parable about an elephant in a dark room. One person touches the trunk and describes the animal as a tree, the next touches the torso and describes the animal as a wall, and the third touches the tail and describes the animal as a rope. My photographs were similarly fragmented. Only pieces, rather than the whole. No grandeur. No force. No sense of power and size.

I was scrolling through the images I had taken—all unsuccessful and unbeautiful—when I felt a tap on my shoulder. I turned so swiftly that I lost my footing. Andrew stood there grinning. His red cap was askew, the gold emblem winking at me. I skidded down the slope, flinging out a hand. Andrew caught my arm. He pulled me up, then yanked me against him. He wrapped me in a hug.

"Poor Melissa," he said. "Always falling down."

"Let me go."

He tightened his hold. My camera was pinned between us, digging into my chest.

"You're hurting me," I said.

He released me, stepping back. I shivered.

There was a scuffle, and Lucy appeared on the hill. I was glad to see her—a novel sensation. She was panting, her cheeks scarlet from exertion. A coil of hair trailed across her cheek. Her expression was mulish.

"You walk too fast," she said to Andrew. "You never wait for me."

"Look who I found," he said.

Lucy glanced up, wiping her brow with her sleeve.

"Oh, mouse girl," she said. "Have you seen any burrowing owls?"

I wasn't sure how to respond to this.

"They're an invasive species," Andrew explained. "They feed on the mice."

"They don't belong here," Lucy said. "We chase them off, but they always come back. It's a constant battle."

"Oh," I said.

She turned away. "Let's check Garbage Gulch, babe. I saw a couple there yesterday."

She did not say goodbye to me. She marched down the slope, her braid swinging behind her. Andrew blew me a kiss.

THAT EVENING, LUCY brought the octopus into the living room. We were all downstairs, as we are every evening, seven bodies crammed into the tiny space, Galen and Forest reading on opposite ends of the couch, Mick scribbling notes about whales in the daily log, Andrew at the table, Charlene washing dishes. I was sitting on the floor, scrolling again through the images on my digital camera, deleting the duds. This is a nightly ritual. It will be months before I will be able to convert my pictures into prints. For now, they remain in a half-real state, glimmering on the screen, stored in electronic impulses in the memory card, more idea than art.

I was aware of Andrew's gaze on my back. Galen's noisy breathing. The odor of Mick's sweat. The restless jiggle of Forest's legs. There is no peace here, no solitude. I have not yet learned to tune out the constant presence of the others. I will have to acquire this skill soon, for the sake of my sanity.

Then Lucy laughed. The sound startled me. She was standing in her bedroom doorway with something cupped in her hands. She set the octopus on the floor. Evidently she had removed him from the aquarium on her bureau. She flicked the damp off her fingers. For a moment, Oliver stayed curled in a protective ball. His suckers were flipped outward, rumpled like lace. One yellow eye gleamed.

He unfolded all at once, a remarkable gesture, eight legs tumbling in every direction. The sac of his body sagged like a deflated balloon. No bones. He had no bones. He began to drag himself right toward me.

I got to my feet, backing away. I bumped into the couch. Oliver changed color, his flesh darkening from sandy ochre to furious red. The same hue as Andrew's stocking cap. His progress made a surprising amount of noise. Suck and slide. Slither and coil. Suddenly, he changed direction. One long arm snaked to the side and tugged. His body rolled over, the skin puckered with dust.

"He can't breathe," I said. "Won't he die?"

Lucy did not answer. She was watching her pet with something like pride. I found that I was standing by Mick, my fingers hooked in his sweater.

"He's fine," Mick said. "They can hold their breath for thirty minutes or so. Look at him run! He's trying to find a way out of here."

There was something both hopeful and hopeless in the scene. The octopus did not know that he was half a mile inland. He did not know about the obstacles he would have to overcome to return to the ocean. Acres of sharp, uneven granite. Gallons of dry, unforgiving air. The predatory seabirds overhead. The detached, amused gaze of the biologists. The octopus was unaware of how trapped he truly was.

"There's no escape," Lucy said.

10

I WISH YOU WERE here. I wish you were anywhere.

Over the years, I have tried to reconcile myself to the fact that I write to you, and you don't write back. I have pretended that there is something therapeutic about all of this, in simply putting pen to paper. I have imagined that by storing up anecdotes for you all day long, I will be able to keep you with me. A relationship is a two-sided thing, both parties reaching toward one another across the empty air. You may be gone, but if I keep reaching, some element of our bond may remain.

I even find myself narrating my own life, in my mind, throughout the hours—notes for my next letter to you. Sometimes it feels as though I'm two different people—the one doing the action and the one describing it afterward.

Pouring a cup of tea, I will think, *The steam billowed over the rim and filled the air with cinnamon.* Taking a walk along the grounds, I will think, *I saw five birds circling the lighthouse, climbing higher and higher on a current of air, their wings open but unmoving, folded and fixed like the flaps of a kite.* This is not the way most adults live their lives: narrating every moment as it occurs, in the past tense, as a detached observer. But for me, the act has become reflexive. I have been writing to you for so long that I don't feel as if something has happened until I have told you about it. The life cycle of any event begins with action, crescendos in observation, and finishes with nouns and verbs. It isn't over until I have recorded it on the page. For you.

But recently, I have not written to you. I have not been able to. Something terrible happened—so terrible that it took away my words.

During that time, I have tried to write. God knows I have tried. But I could never seem to begin. My mind has been empty. I have taken out paper and pencil, sat staring for a while, and walked away, leaving the page blank. The other day I sent my father a post-card that said simply, *Status quo*. A big, fat lie. I could not write the truth. When Charlene has settled deferentially beside me at the kitchen table, asking how I am, I have made noncommittal noises and shaken my head. I have said nothing of consequence. Even my usual narration, internal and constant, has deserted me. Mick and I have taken our customary long walks in the chilly air, pushing through the fog. Holding his arm, steadying myself, I have been as silent as a stone.

IT ALL BEGAN on a November evening. The afternoon was long and exhausting for everyone. A broken window. An injured auklet. A choppy, treacherous ocean that kept Galen and Forest on land against their will with nothing to do but sulk. For my part, I spent the hours on the grounds, attempting to get a few good images of the humpbacks. I was on the coast with Charles, my dear old friend and camera, for far too long, forgetting to eat, straining my ankle on the rocks, freezing myself to the bone. The humpbacks remained unhelpful. Despite my best efforts, they were in a coy mood, bobbing offshore, a glimmer of eyes and flippers. I came home with nothing to show for my efforts except a sore leg and the sniffles.

By dinnertime, we were all worn out. Mick boiled the pasta as Andrew assembled a fruit salad out of the remainder of our canned goods. Every detail of that meal is still illuminated in my mind. Lucy's braid, slung around her shoulders like a snake. Galen's thumb, wrapped in a bandage. Andrew's red stocking cap, with the little flash of gold on the side, a tiny phoenix stitched onto the fabric. How sick I am of seeing that hat. The conversation was rapid and ardent, though a lot of it, even now, zoomed right over my head. Galen and Forest sniped at one another in undecipherable biologist code. Lucy chattered on about common murres. Andrew did not say much. He sat there looking bored. His few comments were a bit risqué, I noticed—the relatively enormous size of a barnacle's penis, the aggressive mating habits of the gulls. I could not tell if he was watching me or if I merely happened to be in his line of sight across the table. Charlene was a spot of color. She mostly asked questions, and I found it reassuring that someone else was confused too. I never asked questions. I was too far behind, left in the dust. *What's a common murre?* I might have inquired, or, *Who cares whether sharks mate for life?* Only blank stares would have resulted.

We had wine. Remember that, because it will be important later. It has never been my habit to drink; I don't particularly like the sharp bite of alcohol, much less the ensuing mental muddle. I am not a person who enjoys a confused mind. But Mick had been storing a few bottles under the porch for weeks, hiding them from everyone. That night, we all needed a little cheering up. That night, I figured that it would be festive to raise a glass—or three, or four— with the rest of them.

I went to bed late. I remember cannoning into my doorjamb, under the impression that it had moved a few inches to the left. I could hear Lucy's soft voice in her bedroom downstairs. Galen, I knew, was out cold on the sofa, a bottle still hooked in his limp fingers. Charlene was in her room with headphones on. She often listened to music before bed, claiming it helped her sleep. In my drunken state, I'd found amusement in watching her work the apparatus over her mane of red.

I heard a sound in the corridor. Mick and Forest were whispering. Then the front door creaked. They were outside on the porch. Evidently they were heading off to whale-watch by starlight. This was a wild risk, but I was too tired to consider its ramifications. The wine had reduced us all to drunken fools. I lay down in bed, feeling that my body was an enormous weight, one I had been carrying far too long. As I drifted off, I caught sight of a shape in the corner of the room. It was moonlight—I was almost sure it was only a streak of moonlight. Pale and gaunt. A suggestion of movement. I was already tumbling into sleep.

My dreams were fitful. I was in a courtroom facing an angry judge. I was being accused of taking a life, an act I held no memory of. The jury seemed to be made up of the biologists on the islands. Lucy, in particular, looked forbidding.

My bedroom was cold at first, but it began to grow warmer until I was sweltering, even sweating. I threw off the sheet without fully waking. The dream shifted. The octopus appeared, slithering over the mattress, groping my flesh with his suckers. I could not get him off me. He was slick and wet, smelling of salt, his tentacles surprisingly rough. The dream changed again. I was undergoing torture now—some medieval device, two slabs of stone crushing me between them, like a flower being pressed and dried. It seemed vital that I remember the name of this device before it took my life. I could not remember it. I could not move my arms.

Gradually I realized that someone else was there. Breath on my cheek. Weight on my chest. Another presence. Something was shaking—the whole island, or else the bed.

It took me a long time to understand what was happening. That was the fault of the wine and the dreams. It was difficult to sift out the reality of the situation. I was still half-aware of the octopus, his suckers palpating my skin. There was pressure on my hips, pain in my belly. I could still hear the rough voices of my torturers, the squeak of their ropes. Then I understood the noise to be the bedsprings.

A man's shape. A man's body on top of mine. The medieval vise was, in fact, his rib cage, squeezing the breath out of me. His face was in shadow.

I was still calm, waiting for the dream to shift again, waiting to wake up. Maybe he would morph back into the octopus, tiny and damp. Maybe he was one of the medieval torturers. Maybe he was a stranger—a stranger had broken into my childhood bedroom—I was not in my father's house—no stranger could have come to the islands. He must be someone I knew. My legs were stuck beneath his. My arms were stuck beneath his. I was no longer dreaming. The octopus and the ropes were gone. But the man remained. The terrible weight of his limbs held me captive.

I should stop there. You can imagine what came next. I will say only that it did not hurt—not exactly. Physically, it was just unpleasant. In retrospect, that does seem odd to me. I would have expected there to be an immediate, protective response: tensed muscles, torn tissue, pain. But my body, stupefied by wine and sleep, had stood aside to let him enter. In such a state, it could not distinguish between what he was doing and the act of love.

Then the sheet slipped off his shoulder. In the moonlight, I saw blond hair. A pale forehead. It was Andrew.

In that moment, everything splintered. I opened my mouth to scream for help. At once, his hand slammed across my lips. A kind of seizure overtook me. I wriggled like an eel, snorting against his fingers. I kicked against the dense, bony burden of his calves. His eyes were lifted above my head, a little dazed; he looked like a man on drugs. His hips went on pumping like a piston, but the rest of him was dead weight. He was in no hurry. He kissed me clumsily on the cheek, like an inexperienced teenager making the first move on a date.

I arched my spine, trying to work my arms free. I could not get even a few fingers loose. His palm was too broad and flat to bite. As rapidly as it had come on, the seizure passed over and left me limp.

After that, it gets harder to remember. Minutes or hours might have passed before he left me. I cannot tell you all the bizarre thoughts that passed through my brain. Lucy asleep in her bedroom downstairs. Charlene hidden inside her music. Galen, who was supposed to know everything that transpires here. Mick and Forest out staring at whales. Explorers on the moon. You—you—you. Your coffin. Your gravesite. Your bones, your musculature, crumbling into the earth. All the material elements that had once made up a living woman. Tiny particles of you, strewn across the world, carried on the rain. How we are broken down to just the essentials.

Andrew was still moving. He was panting and sputtering. I let my gaze roam around the room. I could feel the heat of his breath. I ignored him for a splash of moonlight on the wall. A tall, slim shape. One beam radiated outward like a raised arm. The curtains moved, and the figure trembled.

The ghost was coming into focus. I could almost see the dial swiveling on my mental camera, pulling her into greater and greater clarity. The swing of her nightgown. Her bony wrists. The plane of her cheek.

She was nothing like I had imagined. She was at once more and less real—raw, ethereal, icy. Her body was of an indeterminate density, shifting in the murk and moonlight. Her torso was a pearly smudge, her fingers as distinct as piano keys, her legs lost in a haze. Her eyes were dark holes. There was something weary in her expression, as though corporeality had cost her a great deal.

For the first time, I understood why ghosts were antithetical to photography. I was certain that she would never have turned up on film. She was like a column of salt dropped in water—soluble, permeable, mixing with the surrounding matter. The camera would not have been able to perceive her the way I did. Its mechanism was designed to replicate the action of the human eye—precise and objective—rather than the subjective, suggestible mind. I could not tell whether she was beautiful. Her face was too elemental to register inessential qualities like symmetry or shapeliness. Burning eyes. An oval skull. I could not find her mouth among the shadows. Her hair drifted in a wind I did not feel. Then her arm swung in a gesture of entreaty. The intent was unmistakable. A welcome, from one ghost to another.

11

YOU AND I binge-watched crime shows one winter. I had just turned thirteen. D.C. was an unpleasant place that year, a wasteland of icy pavement and billowing wind. Rain fell by the bucketload. Snow carpeted the parked cars. You and I sheltered on the couch, bowl of popcorn at the ready, watching episodes about cops and crime scene investigators. We would argue about whether the D.A. was on the take, which suspect had committed the violent act, whether the unwholesome brother-in-law might be hiding something. Usually these shows dealt with murder, but sometimes they would shift over to rape.

The attack itself was never handled with sensitivity. You would cover my eyes during the worst of it, but I was still able to get the gist. There was always too much exposed flesh, the camera lingering on a T-shirt being ripped off, lacy lingerie tossed to the floor. You used to comment that it was unsettling and exploitative. Invariably, when the assault was over, the victim would dash into the shower. Even as a child, I found this irritating. Everybody knew about DNA. Everybody knew to go to the hospital, where the nurses would get out the rape kit and find all the evidence written on the body. But no—that would have been too simple. If the victim

had behaved logically, the show would have been over in ten minutes. Instead, she would crouch, shivering, in the shower, scrubbing
beneath her fingernails where her attacker's skin cells had collected
when she scratched him. She would shove the sheets into the washing machine. She would burn the clothes she had been wearing. In
the end, it would be up to the police, our heroes, to verify her story
by interviewing witnesses and double-checking alibis.

That was how things struck me back then. But now I know
better.

My first clear memory after the act is of sitting in the tub,
clutching a sea sponge in both hands. A cold sprinkle pattered
my shoulders. There was only one bathroom in the cabin, and
the shower had plainly been tacked on as an afterthought, held
to the wall by a suction cup. That night, there was no hot water.
We had used it up doing dishes earlier. The frigid stream was peppered with flakes of rust. My teeth were chattering. My fingers
were so numb that it was hard to manage the sponge. If someone
had asked me what I was doing, I am not sure what I would have
answered. Some powerful internal instinct had taken over, and all
I could do was obey. Cleanliness. Safety. A rite of purification. A
little more soap.

When I climbed out, my lips were ghost-blue in the mirror. It
looked as though I had aged a hundred years. I stumbled to the
toilet and threw up. I voided dinner, then lunch, then breakfast. I
sank to the floor and vomited until the sides of my stomach banged
together. It felt good to flush that mess away, watching it swirl
down the drain.

I BARELY REMEMBER the days that followed. By morning, I had come down with a roaring fever. I can tell you this much: I was out of my mind.

The Farallon Islands were not designed for illness. Cuts and bruises, yes. Colds, no. There was no medicine in the cabinets. Our stock of aspirin had expired. I was too sick to go foraging anyway. I lay beneath the covers, limp and bewildered. The light through the blinds was a knife in the temple. The others had no sympathy at all. Galen and Forest refused to get anywhere near me. Even Charlene only poked her head in to flash a cheery grin, maintaining a safe distance.

It was Mick who kept me going. Without him, I probably would have died of malnutrition, dehydration, and loneliness. But he was tireless in his compassion. He came rushing to my aid, toting crackers and soup. He laid his calloused hand on my forehead and assured me that I would be better in no time.

For three days, I did not leave my room. Part of this was the illness—I was almost too weak to stand—but the greater part was Andrew. He had not varied his routine one bit. He was everywhere. He was always in the cabin. I heard him typing. I heard him in his bedroom right below me, humming as he flipped through a book. I heard him in the kitchen laughing with the others. If anything, his spirits seemed lightened.

I cannot explain what it was like to be so close to him. I might as well have been a rabbit trapped in a burrow. All the runs leading straight into the fox's mouth. The fear was overwhelming. Even Mick noticed something amiss. A window would bang shut in another room, and I would jump out of my skin. The only solution

I could come up with was to hide. For those three days, I did not shower. I did not even visit the bathroom. Instead, I made use of the old, dusty bottles and jars that had been scattered around my bedroom for decades. I would fill a glass container with amber liquid, which Mick, believe it or not, obligingly disposed of.

Looking back, I must conclude that Mick was raised by women, rather than men. A pack of three sisters, perhaps. A single mother, maybe. Somebody had taught him the kind of benevolent unselfishness that most women are schooled, in childhood, to offer unquestioningly—and few men ever attain. Throughout my illness, Mick was unflinchingly heroic. He sat on the end of the bed and watched me, making sure I ate my soup. He told me silly jokes to keep my spirits up.

On the third day, my fever spiked. Mick stayed close, bathing my brow with a cool washcloth and wrestling the covers back onto the bed whenever I threw them off. After a while I grew delirious. I shuddered and wept. I told him that I was scared. I said it over and over: *I'm scared, I'm scared.* It seemed vital that he understand this simple fact, yet I could not be sure I was making myself clear. Mick hurried out to soak the washcloth in cool water again. He stroked my hair. He told me that anyone who tried to hurt me would have to go through him first.

"I'll deal with it," he said. "Don't worry, Mel. I'll handle it."

ON THE THIRD night, I ran away. Mick had left me alone, tucking me in and heading off to do a bit of note-taking in the daily log. I lay beneath the quilt, staring out the window in a daze. Throughout my illness, I had continually lost time. It reminded me of the aftermath of your funeral—days torn from the calendar. I would blink and find that an hour had gone by. I would inhale and exhale, and in that instant, the sky would darken. Now I watched the clouds billowing across the horizon, moving with the speed of stop-motion video. The wind brushed the glass.

And then I heard it. A moan. A squeal of bedsprings. A gusty sigh. Andrew and Lucy were having sex downstairs.

I limped down the hall to the bathroom. I leaned over the toilet, attempting to throw up again, but nothing happened. I shuffled back to my room. I was weak enough that even this little jaunt exhausted me. Still, without pause, I bundled myself up under half a dozen sweaters. I hummed under my breath to block out any ambient sounds that might drift up through the floorboards. Gripping the banister, I descended the stairs. I left the cabin through the front door.

Even at the time, I was aware that this was a terrible idea. We all had been warned so many times. It was easy to get turned around at night on Southeast Farallon. The cabin and the coast guard house were not useful landmarks—dark shapes against a dark sky. The swiveling beam of the lighthouse was inconstant, disorienting. The roar of the sea came undistinguished from every point of the compass. There was no paved path. Many of the biologists had been injured, dislocating a knee or fracturing a wrist. I myself had been gutted by a sharp stone, and that was in broad daylight. I still bore the scar. Once, an intern had become so befuddled that he had spent an entire night hunched beside a boulder, unable to locate the cabin again, unwilling to imperil himself further by abandoning the meager shelter he had found. He had nearly succumbed to hypothermia before Galen discovered him the next morning.

And, of course, there were people who had disappeared. In the old days, when the eggers and pirates had overrun the islands, one or two men had vanished every season. They would go for a walk and were never seen again.

After a few minutes, I started shivering. There was a mist in the air, collecting against my skin like gauze. The moon was bright that night, bathing the flat surfaces in a blue glow. I thought I saw a figure ahead of me. It seemed to be moving toward the coast guard house. I squinted, my heart beginning to pound. But the shape melted away. There was no one else on the grounds. The fog often played tricks like this on the mind, tangling the moonlight in bright pockets, coating the air in planes of iridescent sheen.

During my time on the islands, I had, for the most part, ignored the coast guard house, as everyone did. Though it stood only a hundred feet from the cabin, a duplicate of our own home, we all left it alone, treating it like an optical illusion—a mirage in the desert, to be seen but not touched. Mick had told me that it wasn't safe to try the porch steps of this ancient structure, let alone go inside. The floorboards would be rotten after so many years. Even the animals gave the place a wide berth. During the summer months, the gulls nested all over the islands, pitching camp on any free inch of grass. But they did not attempt to penetrate the coast guard house. Only the bats were bold enough to claim those empty rooms and eerie silences for their own.

Now I pushed the door open with a groan of hinges. The floor was spongy beneath my feet. My arrival disturbed the bats, who launched themselves into flight, filling the air with their frenetic wingbeats. The rooms were clean of furniture. A crumpled piece of fabric lay on the floor. It looked a bit like one of Forest's ratty undershirts. The air had a stale quality, like the interior of a cave. I shut the door behind me. At once, I felt better. There is something fundamental in the desire to have a door to close, sealing out the rest of the world.

The exertion of my brief walk had left me dizzy. I was seeing spots. I sat down cross-legged. A bat flitted past my cheek. There were hundreds of them. Maybe thousands. I could not quite see them—gray on black—but I could feel their bustle and flutter. They whirled like an indoor tornado. A swollen moon dangled above the horizon. The beam of the lighthouse swept across the sea. I listened to the pounding of the waves. I smelled mildew and rot. Nature was reclaiming the coast guard house. Mice and insects were in the process of destroying it.

There was a sound. I could not identify it—somewhere between a violin and a siren. It reverberated around the room, then dissipated. It reminded me of something, but I did not have time to consider the matter. The energy of the bats was increasing. They were moving fast, rocketing past my body, clipping me with their wings, brushing my cheek. They touched me over and over.

The bats began to rise. It happened all at once, as though they had received a command. I could see them spiraling upward in a column of smoky gray. Their wings shook the air. Everything seemed to be vibrating. My mouth was open. My palms burned. I watched the flock pour out through a broken window. Their numbers were enough to blacken the stars. They erased the moon.

Then I heard the sound again. A call. A keening.

It was the whales. This time I recognized their music. The breeze came through the window, battering my hair out of my face. The bats swirled inside the gust. I could not get my bearings. I could not catch my breath. The harmony grew louder and louder until it thundered in my ears. The coast guard house seemed to be moving around me, or else I was moving inside it. For a moment I thought I was underwater. I screamed. My voice was lost in the song. I could feel the waves crashing over me—or the wind—or the bats. I thought the whales were there too. Something was surging in the darkness, sending out pulses of noise and motion. Massive bodies rolling in the tide. Their flippers disarranging the swell of the surf, knocking me off balance. Their tails scooping holes in the material of the world. They were coming for me. Their music made my body tremble, struck like a tuning fork. The sound was mournful and otherworldly, almost human, like a cry of pleasure or pain.

I must have dozed off. Maybe I fainted. When I came to, the coast guard house was empty and dark. In the stillness, I was alone.

12

I MIGHT EVENTUALLY HAVE made a more concerted break for freedom. I might have pushed the rowboat out on my own and headed for the mainland. (The *Janus* would have been smarter, but I could never have started that motor without aid.) I might have told someone what had happened. I might have told Mick, however daunting it would be, stepping into the bright glare of a spotlight, all my wounds exposed. I might have smashed Andrew's head in with a rock. I might have leapt from my bedroom window, like a dewy chick tumbling from the cliff's edge, not yet able to fly.

But on the morning of the fourth day, everything changed.

The sun was high when I awoke. Dimly, I was aware of some kind of disturbance. For a moment I thought I was still in the coast guard house—but no, during the night I had made it back somehow. My fever was undiminished. Sweating beneath the blankets, I slid in and out of a hot, honey-colored dream. A persistent banging roused me. Someone was hammering on my bedroom door.

"Get up!" Mick shouted. "Galen wants all hands on deck."

"I'm too sick," I called back.

The door flew open, and Mick strode into the room. He looked even larger than usual today, his girth increased by a heavy vest.

"Get up," he said. "We need you."

He gazed down at me for a moment. Then he yanked the covers away. I shrieked as he hefted me out of bed. Boots were shoved over my pajamas. He tugged a sweater onto my torso. Before I could gather my wits, he had frog-marched me out of the room and down the stairs. My heart was thumping so wildly that I thought I might pass out. A shape flicked by—I almost screamed—but it was only Charlene, wrapping a scarf around her neck as she raced out the front door. Her expression was grave.

"What's going on?" I said.

"Something at Sea Pigeon Gulch," Mick said. "I don't know what. I just heard Galen yelling. Something bad."

Out on the slope, I felt like an overstimulated newborn, startled by the most ordinary things. The sun was too big and bright. The wind was a bucket of ice water, upended over my head. Mick kept his arm looped through mine, preventing me from bolting. In the distance, I saw the coast guard house bobbing along as I stumbled forward. Maybe I could head back there now, shut the door behind me, and never come out again.

A group was gathered at the water's edge. Sea Pigeon Gulch was a tiny inlet, a crevice with high, granite walls. The sun never shone into that cold gorge. My heart was now pounding hard enough that it interfered with my vision. At the crescendo of each beat, the world danced a little.

Mick picked up the pace, frowning. Forest turned and grimaced at us. He lifted a hand. It was a strange, indeterminate gesture, as though he were waving us away and summoning us onward simultaneously.

"I'm not sure you should—" he called, then paused. "It might be better for you to . . . Or else maybe . . ."

I was surprised; I had never seen him at a loss for words before. After a moment, he turned helplessly to Galen.

"Let them come," Galen said.

Mick broke into a run. He let go of my hand. In his wake, I lost my balance and stumbled. Lucy was on her knees, rocking back and forth. As I watched, she gave a high-pitched, inhuman sound, an ambulance's wail. Charlene crouched beside her, but Lucy batted away her embrace. Charlene, too, was wiping away tears.

"Oh, no," Mick said, gazing into the gorge. "Oh, man."

I moved forward slowly. It was an odd sensation. I did not seem to be walking, but rather drifting on a current, carried inexorably toward the shore. Galen stepped aside to let me pass. The stone opened outward in a jagged vee. Inside, the sea was dark and frothy, sucking at the walls.

There was someone in the water. Facedown. The waves jiggled him from side to side, his arms and fingers bobbing on the wash. I stared for a while, making sure. I knew that rangy frame all too well, the marble skin, the broad shoulders. He had been in the water long enough that he did not look completely human anymore. He might have been a clever simulacrum—a blow-up doll or a crash-test dummy. His blond hair was disfigured by dirt and blood. For once, he was not wearing his red stocking cap. Squinting closer, I saw a nasty wound on the back of his skull. His pants were torn. His ankle looked swollen. Andrew wore only one shoe.

13

I SOMETIMES WONDER HOW much about you I really remember. I have held on to what I can, of course, over the years. There was the day you and I had a picnic on the National Mall. I remember the heat of that golden afternoon, the glare on the dry grass, the drone of honeybees. There was the evening you and Dad got into such a terrible fight that it woke me up. I remember creeping down the hallway in my nightgown, trembling with cold and nerves, listening to your voices in the kitchen. You lost your temper to such an extent that you hurled a tomato across the room, leaving a splotch on the paint (scary at the time, hilarious in retrospect). There was the morning I found a rabbit in the backyard, its throat worried and bloody. For the next few hours, you and I worked in vain to save it, bent over its small form like doctors in the ER. I remember the day you spilled coffee down a brand-new skirt and cried. I remember the evening you and I made a mobile out of rainbow pipe cleaners. I remember events. I remember stories, since they can be told and retold, memorized like poetry for a recital.

And yet a great deal has been lost. Nowadays, I can't call up the exact timbre of your voice. I am not sure whether your eyes were hazel or unmottled green. Was it you who liked to take the time to give yourself a full pedicure, separating each toe with a roll of cotton and applying several meticulous coats? Or was that a character from a TV show? Was it you who watched the presidential debates before each election with a beady eye, hunched in front of the television, hollering out your own questions and rebuttals? Or am I remembering the mother of a friend? I have lost so many details. Whether you wore earrings. Whether you were afraid of spiders. Whether you had inside jokes from childhood with your twin sisters. Many things are gone forever. If time is a river, these are the memories that have slipped to the bottom, too heavy to be carried on the current any longer—tumbled in the dirt, hidden in the silt.

I even wonder what parts of your personality I may have fabricated. It was all so long ago. Surely, some of what I recall must be my own creation. Maybe you didn't spill coffee on an expensive new skirt and burst into tears in the middle of the street. That recollection might have come from a nightmare; it does have a lurid, dreamlike quality in my mind. Perhaps we never found an injured rabbit in our backyard. Come to think of it, that does sound like the plot of a short story I once read.

Each time we remember something, we change it. This is the nature of the brain. I imagine my recollections like rooms in a house. I can't help but alter things when I step inside—tracking mud on the floor, moving furniture out of alignment, kicking up swirls of dust. Over time, these small alterations add up.

Photographs speed this undoing. My work is the enemy of memory. People often imagine that taking pictures will help them recall exactly what happened. In fact, the opposite is true. I have learned to leave my camera in the drawer at important events, since snapshots have a way of superseding my recollections. I can either have the impression in my brain or the image in my hand—not both.

To remember is to rewrite. To photograph is to replace. The only reliable memories, I suppose, are the ones that have been forgotten. They are the dark rooms of the mind. Unopened, untouched, and uncorrupted.

One thing I am sure of—one thing I *do* remember—is that you believed in God. I am as certain of that as I am of anything. You and Dad used to debate the matter, working yourselves up into a lather of erudite references and philosophical rhetoric. My father was (and is) a devout agnostic. He stands firm in the conviction that he doesn't know everything and never will. You, on the other hand, went to church every Sunday. I remember the long, sleepy mornings I spent at your side, watching the light shift through the stained glass. I remember those uncomfortable patent leather shoes. The rise and fall of the minister's voice. The pungent odor of floor wax. I remember the look on your face during services—elated, confident, as radiant as a bride. You would follow every word of the sermon, nodding in agreement like a student in class. You sang the hymns with gusto, your voice sweet but out of tune.

Church was coal for the furnace of your mind. You would spend the rest of every Sunday mulling over higher matters. All three of us would head home and settle in the living room. Dad reading the newspaper. Me perusing the comics section. You chewing on your pencil, thinking and thinking and thinking.

Back then, it bothered me that I did not share your conviction. I could not revel along with you. You prayed often, sitting with your face turned toward the sun, eyes closed. When Aunt Janine was having trouble at work, you gave her a gold cross on a necklace to support and sustain her. I remember hearing you on the phone with Aunt Kim, urging her to have faith. You offered me the same advice when things were not going well at school. It gave me a squirmy feeling.

Even then, I was in my father's camp all the way. The Bible stories were silly. Sunday school was a bore. The sermons contradicted each other. Sitting in the quiet, sun-drenched church, I felt nothing, no power, no release. The hymns left my soul unmoved. In short, I have never believed in God.

That is, until Andrew.

NOW, LOOKING BACK, I can tell you what I felt that day. At the time, standing at the edge of Sea Pigeon Gulch, it was just a rush of emotion, like a bonfire on a frozen winter night, almost too much relief. I took one last glance at Andrew's pale, swollen figure, and then I turned away. Every step on the packed ground felt like a revelation. Every gust of wind was a sweet caress. Galen and Mick were with me. Someone's arm was linked through mine in a steadying manner. I remember seeing Forest's silhouette on the landscape ahead, hurrying toward the cabin. The sun touched the high clouds with light. A seabird winged by, braying noisily. Somewhere in the background, Lucy was sobbing. Charlene was supporting her, murmuring to her.

In that moment, I may well have been converted. It was enough to make a person believe. There seemed to be no other explanation. Andrew had been a foul thing, a wicked creature, and so God had erased him, exactly as I myself might have removed a blot from a sheet of clean, white paper.

14

THE POLICE CAME. I suppose I shouldn't have been surprised, and yet I was. After four months of isolation, I had come to think of the islands as an impenetrable fortress. Only Captain Joe was intrepid enough to find us on a map, let alone make the arduous journey to our shores. I had lost touch with the simple fact that California was only thirty miles away. All it took to attract the attention of the civilized world was a call on the radiophone. At once, a helicopter was dispatched to our location.

I was in my bedroom—Mick had deposited me there—when I saw a wisp of movement, a shadow on the glittering sea. The helicopter crossed the horizon. Downstairs, the biologists were coming and going, voices raised, doors slamming. I remained unconcerned. I perched there in a pleasant dream.

Andrew's body was still in the water. None of us could have reached it, even if we had wanted to. The tide was coming in. From a police standpoint, this was fortunate. Andrew's corpse would be pushed toward shore; he might bang himself up on the rocks, but at least he would not be carried out to sea before anyone could get to him. In truth, he had chosen an ideal time and place to drown. A few hours later—a different gorge—and the marine life would have made short work of him. His remains might never have been discovered.

My flu was gone. It had been carried away as rapidly and finally as a fetid odor on the breeze. The fever had broken. The headache had disappeared. Only a residual weakness remained, a tremor in my extremities. I was now ravenous. For three days, I had imbibed nothing but clear fluids. Yet it seemed indelicate to raid the kitchen at this juncture, stuffing my face with crackers and canned fruit as Andrew's body floated in the surf and Lucy lay in her bedroom. I could hear her crying. Sometimes it was sobs, like a kitten mewing, and sometimes it was deep, wracking breaths, like a woman in labor. From what I gathered, Mick and Charlene were in there with her, making futile attempts to soothe her pain with stale cookies and hot tea.

Beyond the window, Galen and Forest appeared, striding together up the hill. As I watched, they stationed themselves by the helipad to wait. The helicopter was closer now. It moved with startling speed, the whirl of the blades disturbing the sea beneath. There was the suggestion of a dragonfly about its contours. It breached our perimeter, whizzing along the shoreline, casting its shadow on the grass. I saw a trickle of movement amid the green: mice bolting in panic. That glowing bubble maneuvered downward. It alighted in the center of the rectangle of pavement.

Figures began to emerge from inside. The metallic husk disgorged them one at a time, each ducking low, apparently to avoid the blades, though these were at least ten feet off the ground. The rotor slowed, spinning lazily, sending out pulses of breath that shook the grass. I had been expecting blue uniforms, but the policemen were in plain clothes. Galen and Forest hurried forward. There was a round of handshakes. I watched as the group collected by Sea Pigeon Gulch.

There were two officers, plus a doctor, distinguishable by his silver kit. Galen and Forest lingered outside this knot of official-dom. The policemen were plainly having trouble figuring out how to get Andrew onto dry land. He could not be reached by boat; there was nothing on the islands that could maneuver into that narrow inlet. Nor would it be safe for a diver to attempt it; the tide was too strong. The policemen adopted thoughtful poses, stroking their chins and rumpling their hair. It reminded me of the way men would gather around a car that had stalled on the road.

Eventually the group came up with a complicated solution— something to do with ropes and a surfboard. At first I watched the proceedings eagerly. Forest and Galen had taken charge, giving instructions with sweeping gestures. The policemen hurried to obey. The doctor stood to one side, visibly fretting, checking his watch every few minutes. The surfboard was lowered down on a system of rigging. Everyone was working together, shouting encourage-ment. But it was hard going. From what I could tell, they were trying to work the surfboard under Andrew's limp form and hoist him upward. This required timing their industry with the surging tide and shifting waves. After their fifth failed attempt, I left the window. I lay down on the bed.

Hours later, Charlene woke me.

"Dinnertime," she said softly, leaning in at my door.

I sat up, yawning. Through the window, the sky had turned a muted gold, the sun low above the horizon. The helicopter was still in evidence, its bulbous belly refracting the light. The ground was shadowed, the coast guard house a dark, rectangular stain. It seemed remarkable that I had once felt the need to escape to that hulking relic. Now that the fear was gone, the threat removed, I could chastise myself for my carelessness. I was lucky to have escaped with nothing more than a chill.

"How are you feeling?" Charlene asked as we headed down the stairs.

"Great," I said. "Fine," I amended, catching her startled look.

The meal was an odd one. The police ate with us, as did the medical examiner, whose name appeared to be Dr. Alfred. None of them were delighted by our repast of macaroni and cheese with canned tuna mixed in. They picked at their plates, peering around the kitchen at the mismatched chairs, chipped cups, and warped utensils, all of which—to me—brought back amiable echoes of dorm life. Mick ate heartily, shoveling pasta into his mouth. I consumed at least twice my share. Forest and Galen engaged in polite conversation with our visitors. Charlene seemed anxious, her dark eyes wider than usual, a deer in the headlights. Lucy was not there.

Gradually I became aware that the two policemen were not policemen at all—they were federal agents. The islands were a refuge with congressionally designated wilderness status. Accordingly, the place fell under the jurisdiction of the men in black. This intrigued me. I had never been around government agents, and I would have expected something more polished, less homey. They were a mismatched pair, clearly alpha and beta. The latter was young, with a mousy, ineffectual beard. The former was a tanned, leathery fellow, a lattice of wrinkles scored across his forehead.

By common consent, we did not discuss the matter at hand. Andrew had been disinterred from his watery grave and was now reposing in a refrigerated unit on board the helicopter; that much I had learned from Charlene as we had slipped downstairs together. During the meal, however, we all spoke instead about the San Francisco beat. Galen seemed to know a great deal about the law. (Of course Galen knew a great deal about *everything*.) Mick joined in, and they reminisced about a few cases that had been splashed over the newspapers during the past couple of years.

I was quiet. As I helped myself to more pasta, I wondered for the first time what had actually happened to Andrew. Oddly enough, this question had not occurred to me. I had been so overwhelmed by the shock of my reprieve that the reasons behind it had seemed unimportant.

His corpse had been discovered at eleven a.m., which suggested that he had taken a morning walk. It was unlike him to do so—but stranger things had happened. Perhaps he had headed off to do a little fieldwork for once. He might have been gazing too avidly through his binoculars, not looking where he was going. Nobody had been a witness to the accident, which was hardly surprising. Galen and Forest had been on the water that morning, Mick in the lighthouse, Lucy and Charlene near Breaker Cove. I had been in bed, asleep. It would have been a matter of seconds for Andrew to lose his footing, knock himself unconscious on the rocks, and drop into the drink.

After dinner, the two agents asked us to step into the living room. We distributed ourselves in our usual positions: on the couch, in the armchair, on a few ratty old pillows that were strewn across the rug. Both officers, however, stayed standing. I wondered whether this was intentional; we all had to literally look up at them. Hands on hips, the alpha agent launched into what sounded like a prepared speech, delivered many times before.

"You've all had a trying day," he said. "I'm sorry for your loss. As you can imagine, we need to get as much information as possible before we head back to California. It's our procedure—"

He broke off. A door had opened. I turned to see Lucy emerging from her bedroom. There were purple crescents beneath her eyes. A blanket was wrapped around her shoulders, trailing across the ground.

"Sorry," she murmured. Her gaze lingered on the empty spot on the couch beside me, but after a moment she sank unsteadily to the floor, next to Forest. Her arrival had all the ceremony of a stage entrance. Everyone gaped at her. Even the alpha agent's bureaucratic manner was momentarily derailed. He stood scratching his cheek before continuing, "Galen here—Mr. McNab, I should say— has offered to let us use his bedroom for our interviews. We'll have a bit more privacy there. I'll be asking each of you to—"

Galen interrupted. "Do you have a cause of death?"

"Beg pardon?"

"Cause of *death*."

It was Dr. Alfred who answered. He was settled on a chair in the corner, and he looked up from his clipboard. "Drowning. Foam in the lungs. Petechial hemorrhaging. No question."

Lucy gave a barely visible shudder. I saw Forest reach toward her. Then he thought better of it and withdrew his hand.

"The wound on the head?" Galen asked. "The broken ankle? It was broken, wasn't it?"

"A fall," the doctor said. "That's what it looks like now. I'll find out more at the autopsy."

"There will be an autopsy, then?"

"Oh, yes."

Once again, Lucy shivered. It was a convulsive movement, like a dog shaking off water.

"And the time of death?" Galen asked.

Dr. Alfred glanced at the alpha agent, who gave a barely perceptible nod. The doctor pursed his lips and said, "Between midnight and two a.m. last night, based on the liver temperature. My best estimate."

In that moment, something happened to me. Even before I'd had time to process his words, I felt the room beginning to pivot. The floorboards swung under my feet. I gasped a little. I could not help it.

Someone was speaking—Forest, asking a technical question. Something else about Andrew's ankle. Mick had his hand raised like a child in school. They were biologists, after all, unfazed by blood and injury, interested only in the mechanisms and specificities of death. They had spent years practicing this habit of mind. Clinical distance. Emotional detachment. Facts, not feelings.

My brain was in a tumble. Andrew had been on the grounds at midnight. I had been on the grounds at eleven p.m. I had lingered

in the coast guard house for at least half an hour. In my wildest
dreams, I had never imagined that my late-night trek could have
had anything to do with Andrew's demise. The two events had
seemed entirely unconnected. I had gone to the coast guard house.
He had gone for a stroll. Naturally, I had imagined a morning stroll
taking place well after dawn.

Now my breath came strangely, stifled in my chest. When I
had departed the cabin last night, during the witching hour, I had
been aware that I was putting myself in a certain amount of jeop-
ardy. I had been willing to risk losing my way, exacerbating my
flu, even wrenching my bad ankle. Evidently, however, it had been
a greater gamble than I knew. In a million years, I would never
have risked seeing Andrew alone. We had been ships in the night,
missing one another by minutes. My nausea returned, and for a
moment it seemed likely that I would vomit on the beta agent's
shoes. But I controlled myself. I took a deep breath and sat up
straight again.

"—definitely broken," Dr. Alfred was saying. "The right tibia.
It happened antemortem, but just barely. I would say the bone was
fractured a few minutes before death. That would be consistent
with a fall."

"He had some scratches," Forest volunteered. "What does that
mean?"

"Oh, drowning victims usually do," the doctor said. "The body
floats facedown, and the arms are dragged over the bottom. It's
common to see many kinds of wounds. Those would be inflicted
after death."

At this point, the alpha agent cleared his throat.

"As I said," he announced, "we've got to head back to the mainland soon. No time to waste. This is a bit unorthodox, you understand. Normally we'd do things differently. But here, on the islands—" He sucked in a breath, looking around with a pained expression. "We'll be asking each of you to come up in turn." He indicated Lucy, who was sitting with a blanket clutched around her shoulders. "Ms. Crayle, I guess we'll start with you."

OUTSIDE, THE SKY darkened by degrees. The clock ticked in the corner. A breeze rattled the panes and set the front door to rocking in an arrhythmic rattle. Ordinarily, we would have been preparing for bed now. There would have been the usual squabble over who would have the first shower before the hot water ran out completely. Forest might accuse Mick of swiping his toothpaste. Galen might settle himself at the kitchen table, chin on fist, flipping through the tidal chart.

Tonight, however, we remained cloistered in the living room. The mood was both listless and tense. The rumor of voices filtered through the ceiling. Normally, I was sure, the federal agents would have had hours, even days, in which to collect information. Normally they would not dine with their witnesses, then take statements in somebody's bedroom. But the islands, as usual, had made everything more difficult. Time was precious; space was limited. The agents could not urge us all to stop by their offices when we were feeling a bit calmer. They could not plan to return for a chat.

Unless they felt like commandeering the helicopter again—unless we felt like spending twelve hours on board the ferry, there and back—this had to be done now.

The tension affected everyone differently. Any conversation that might have arisen between us was constrained by the presence of the doctor, who had remained in his corner, scribbling away on his clipboard. Mick was at the window, peering out at the sunset. Charlene was on the floor, slumped against the wall, as pale as I had ever seen her. Her freckles stood out like chips of sand caught in ice. She had not said a word since dinner. Forest, on the other hand, was frenzied. He was pacing like an expectant father. His movements were so rapid that I kept thinking he would barge straight into the wall. Instead, he pivoted on his heel. I had never been able to get a handle on Forest. Clearly he was in the grip of some strong emotion, but whether it was anxiety, or anger, or ghoulish enjoyment, I could not tell.

In the past, I had always assumed that there were only two mental states: waking and dreaming. The former was conscious, logical, and sane. The latter was chaotic and bizarre. I had never confused the two before. But in recent days, I seemed to have stumbled on a third state of being: a twilight haze, somewhere in between. In this half-lit realm, everything around me looked and felt like the reality I had always known. The ocean and sky still met in a precise line. Gravity functioned. The laws of daily life continued unabated. And yet monsters walked abroad. Rape, drowning, Andrew himself—these things belonged in the land of nightmares. Waking and dreaming were no longer distinct. Now the moon, the cabin, and

Mick at the window were all happy reminders of the wide-awake world. But the federal agents, the helicopter, and Andrew's dead body had sprung out of a bad dream.

After a while, Galen got to his feet. He shot me a searching glance, which I pretended not to notice. He wandered over to Dr. Alfred.

"Well," he said. "You're definitely doing an autopsy, then?"

"Oh yes," the doctor said.

"I must say, I don't see why. It seems like a clear-cut case of accidental death to me."

Dr. Alfred set his pencil aside with an impatient gesture. "These things can be interpreted many different ways. We never want to rush to judgment."

"There's only one interpretation here, surely," Galen said.

"In layman's terms—" Dr. Alfred began.

At that moment, there was a clatter on the stairs. Lucy was descending. She had divested herself of her blanket, and without that sweeping cape, she looked smaller than usual. Normally there was a solidity about her hips, but now her frame seemed to have shrunk like a doll left in the wash. She kept her head bowed, her hair falling in her face, and slipped into her bedroom without speaking to any of us.

"Mr. Audino?" called a voice from upstairs.

"That's me," Mick said. "Jesus, this is awful."

The rest of the evening passed that way. One by one, we were summoned. The use of everyone's last names lent a formality to the proceedings. Mick came down after a few minutes. He shot me a consoling wink, then he picked up a book and began to read. Forest was called up next—Mr. Cohen, I should say. A few moments afterward, Charlene was sent for—Ms. Westerman, that is.

I got to my feet and went to the window. Lighthouse Hill stood against a watercolor sky. A few boulders were silhouetted, spills of ink. Two seabirds were calling in harsh voices, back and forth, like a married couple engaging in a well-rehearsed spat. The sea roared. The clock ticked like thunder. The doctor was dozing, his chin sunk onto his chest. His glasses were sliding down his nose, millimeter by millimeter. I wondered whether it was worth it to wake him or whether I should let the inevitable happen and hope the fall didn't break the fragile frame.

Soon Galen succumbed to habit. At the table, he got out a small green notebook. Murmuring to himself, he made some notes. Mick went up to bed. Forest went with him. I heard feet in the corridor. There was a whooshing in the pipes—teeth cleaned, toilet flushed. They shared a room at the end of the hallway, and for a while there was shuffling and banging in there. Then two bunks squealed audibly.

But I was wide awake. I lifted a hand and touched the window, as cold and slick as a sheet of ice. In the distance, a seabird gave one last cry, the final word in the argument. I barely noticed when Charlene came back downstairs, sniffling a bit, and disappeared into her bedroom beside the front door.

I was thinking about the whales. Mick had recently told me an interesting fact. Humpbacks are known for their family life. They play games with their calves, make lasting mates, follow one strong leader, and sing without cessation. They stick together. But over the years, whalers noticed something odd. (Mick can't say the word *whalers* without grimacing. He knows a lot about them. Too much.) Whenever a humpback was harpooned, its pod would swim off and leave it. For a time, the sailors believed that humpbacks were incapable of affection. The animals smelled blood in the water, heard cries of pain, and did not stay to render aid or comfort.

Yet the truth was more complicated. Human beings are visual creatures. The whalers imagined that because they couldn't see the pod anymore, the wounded animal had been abandoned for good. But Mick knows better. Whales are tactile, auditory, alive to sonar and magnetism. The harpooned creature would be pulled away, salting the sea with its blood. As it was dragged into shallow water, where the worst of fates awaited it, its pod would keep pace nearby—staying deep, out of sight of the sailors—and sing to it. They would sing until the very end.

"Excuse me," someone said.

I spun around. The beta agent was standing behind me, hand outstretched, as though about to tap my shoulder. He had plainly been trying to get my attention for some time.

"We're ready for you now," he said. "Ms.—I'm sorry—"

He fumbled for the clipboard in his hand, running his finger down a list. I sighed. No one on the islands seemed able to keep track of my identity.

"Her name is Miranda," Galen said.

His voice was quiet but firm, carrying from the table where he sat. I looked at him in consternation. It had been a while since I had heard my real name. I almost didn't recognize it. At the expression on my face, Galen smiled.

"Wonderful," he said. "Worthy of admiration."

"What?" I said.

"Miranda," he said. "That's what it means."

15

YOU MIGHT BE surprised to hear that I still find joy in the islands. In truth, I love this place as I have never loved anything else. (Except for you, of course.) Every morning, I climb out of bed and smile involuntarily at the view. The landscape is a charcoal drawing, varying from smudgy black to ash gray. The tumbled shoreline. The granite of the nearby islets. The flicker and dart of the mice. The clouds are gauzy. The sea lions are the hue of slate. Distant whales pass by like metallic submarines. It is a colorless world, yet I find it as beautiful as a rainbow. My affection for the islands has only deepened in the past few weeks. I have come to see the archipelago as more than eerie, more than wild. It is a nurturing, protective place.

I have felt this way since the night Andrew assaulted me. My alleged friends and companions were nowhere to be found then. No one defended me. Galen drank himself into a blackout state. Charlene put on headphones and stopped listening. Mick and Forest left the premises, abandoning me completely. And Lucy was asleep. Andrew used to joke about how she went down like a ton of bricks. It would happen suddenly, sometimes midsentence. Her normal whirl of energy used up so much juice that she would remain in a near coma until morning. (Apparently hummingbirds were the same way. During the daylight hours, their wings moved in a blur and their hearts beat several times each second. At night, however, they dropped into a temporary hibernation. Their hearts slowed to one beat per minute.) Lucy the hummingbird slept right through my ordeal.

But the islands were awake. The islands were listening.

I often imagine Andrew's death. In fact, I like imagining it. The islands paid attention when no one else did. They protected me when no one else would. Andrew hurt me, so the islands took care of it. They took him away.

Lately I have been studying the others here. For once, I am the biologist, and they are the specimens. Everyone has reacted differently to Andrew's passing. Mick has grown louder, more jovial. His bonhomie is almost painful in its intensity. Charlene, on the other hand, has withdrawn. She has always been quiet—cowed by the others—but now she has melted into the wallpaper. More than once, I have entered a room, found it empty, settled down with a book, and just about had a heart attack half an hour later when a cough or sigh behind me indicated that Charlene had been there all along. Watching me or lost in thought, I cannot tell.

For his part, Forest has become an automaton. His steely focus has increased by an order of magnitude. It is December, rainy and cold. There are only a few more weeks before the last of the sharks will depart for warmer climes. I have begun to hear Forest's alarm clock going off at three in the morning. Mick, his roommate, will toss and turn, the squeal of bedsprings echoing down the hallway. Even before the sun is up, Forest wants to be in the lighthouse, on call.

And Galen—poor Galen—seems a little lost. For the first time, I can see that he is a man in his sixties, twice the age of anyone else here. He has become absent-minded. Sometimes he seems to be on the verge of asking me a question, but decides against it, averting his gaze. I have come across him wandering around the kitchen, looking everywhere for his reading glasses, unaware that they are perched on his brow. He trails off in the middle of telling stories, staring at me.

If I were a fanciful person, I would say that in those moments, he hears death speaking to him. More than ever before, death is with us on the Farallon Islands. In the past, it was like the sound of the sea caught in a shell's curl—distant, vague, half-imagined. Now, however, death is front and center. It is there at the breakfast table. It appears amid the silences in an everyday conversation. It lingers outside the window in the evenings. Perhaps Galen is distracted by that cloaked figure, barely glimpsed out of the corner of the eye. Another ghost in an already-crowded cabin.

The days are growing shorter. The constellations have pivoted, the autumn shapes dipping beneath the horizon, the winter stars shining with greater urgency. The sea seems different too. The islands sit on the edge of the coastal plateau. To the west, the ocean floor plummets into black depths. Storms blow in now from the deeper water. They do not last long; they are brief, vicious squalls that have stripped our two little trees of leaves. Rain has battered the cabin and soaked the porch. We have all taken to wearing ponchos around even when the sky is clear, just in case.

I am still expecting Lucy to leave. Indeed, I am amazed that she is not gone already—that she did not board the helicopter with the federal agents and flee without a backward glance. But instead she is hard at work. She is on a mission to tag more birds than anyone else on the planet ever has. She does not eat; she barely sleeps. Her hummingbird energy seems perilous now. The mechanism that drives her is clearly working beyond its capacities. I can just about smell the smoke from the overheated gears. Lucy continues, each evening, to scrub and mop the house; I have woken in the night to hear the vacuum cleaner running. She polishes the knives and wipes the countertops as though the grime and dust are the physical manifestations of her own sorrow. By eradicating mold, by making each countertop shine, she might wash her soul clean of suffering, leaving herself burnished and bright.

A FEW DAYS ago, I lay in bed, awake. I had been dreaming about the whales again—their slippery weight, their unearthly song. The sun was rising. My room brimmed with light like a wood stove. I had grown accustomed to perching in the bedroom like a spider on a web, determining where the others might be by the shake of floorboards, the chime of voices. Today there was someone in the kitchen. I caught the scrape of a chair. Someone was making coffee; that earthy odor wafted up the stairs. Forest and Galen were out on the grounds. I could hear them calling to one another.

Getting to my feet, I saw that a slip of paper had been pushed under my door. On one side, my name was printed in block letters. *MELISSA*—my name here. On the other side was written, *Lucy*

Crayle would appreciate your attendance at a memorial service for Andrew Metzger. It will be held at sunset on Friday.

I read it twice. I could imagine Lucy cutting up a sheet of paper; there was a faint pencil mark where she had measured it out. She had evidently made formal invitations for each of us. I was aware that she would not be attending Andrew's real funeral. His family was in Maine, and the trip would be too long, too expensive. This, apparently, was her solution. I stood there for a long while, holding the square of paper, a lump in my throat.

THERE WAS SOME excitement that afternoon. Mick, Forest, and I walked to the Tit—a rotund promontory on the northern shore—to get a look at a pod of gray whales that were frolicking there. The day was chilly. I positioned myself on the plateau with my tripod. The granite seemed especially loose, sliding and crunching beneath my shoes like melting ice. I leaned forward, eye to the viewfinder, and I experienced the mental shift I always feel in those moments— the physical falling away, my sensory organs dimming, aware of nothing but color and exposure and light.

The gray whales were in an obliging mood. There were ten or twelve of them in the group, and they seemed to be playing. I captured a flash of baleen slats, glistening inside a wide mouth. I caught an image of several tails cresting together, flinging a tsunami of droplets upward. The animals lived up to their name, deep gray, patched with white like a cloudy sky. For the first time, I was able to get what I wanted from the whales on film. The size of them.

Their breath climbing in columns of steam. Their enormous flippers. Their elegance. Their mystery.

Mick and Forest were standing by the water's edge. From what I could tell, they were arguing. Mick had the daily log in his hands. Forest had been deputized as his assistant and note-taker. This was the way of things on the islands. No one ever had time off. All the biologists had seasons in which they could focus on their areas of expertise (when their animals ruled the roost) and seasons when they were required to help the others (when their animals were absent). During the summer, Forest, the shark specialist, had been in command. He and Galen had given orders, and everyone else had jumped to obey. But autumn had brought the whales, and winter would give way to Seal Season, which would be followed by Bird Season. Each biologist had a moment in the sun. This was Mick's time to shine.

Just then, one of the gray whales decided to "spy-hop." It was a behavior Mick had described to me, but one I hadn't expected to see in person. The creature poked his monstrous head out of the water. He rose vertically, perhaps ten feet in the air. Then he began to rotate. He pivoted on the spot like a barber pole. Camera in hand, I clicked gleefully away. I knew what he was doing—scouting the surrounding area—but there was such beauty and strangeness in the action that for a moment I felt that he was dancing for me. He was performing for the camera.

I heard a shout. Mick was waving in my direction. Forest appeared to be injured; he was bent double, holding his calf and grimacing.

"What happened?" I cried.

"He lost his balance," Mick said. "He wasn't listening to me."

"Don't start," Forest said.

I hurried over, my camera bouncing on my chest. Forest's pant leg was stained crimson. He had left smudges on the rocks, marking his path in blood.

Mick and I organized ourselves into makeshift crutches, one on either side of him. With my arm around Forest's waist, I could feel his thinness. He was a surfboard of a man. His ropy musculature flexed beneath my fingers. His ribs were iron bars. He limped and winced, and we steadied him all the way home.

Back at the cabin, Mick stitched him up. First a shot of anesthetic, then the needle and thread. I knew the drill now. It had been the same for me. Forest sat at the table, reading a book, leg extended, as Mick worked away with reading glasses perched on his nose. Forest turned a page. Mick sewed in silence. I could not tell if Forest was genuinely uninterested in the progress of his injury—so accustomed to wounds, to stitches and scars, that he could not be bothered to attend—or whether he was keeping his mind occupied out of a dislike of syringes and blood.

I myself felt oddly detached. The sight of that pulpy gash, the trickle of red—I found these things engaging, rather than upsetting. I was glad to see Forest injured. Hurt, not killed. Already beginning to heal. He'd been dinged—Mick's phrase. The islands were dangerous, but they did not have to be deadly.

At last Mick leaned forward and severed the thread with his teeth.

"Done."

"Thanks," Forest said.

He glanced down at his wound. He flexed his ankle, teeth bared in discomfort.

This is how we know we're alive, I guess: we continue to feel pain.

16

YOUR DEATH MADE me into a nature photographer.

I was always going to be an artist. There was never any question about that. I need to take pictures of the world around me the way a whale needs to come up for air. For as long as I can remember, I have been driven by beauty. I am talented; I don't mind saying it. Photography was a given. Nature was the wild card.

If I were a different sort of person, I could have made my bones on babies and anniversaries. I could have been a wedding photographer or a portraitist. I would have been happy enough. Beauty is in the eye of the beholder, after all. The camera is nothing more than an eye that records what it sees. I could have found beauty in an ordinary life. I could have settled down. I could have had stillness and permanence. I could have mined art out of the raw ore of the visible realm.

But you died. That changed everything. Your death sent me skimming over the planet like a rock across a pond. A nomad. A lost soul.

For most of my life, I have been interested in the journey, rather than any particular destination. I never cared where I ended up as long as it was somewhere new. I like feeling rootless. I like airplanes and buses. I like waking up without being certain where I am. I like owning next to nothing. Six cameras (now five). A light meter. A tripod. A changing bag. A couple pairs of jeans. Nothing more.

I have enjoyed what travel does to my mind, too. My mental baggage is as spare and well-organized as my suitcase. I don't have romantic relationships, only brief, incandescent trysts. I don't have friends, only coworkers. Every new connection has come with a built-in expiration date. This is fine with me.

After all, I have you. You know me better than anyone else ever could. While you were alive, I loved you as passionately as a daughter can love a mother. Ever since your death, I have written to you ceaselessly. I have told you everything. I have left nothing out. I have had no desire to bond with the people around me—braving those awkward getting-to-know you sessions, figuring out the equilibrium of the relationship, calibrating the level of intelligence and compassion on both sides, stumbling toward shared experiences, whispering secrets, getting attached. I have never had to bother with all that. Not when I could write to you instead.

Your death taught me what happens after love. I have no interest in reencountering that depth of loss.

So I have moved and moved again. I have moved here.

I FOUND MYSELF considering this matter today during a conversation with Mick.

I had planned to lounge around the cabin, reading and napping at intervals. Sleep and I are renewing our relationship with open arms. Any horizontal surface seems to whisper to me, enticing me to lie down and rest for a minute, or maybe an hour. Time is still fluid for me, hard to keep track of, but it is getting better, clearer.

Mick, however, had plans. I was stretched out on the couch, book in lap, when he approached. I was feeling a bit nauseous, probably due to the food. As usual, we had been noshing on snacks of dubious origin and date. The previous night's dinner had been canned chickpeas and Spam, with canned mushrooms thrown in for good measure. The radiators were clanking, warming my toes. Dust motes twirled on the air. Somewhere nearby a mouse was gnawing and scratching inside the wall. Mick asked me to accompany him with all the chivalry of a swain requesting a place on his lady love's dance card. I sat up, brushing the hair out of my eyes.

"Yes, please," I said.

He kicked at the carpet. "If I don't get out of this cabin, I'm going to go stark raving mad. Everyone is working. There's a hole in the rowboat. A catastrophe. Galen and Forest are out there fixing it. They've got Charlene with them. And Lucy—she's busy. You've got to come with me. It's got to be you."

I held up a hand.

"Stop trying to convince me," I said. "You've already made the sale."

An hour later, I was shivering beneath my coat. The *Janus* trolled over waves the size and shape of desert dunes. The roll and plunge, the tug of the current, seemed to be doing some damage to my equilibrium. I gripped the bulwark so I would not fall over. Mick was oblivious. A little distance from the cabin had worked like a tonic on his mood. We were heading toward Asia, leaving the

archipelago in our wake. The line of islets had become tiny once
more. It was disconcerting. For the past few months, those shore-
lines had encompassed what felt like the whole world, the borders
of the knowable universe. From this vantage point, however, the
islands looked scrawny, insubstantial, like a row of rubber ducks
in a bathtub.

"Sit by me," Mick shouted. He was settled at the rudder, steer-
ing with a practiced hand. I staggered over and collapsed on the
bench. I wished I had thought to bring a hat. A warm stocking cap
would have helped ward off the chill.

"I don't see any whales," I said.

"They'll be by," he said serenely. Then he did a double-take, his
eyes narrowing. He looked me over, head to toe.

"What?" I said.

"Mel," he said slowly. "You didn't bring your camera."

I groped for the strap that I habitually wore around my neck
like a favorite locket. I had transported six cameras to the Farallon
Islands in all. One had perished, of course. Dead and gone and
buried. During any given week, I would rotate through the five that
remained, depending on my mood, depending on the circumstances.
Jewel, for instance, was a large-format camera. To use it, I had to
first lug massive, heavy equipment over the rocks—my tripod, my
light-tight film boxes, my changing bag, my light meter. Each shot
required preparation. I would duck under the dark cloak. The rest
of the world would fall away, sounds muffled, erased by the cloth. I
would breathe in the musty air. For a moment, only the image and
I would exist—a glimmering rectangle, the horizon flipped upside

down, a meditation on vision and light. I would never have brought
Jewel onto one of the boats. Normally I would have taken one of
my digital SLR cameras along—Gremlin or Fish Face. But none of
these precious instruments was with me now.

"It's like you're missing an arm," Mick said.

"I feel naked," I cried.

He snickered. "Plus, you might get in trouble. I assume somebody's paying you to be here. They'll be mad that you missed the
whales."

He pivoted the wheel, and we swung to the left, my stomach
lurching. Then he frowned, his brow knotted. I watched what
seemed to be a ponderous internal conversation going on in his
brain.

"What *are* you doing here?" he said.

"You've never asked me that before," I said. "Nobody has,
actually. Except Galen."

"I'm asking you now," Mick said.

His tone was aggressive, almost suspicious. I looked at him in
surprise.

"Fine," I said. "The way it usually works is that I get an assign-
ment. I'll be sent to a specific place to get specific images. I've traveled all over—the mountains, the arctic, the desert. But this time
it was my choice. *I* wanted to come here. Nobody asked me to. I
made it happen myself."

"Fair enough," he said.

"I applied for a grant to do a personal project," I said. "The
islands aren't that expensive. One of the cheapest places I've ever

stayed. I'll have to coast on my savings for some of it. There's a gallery in D.C. where I'll be able to show my photos when I'm done. I'll make the circuit of the usual arts-and-crafts fairs, too. I might even be able to get a book together. I was lucky. I rarely get to stay anywhere this long."

"Bird lice. No hot water. Spam. Lucky mouse girl!"

"This is the beat I wanted," I said, staring at the waves.

Mick nodded. I fell silent. There was more I wanted to say, but I found that I could not quite explain.

Over a year ago, I had first glimpsed an image of the archipelago. On a lazy afternoon, I had stumbled onto a snapshot—and that was all it took. Saddle Rock, silhouetted against the sea. White spray breaking on the cliffs. Islets of bare stone, like the skeleton of some massive sea creature, long extinct. I had gazed at that image, stunned and enthralled. It might have been a photograph of loneliness. The Islands of the Dead—they had taken my breath away.

For the first time, I had been pulled *to* somewhere. In the past, I had craved motion for its own sake. To go *from*. To go elsewhere, anywhere, away. But the call of the islands had been unmistakable. It was magnetic. It was gravitational.

I could not say these things to Mick. In truth, I did not understand it myself. I had to come here. It was that simple. It never felt like a desire or a wish; it was a requirement, a command. I'd begun to do research, and everything I had learned only made me want it more. Mist without end. Blood in the water. Tetchy biologists. A hundred thousand mice. Sea lions birthing their pups on the granite.

Storms like the judgment of a vengeful deity. Shark Season. Boats that had to be lowered into the sea by crane. Mysterious deaths. A lighthouse beacon crying out to an empty ocean. I wanted it all. I was a woman possessed. I was falling in love.

The archipelago was the answer to a question I had not realized I was asking. It was the home I had not known I was looking for, all along.

Now I sighed, remembering how hard I had fought to come here. I had written dozens of letters detailing my love of nature, my résumé, my awareness of how to conduct myself in a marine sanctuary. The biologists who lived on the Farallon Islands had their room and board provided for, as well as their equipment. Nothing more. They took their payment in life experiences and earned no salary. But even their meager government stipend, which kept the cabin's electricity on and paid Captain Joe's fare, did not extend to me. As a photographer, I was not eligible to take part. The powers that be—which I now knew to be Galen—had looked askance at my desire to live among these scientists, interfering with their righteous labor.

So I had pleaded. I had cajoled. Into each envelope, I had stuffed dozens of my photographs—rainforest trees, rare animals, polar ice caps, anything that might help my case. I had explained that I was hoping to document, to observe—not to touch or interfere. Photography, like biology, was fundamentally passive. I had filled out so many forms that I could have papered the walls of my father's house with them. I had done everything but fall to my knees and beg.

At last, after nearly six months, a letter had come in the mail, as lovely as a summer air. It was decorated with Galen's signature. *Your application for residency is approved. I look forward to meeting you in person.*

"There's a market for this kind of work right now," I said. "Endangered species. Vanishing places."

"Poof," Mick said, waving a hand at the islands.

"Global warming," I said. "Climate change. If the ocean rises by about half an inch, they'll be gone."

He nodded. "If it's too late to save them, we might as well get a few photos of them. You're a witness to the end of days."

I leaned back against the railing.

"I showed you mine," I said. "Now show me yours. Why did *you* come here?"

"Ask me no questions and I'll tell you no lies."

I opened my mouth and shut it again. His expression was a closed door.

There was a pause, the boat rising and dipping on the waves. Mick stroked his nose thoughtfully. I found myself admiring anew his thatch of bristling hair, the curved brow, the strong bones of his jaw. He was, without question, a fine specimen of humanity. I could see this now without feeling the smallest inkling of desire for him. The timeline of my life was divided into two distinct periods: Before Andrew and After Andrew. Before Andrew, I had nursed a crush on Mick. After Andrew, everything was different.

Without warning, Mick punched me in the shoulder.

"Ho!" he cried.

Rubbing my arm, I pivoted in my seat.

At first I thought it was not a whale at all. It was gray and slimy, the size of a dinghy. It was floating on the surface. We were far enough away that it did not seem to pose an immediate threat. Its hide was disfigured by scars and bulges, warty lumps of barnacles. For a minute or two, I thought it was dead—a dead elephant, drifting over from Asia on some strange current—but then it reared. The tail came out of the sea, a cleft fly swatter. A wash of droplets fell like rain. The beast exhaled. An orifice in its back opened, coughing steam. The wind carried the cloud toward us. I can honestly say that I have never smelled anything so foul. A row of Porta-Potties standing in the hot sun would not have come close. I clapped a hand over my nose.

Mick chuckled. "What did Queen Victoria say? 'We are not amused'?"

And then the sea was filled with them. In every direction, gray bodies appeared, thrusting upward, burst after burst of spray. The entire pod seemed to come up for breath at the same time. They penetrated the surface any old way, upside down, sideways. Massive fins swiveled. Tails poked upward and sank into the ocean again. For an instant, I wondered if I was dreaming. I had been here before, lost at sea, surrounded by animals the size of houses. Their bellies were scored with deep grooves, ridged like the roof of a mouth. Unlike sharks, they had no dorsal fins, which made it hard to tell which end was up. Their faces were oddly expressionless. No nostrils. No ears. Tiny eyes. Some of the whales were an acceptable size—they might have been the juveniles—while others appeared too huge to be real.

As they rose and sank, they disarranged the organized flow of waves. The humpbacks rolled in the surf, and the boat sloshed back and forth. Everywhere I looked, there was a nose, a blowhole, a rim of tail. The animals had skin that was topographical—scarred, seamed, patched with rocky barnacles. The overall impression was one of a new archipelago in the process of forming.

Mick began to lecture me. This was not unexpected. Over the past months, I had been lectured by everyone; they couldn't help themselves. Diet. Mating habits. Anatomy. Mick was nicer about it than Lucy usually was. He did not make me feel ignorant. I *was* ignorant, of course. But Mick had a way of explaining things as though he was just thinking out loud.

He told me that the humpbacks had the most complex and beautiful songs of all cetaceans. He told me that they named their children, addressing each calf with a specific chord progression. I was scarcely able to listen. So much was happening. A whale yawned— our entire boat could have fit inside that maw—and I saw the bony struts of baleen. It coughed a wet spume, which climbed against the sky. Ten feet high. Twelve feet. Mick told me that the pod navigated hundreds of miles of open sea. Yet the whales did not use sonar, and they did not use the position of the sun—not exclusively, anyway. The earth's magnetic field might have had something to do with it. No one knew exactly how they managed to find their way without landmarks, without any visible oceanic bottom, just the wide, blank blue.

At this point, one of the beasts decided to jump completely out of the water. The snout, then the torso, then the tail rose into the air. It blocked the sun. I screamed. I could not help it. In that moment, I wanted my camera—partly so that I could get it on film, but mostly so that I would have a measure of distance against the fact of such raw wildness. Without that intermediate shield of glass, it was not safe for me to be so close to such things. I had been right on top of untamed animals before—the Sister, with her splintered rows of shimmering teeth, sprang to mind—but despite this physical proximity, I had always had a degree of intellectual remoteness, the keen observer's eye overriding every other concern. I could not feel afraid when I was considering how best to frame the shot. Now there was nothing to insulate me.

The whale rotated in midair, thirty feet away, the fins flung balletically outward. It might have been alive since the world was new. The shadow dwarfed our boat. As I watched, the creature seemed to fall in slow motion. The crash came like thunder. I grabbed at the railing, too stunned to scream. A wall of spray climbed above the waves. The boat rocked perilously. I staggered backward, colliding with Mick.

"Relax," he said, in my ear. "That's just how they scratch an itch."

THAT EVENING, WE came upon Sea Pigeon Gulch. We were strolling toward the cabin, each hefting a carton of gear. I had not been paying attention to where we were going. My mind was still packed with a throng of whales. Mick and I were arguing happily about whether cetaceans might be sentient. There was evidence on both sides of the question. Then he stopped dead. We had reached the edge of the water. Sea Pigeon Gulch was its usual, sinister self. A shadowy chasm, filled with restless ocean. I had not been near the place since the discovery of Andrew's body.

I froze. Mick flushed a dark red. He grabbed my arm and tugged me away.

"I can't believe they're doing an autopsy," he said, pelting along as though his life depended on it.

"What?"

"Nothing. Nothing."

"No, tell me," I said eagerly. "Galen said the same exact thing when he was talking to the doctor."

"Uh-huh."

I cast my mind back, trying to recall Galen's phrasing. "Don't they always do an autopsy when somebody dies?"

"Only on TV," Mick said. "In real life, not so much. If it's obviously natural causes, like a heart attack or old age, they don't bother. But in this case—oh, hell."

In his urgency, he had begun to outpace me. I doubled my strides to keep up, trotting in his wake like a poodle on a leash.

"Think about it," he said. "There are two ways the thing could have happened. Andrew is strolling by the sea. He slips. His ankle breaks. He falls, banging his head. He lands in the water. He drowns."

"Yes," I said. "Exactly."

"That's *one* interpretation," Mick said sourly. "The other is that someone whacks him on the head first. That's *why* he goes down. He's already unconscious when he hits the sea."

I paused in shock. For a minute, I did not even draw breath. Mick strode onward, and I gathered my wits, jogging after his retreating form. We reached the porch together. He threw himself into a deck chair, gripping the armrests. I sank onto a bench beside him, setting down my carton of gear.

"You get what's coming to you," he said. "I believe that."

"What?"

"I never liked Andrew. It's not much of a loss, in my opinion."

There was a small silence. Then Mick stood up with a sudden movement.

"I'm heading in," he said. "You coming?"

I shook my head. I did not watch him go. He slammed the door hard enough that the entire cabin shook. There was a band of gold above the water. The sun was a crimson orb, its contours disfigured and distended by the clouds. When that fiery ball touched the sea, a bright arrow streaked toward me, a pointing finger, the reflection broken up by waves.

17

I T IS MID-DECEMBER. In Washington, D.C., this is the heart
of winter. The sky over Dupont Circle will become as gray and
smooth as a length of linen. The streets will be filthy, disfigured
by mud and fallen leaves. The schools will occasionally close, not
because of snow, but because of rain.

I remember, as a child, strolling with you on a winter afternoon,
right down the middle of the street. That was the only patch of solid
ground left. You walked in front and I clutched at the hem of your
poncho. The downpour hammered my umbrella. The sewers had
been overwhelmed by the tempest, unable to accommodate so much
liquid. The gutters had filled. The sidewalks had flooded. Cars had
turned into islands, their wheels submerged. Water brimmed against
shop windows and doorways, and the rain turned the pools into
mosaics of light. There was a row of pedestrians moving along the
double yellow line together like a parade, albeit a hurried and commonplace one, schoolchildren, mothers with shopping bags, and
men in suits, all rushing to get home before the storm worsened. I
remember that day perfectly. I remember that when night fell and
the temperature dropped, the overspill left standing on the pavement froze solid. I woke to a glassy wilderness. That is winter to me:
a lingering drizzle, the glitter of ice, and the schools closed, again.

But in California—or rather, off the coast of California—there is no true winter. The season has changed, but not in any way I recognize. The nights are a little cooler, the wind a little wilder. The fog has become semipermanent. It begins in the morning, just a tuft or two on the ocean. In the afternoon it thickens, pale and bright. In the evening it smothers the house in an impenetrable blanket, every window rendered blind.

I have dreamed of sharks. I dream of whales now.

A month has passed. It has been a month since Andrew's assault, and I am still here. Recently I walked outside barefoot. I put on gloves, a coat, even a hat—but halfway to Breaker Cove I glanced down and observed my poor, pale toes caked in mud. It took the shock of the cold to alert me to my error. One day I brushed my teeth with liquid soap rather than toothpaste. One day I fought with the coat rack. As I came in the front door, it seemed to lunge out at me, a bulky, man-sized shape. I struck it with both hands, knocking it sideways and sending the jackets thudding to the floor. I have found it difficult, too, to keep track of time. Andrew's attack seems to have done some damage to my internal chronometer. I often find myself surprised by the sunset or startled by a meal being put on the table, unaware of the hour.

Then there was the day I got into a screaming match with Forest. The conversation began civilly enough, a chat about the female white sharks. The Sisters had left for balmier waters, and Forest suggested that perhaps there would be a change in their breeding patterns soon. Global warming had begun to alter the character of entire oceans, reshaping the tides. Without warning, I flew into a rage. There in the kitchen, I shrieked that I was tired of hearing about the Sisters. I was tired of biologists in general. There had to be something more to talk about in the world than sharks, whales, seals, and birds. At this point, Mick intervened, marching me into the kitchen and force-feeding me cookies and tea. Forest slipped away, and the whole thing blew over. Still, I was shaken afterward. That anger had come out of nowhere, as unstoppable as a volcanic eruption, surprising even me.

But an outside observer would not necessarily see a marked alteration in my behavior, a change from Before Andrew to After Andrew. My temper might be raw now, flaring on a hair trigger. I am sometimes antisocial, hiding in my room. I sleep a little more. I feel curiously absent, almost insubstantial, and I eat like a fur seal filling its belly with stones, trying to anchor myself to the earth.

Still, it is easier than I would have imagined to feign normalcy. Every day, I walk the grounds, taking pictures. One morning I caught an albatross wheeling against the sky. Another day I found a flock of gulls circulating in an aggressive, erratic pattern, some close enough to touch, others so far away that they resembled snowflakes. Once, I captured a pod of dolphins, perhaps forty feet offshore, visible only through my telephoto lens. They were playing some elaborate game—leaping joyously out of the water, not spontaneously, but in predetermined groups, three or four at a time, with the sort of precise unison that synchronized swimmers could only dream of. Though I enjoy the ease and portability of my digital cameras, I have found myself more attached than ever to Jewel, my large-format behemoth. There is a wonderful ritual to using it: framing the shot, setting up the tripod, inserting the film, and throwing the cloak over my head. In the darkness under the cloth, I feel childlike, a kid hiding beneath a blanket. The image will appear before me, glowing in the gloom. The known, familiar world will be flipped over. The sky on the bottom. The sun shining at my feet. The sea rising above me—a gray, solid wall.

We did eventually get word from the mainland, by the way. This was a few days back, on a gusty morning, the cabin whistling and sighing like a ship at sea. The federal agents had finished their work. Andrew's body had been duly dissected. The verdict had been handed down. Galen received a call on the radiophone, and over breakfast he told us the news.

"The autopsy—" he said, then cleared his throat and began again, booming over the breeze. "The results were inconclusive. That happens sometimes, apparently. But they ruled it an accidental death. The case is closed."

On Friday, Lucy held her memorial service. She waited until the workday was done. First Forest and Galen came home in a black humor. Their video camera was on the fritz again. Given my experience, I was deputized to help fix it, and soon the entire table was covered with viewfinders, memory cards, fiddly plastic shapes, tiny circuit boards, and pages of the falling-apart instruction manual. Galen kept reading passages of this useless document aloud to us. Forest and I treated the whole thing like a jigsaw puzzle, starting at the middle and working toward the edges. Mick emerged a while later, whistling cheerfully, having spotted a few elephant seals frolicking in the surf. He tried to participate in the great camera adventure, but almost immediately he snapped a section of the casing in two. As I taped it back together, he retreated in shame.

"You men with your big, clumsy fingers," Forest said unexpectedly in a Southern drawl. Mick hid a smile in his palm.

For the rest of the afternoon, the four of us sheltered there. Forest and I reassembled the video camera. Galen complained that the manual shifted from English into French and then into what looked like Portuguese. Mick, in the corner, raved about the elephant seals. The room was filled with a cheery glow. The kitchen had always been the homey heart of the cabin to me.

At sunset, we had finally finished putting the camera back together—minus a few cogs that Forest suspected were actually part of the toaster, which had been dismantled in the same spot a few weeks earlier. By this time, the sky was the color of a bruised plum. A sliver of moon had crested the horizon.

Then Lucy strode out of her bedroom, followed by Charlene. I was unaware that they'd been in the house at all. Lucy held a bundle of long, slim, ivory candles. As Forest hastily tucked the camera out of the way, she distributed these tapers in silence, one for each of us. Charlene had a handful of round origami shapes—the sort that could be blown up like balloons. Lucy explained that these paper globes would shield our candles from the wind as we walked in procession down to the sea.

I noticed that both women were dressed in dark hues. I wondered if I ought to change out of my hot-pink T-shirt—but it was

too late, Lucy had whipped a lighter out of her pocket. Soon each
of us held a dancing flame. It took a bit of work to attach the
paper spheres to the top of the candles without setting the parch-
ment alight. Galen was unsuccessful. There was a sudden flare,
followed by a few curses, and a charred butterfly floated down to
the floor.

"We made extra," Charlene said.

The evening was suffused with a wintry chill. We moved toward
the water in single file, Charlene and Lucy both hefting a satchel
in their free hands. Despite my skepticism, I could not help but
be impressed by the stateliness of our dark shapes, each bearing a
glowing orb. There was a grandeur about the proceedings. We gave
Sea Pigeon Gulch a wide berth. We headed toward Mussel Flat
instead, where the shoreline was a gentle mound.

At the water's edge, Lucy turned. We gathered in a semicircle in
front of her. Her face looked different, lit from beneath with gold.

"Thank you all for coming," she said.

There was a round of murmurs.

"This was Andrew's favorite time of day," she said. "He liked
the evening. I thought that we might—" Her voice broke, and she
paused. "Charlene has been kind enough to help me gather up
some of his things. If we could—" She paused again. Hastily, she
wiped her eyes.

Lucy had been like a leaking sponge since Andrew's death,
spouting tears at the slightest provocation. I, on the other hand,
had not cried once, though it seemed to me that I had greater cause.
All this gushing emotion was indulgent. Even as a child, I had never

been a crier. I ducked my head, letting the wind carry my hair across my cheek. Drawing a shaky breath, Lucy pulled herself together.

"Galen let me have one of his model ships," she said. "We'll load it up with Andrew's things and sail it out to sea. I think that's fitting. A Viking burial for his best possessions."

She made a gesture, and Charlene bent over the bags, lifting out a miniature clipper ship, complete with rigging. In the past, this had sat on the mantelpiece, adding an extra bit of nautical flair to the living room. Now Lucy looked it over. She brushed a speck of dust off the hull. Charlene pulled out a yellow T-shirt. With a shudder, I recognized it as Andrew's; I had often glimpsed that splash of ochre inside the collar of his jacket. There followed a bottle of cologne and a wristwatch. A fountain pen. A battered copy of *The Catcher in the Rye*. A pack of gum. Each item was settled importantly on the deck.

At last it was done. Lucy turned to us again.

"I wish we had his red hat," she said. "His lucky hat. It's the one thing I couldn't find. The waves must have washed it away."

She and Charlene walked down to the water, holding the little boat between them. They set it in the shallows. Lucy gave it a push, and the tiny craft bobbed away, rotating to port, heading for Saddle Rock. The sea was coated with the last of the day's light. The ship's silhouette made a hole in that shimmering, silvery glaze. We all had our eyes fixed on it. From what I could tell, Mick was holding his breath, willing the thing onward. It traveled farther than I had expected. Finally the sea took matters into its own hands. The craft tilted to one side. It sank abruptly, as though a miniature submarine had breached its hull with a torpedo. Andrew's T-shirt remained for a minute or two, drifting on the surface. Then it, too, slid underwater.

"We'll say a prayer," Lucy said huskily. "I wasn't raised in a religious environment. Andrew wasn't either. Honestly, I don't even know if he'd like us to pray for him. But I thought it would be appropriate. Just repeat after me, okay?"

She bent her head over her guttering candle. The others raised their voices in an atonal chorus, Charlene's soprano clashing against Galen's growl. I did not pay much attention to the phrasing: *God full of mercy—perfect rest—holy and pure—the soul of Andrew Metzger*. Charlene had gone a little teary, a gleam around her eyes. As for me, I kept my lips closed. I did not say a word.

SEAL SEASON

18

THERE WAS BLOOD on the rocks. The elephant seals were fighting again. I stood a safe distance away, eye to the viewfinder, framing the shot.

This is a daily ritual now, in cold December, beneath clotted clouds. Dozens of male elephant seals have come on land to make war with one another. They have claimed Marine Terrace and Mirounga Bay. They have filled the air with their thundering cries. They are monstrous creatures. Mick has told me their dimensions: thirteen feet from nose to tail, two tons in weight. But the data don't do justice to the animals' physical presence, their unique combination of ferocity and silliness. The males have blubbery, lolling bodies. Their heads are misshapen—distorted by a limp, waggling nose, a kind of prototrunk. The elephant seals lumber around the beaches, posturing at one another, swinging their headgear aggressively. They are making a hierarchy. They are preparing for the females to arrive.

Their fights make for excellent photographs. Each confrontation begins with a display. One male will lift the top half of his body completely into the air and torque on the spot, showing off his bulk. A few feet away, a second elephant seal will do the same. Their noses will inflate, and they will bellow—a sharp, clapping cry, the pinniped version of a sonic boom. Often, the smaller male will concede at this stage.

If not, however, the two will engage. These scuffles are brief, brutal things. Full contact. They fling and thrust with their immense torsos. They slash with their vicious teeth. Each elephant seal wears a chest plate of scar tissue. They are gray animals, ocean-colored, but their torsos are pink, veiny, and raw. The flesh there is enough to make me wince. After exchanging blows, the winner will pose and boom triumphantly. The loser will slink away, painting the stones with red.

I have been using my large-format camera to photograph them. Each morning, I set up my tripod and slip the dark cloak over my head. This gives me the illusion of safety, as though I have been rendered invisible, my physical person erased by the fall of fabric. (In reality, of course, a photographer using this kind of instrument is thoroughly conspicuous: a hooded figure framed against the slope, shrouded in black like the specter of death.) On the viewfinder, the animals come into focus. This camera flips the world upside down: a granite sky, the earth made of clouds, the elephant seals floating above the horizon. I love the unreality of it.

Jewel is my favorite instrument. No question. A large-format mechanism requires effort and time, but in the moments when I am hidden beneath the cloth, the whole universe is condensed into the bright image in front of me. My brain is awash with shadow and movement. I don't see the islands as they really are. The truth is obscured by a wall of black. I can only see what I want to see—what I choose to observe through my lens—what I decide to record for posterity.

There is no darkroom on the islands. I cannot develop my photographs here. Instead, I must remove the film from the camera and place it in a light-tight box. I do this by feel, rather than sight, my hands inside the changing bag that keeps my equipment protected from the sun. I open Jewel up and detach its precious cargo. With my eyes closed, I palpate the film, transferring it into the container that will hold it for the next few months. Then I dust off my hands and walk away.

When using my other cameras—my digital instruments—I have a particular routine. Each evening, I look over all the images from the day, systematically erasing the ones that don't satisfy me. On the weekends, I go through the whole memory card, doing the same thing on a grander scale, reviewing all the photographs I have taken during my entire time on the islands. This allows me to maintain an active dialogue with my catalog of pictures, to see what I have done and what I have yet to do. It also allows me to gain a bit of distance from myself. Sometimes an image will seem lovely the day it was taken, but after a week or two it will fade. It can be difficult, at first, to separate my mind from the camera. I know so well what I hoped to capture in each snapshot—the light, the energy, the atmosphere— that when I look at my own work, I will sometimes see what isn't there. I will see what I wanted to make, rather than what I actually made. I need time and space to be able to perceive my images with an objective eye, as though they belong to someone else.

When it comes to my large-format camera, however, I do not have the option of viewing my photographs. Not yet. This kind of film requires a pool of chemicals and a darkroom to come into being. I can't turn the camera over and peer at the back. I will have to return to the mainland, to civilization, before I can develop these images. For now, the film is stored beneath my bed in watertight tubs. Each week I add more treasure to the supply, like a dragon hoarding gold. Sometimes I cannot bear to wait. It seems impossible that months will pass before I can see my pictures.

But sometimes, instead, I relish the feeling of hope, of expectation. Like a fetus in the womb, my photographs are gestating in darkness. I am curious to see what will be born.

ON A DAMP December morning, I saw my first elephant seal pup. Only a few females have come ashore, so there have been no babies—until now.

Mick has been rising early in anticipation. He is the expert on these animals, as he is on so many things. Marine mammals of every sort are his province, cetaceans and pinnipeds in particular. Seal Season is his favorite time of year. He has been in a jubilant mood.

The females will continue to make landfall over the next few weeks. The males are frantically establishing their hierarchy. The alphas will mate over and over. The betas will assist and obey the alphas in hopes of being allowed to breed as well. The gammas—the ultimate losers—will spend the winter in a state of barren frustration. This is a fraught period on the islands. The males have whipped themselves into a fever of expectation. Their guttural cries fill the wind. Their immense gray bodies are always in motion, lurching up and down the coastline, coated in spray. I have to be careful where I go. I have to maintain my distance. An elephant seal could run me over like a steamroller. It could snap me in half with its teeth.

Mick has told me about the strange life of these creatures. The males do not eat while they're on land—and they are on land for months, throughout the whole of Seal Season. They will drop half their body weight before the end of winter. They have spent the rest of the year fattening up in preparation.

When the females arrive, the entire world will change. They come to the islands to give birth, then get pregnant. They are single-minded and efficient. They gestate for eleven months, during which time they live an aquatic existence. Little is known about their experience at sea, since they are capable of holding their breath for hours and diving to depths of more than a mile. Human beings can't follow them where they go. Maybe they eat octopuses. Maybe they eat small sharks. Maybe they stay near the islands. Maybe they travel into the deep ocean. Maybe they remain in family groupings. Maybe they voyage alone. No one can be sure. At last they come ashore, pregnant with a sixty-pound fetus. They deliver immediately.

I was on the grounds with Mick when we came across the seal pup. We were on our way to Dead Sea Lion Beach, where the first females had finally emerged on land. The air was thick with a combination of rain and mist. I had not brought my camera with me, unwilling to risk the damp. Mick and I were both draped in ponchos that rustled as we moved. My eyelids were beaded with wet. He had a hand on my arm, steadying me as we slipped and crunched across the granite.

I heard it before I saw it. The baby's call was like nothing I'd ever encountered—at once tremulous and gravelly, somewhere between the whine of a kitten and the cough of a bear. Mick's fingers tightened on my shoulder.

"Oh no," he whispered.

We held still. Through the fog, a shape appeared. It was jet black. It moved hesitantly, shuffling and pausing. The fur was soft, the eyes brimming, the nose aquiver with whiskers. Though the pup was large, about half my size, it still managed to be cute in that distinctly mammalian way. It lifted its maw, keening.

Involuntarily I took a step forward, reaching for it.

"No," Mick said.

"It's lost," I said. "It's going the wrong way."

"That happens."

The baby wailed again. The sound tugged at my gut. Somewhere its mother was making an answering call, lost in the wind and the waves.

The pup lumbered toward us. There was a suggestion of exhaustion in its manner. I sucked in a breath. It would have been the work of a moment to pick the baby up and turn it around, pointing it back toward the sea, toward its family, toward safety. All it needed was a nudge in the right direction.

"Can't we just—" I began.

"No." Mick's hand was a vise, keeping me in place. "If it dies, it dies."

I moaned. The strength of my own impulse surprised me. I wanted the pup close to me, cradled in my arms. The loneliness of that little figure was unbearable. I could not tell if I was crying. It might have been the cold rain on my cheeks. Mick held on, unrelenting. We watched as the baby headed further inland, struggling through the mist, crying out to no one, until the gauzy air swallowed it up.

19

WHEN IT COMES to you, I am sometimes tempted to play the What If Game. This is a dangerous game, no question—but in low moments, I do find it appealing. What if you had lived? What if?

It opens up a world of possibilities. If you had lived, I might not have become a nature photographer at all. I might never have been afflicted by wanderlust. I might have had a home of my own by now. I might have had a dog, or two, or three. I can imagine myself kneeling in a garden, elbow-deep in earth, my face shaded by a straw hat, my mind clear. I might have hosted dinner parties. I might have woken up every morning of my life knowing where I was. Everything about me might have been different, refracted through the lens of What If.

If you had lived, I might have had friends—not coworkers, not colleagues, but dear companions. I might have had a romantic relationship, at least once in my life, that lasted more than a few tempestuous months. I might have been able to fall in love with a man the way I have fallen in love with the islands. I might have formed human attachments, rather than spending my affection on the sky, the waves, the elephant seals, the mist, and the cold. I can imagine myself writing letters to a pen pal. Not a ghost, but a living person. Someone who would write back.

If you had lived, I might never have come to the Farallon Islands. I would never have crossed Andrew's path. I can draw a direct line from your death to my assault. If you had lived, I might have been protected, nurtured, safe.

I might have been happy. The core of my nature might have been joy, rather than loss.

If you had lived, I would have been able to forget you sometimes. This is how normal people seem to think. I can imagine—just barely—a reality in which I might take my mother for granted, in which you would be a backdrop, like the blurred middle ground of a photograph, important but unremarked.

The What If Game applies to my father too. I can imagine a circumstance in which he might be less focused on his work, less absent mentally. He might not turn on the TV every night with the weary, glazed expression of an alcoholic reaching for the bottle. For years now, he and I have been like roommates, like acquaintances. Whenever I am home between assignments, we fall into the same old grooves, deep ruts that run parallel but do not touch. He has his poker game on Friday nights. I stop by the farmers' market on Wednesdays. He goes for a jog every morning. I take long, hot baths in the afternoons. We each have our own shelf in the cabinet, in the fridge. We each have our own hobbies—I do crossword puzzles, he does sudoku. We each have our own routines for sleeping and waking, drifting past each other in the hallway in our bathrobes without bothering to make eye contact.

If you had lived, all this might have been different. Dad and I would not move around each other with this gentle brand of detachment. We would not spend hours together in a concentrated silence, each of us preoccupied and withdrawn, as alone as it is possible for two people in one room to be.

I did try to discuss this very matter with my father once. I remember it well. He and I were sitting in the living room, in our usual stillness. The wind filled the trees outside. It was evening, and the robins, the first birds to stir in the morning and the last to sound at night, were twittering. Dad was frowning at a file in his lap as I flipped through a catalog of photographic equipment in a desultory way.

At last I cleared my throat. "Hey."

He glanced at me, then back at his file.

"About Mom," I said.

He nodded, though he kept his gaze fixed on the page.

"If she hadn't died," I said, "do you think you and I would have been closer? That we would have been able to talk more, maybe?"

A pause. A long pause.

"We'll never know," he said.

CHRISTMAS IS ON the horizon. This has brought out a previously unseen side of Charlene. She has gone on a holiday rampage. In some back closet, she found a blow-up Christmas tree, the sort of cheap, rubber affair that could serve in an emergency as a flotation device. The greenery is the hue of Astroturf, the baubles painted

right onto the plastic. It smells like a child's wading pool. It is an
abomination. Charlene blew it up herself, puff by puff, and set it
in the middle of the living room. We all have to walk around it a
dozen times a day. She has taken to wearing a Santa hat around,
which she apparently brought to the islands specially, packing it
into her luggage months in advance. The red clashes magnificently
with her auburn hair. And she has not stopped there. A few days
ago she rooted through the garbage, unearthing any bits of metal
she could get her hands on. The girl has made tinsel out of empty
cans.

Our ancient television now blares day and night. The old
Christmas standbys are playing on a loop. The TV screen is officially broken; if any of us stares for too long into that chaos of
static, we might go blind. Yet Charlene does not appear to care.
Legs folded, smiling, she sits in an armchair and listens with her
eyes closed. She seems to know each film by heart, laughing at bits
of unseen slapstick, tearing up during a romantic moment that is
invisible to the rest of us.

I, of course, am not a holiday person. Dead mothers are not
festive. Christmas has meant very little to me over the past twenty
years.

But Mick has gotten into the swing of things. He and Charlene
recently organized a Secret Santa. They urged me to pluck a name
from a hat. In vain did I remind them that there were no stores to be
found on the Farallon Islands, nowhere for me to get a little shopping done. Mick and Charlene were undaunted. I anticipate that we
will all be getting a shark tooth, or a box of crackers, or a stapler,

or a worn pair of socks, each gift festively wrapped in moldering newspaper and tied with filthy string.

This is a busy time for all of us. As the elephant seals have come ashore in greater and greater numbers, Mick has been run off his feet. But the other biologists have their own work to do as well. Though the white sharks are out of the picture, Forest and Galen must now tally up the data they collected during the summer. How many kills. How many Sisters. How many members of the Rat Pack. Everything has to be cataloged. Forest has been making copies of all his videos, ready to be shipped to the mainland. Galen has been filling out forms, which he hates. He will sit at the table, running his hands through his hair in exasperation until that white crown stands up in tufts. At his side, Forest will gently correct his work: "No, that was Thursday, not Wednesday. Hand me the eraser and I'll fix it."

Lucy, the bird girl, has been taken up with the storm-petrels. This has caused her a certain amount of angst. Normally she would have been able to assist Mick throughout Seal Season. That has been the pattern in the past. Normally Andrew would be in charge of the winter birds, which were his area of expertise. But Lucy must fill in for him now. She has been paler than usual, circles under her eyes.

I did not know there were storm-petrels on the islands at all—but in this case, my ignorance is not my fault. Storm-petrels do not make visible nests. They live in burrows in a sheer cliff face at the water's edge. In addition, they are nocturnal. Their eerie voices echo all night long. When Lucy mimicked them for me, I realized that I had heard that cry without fully registering it, the sound woven throughout my dreams. The storm-petrels skim over the sea in the darkness, hunting what Lucy refers to as "planktonic animals," returning to their burrows only at dawn. In the breeding season, they will coordinate their parenting with the phases of the moon, fledging their chicks during the brighter lunar periods. Now, however, they are childless. They are practically phantoms. A few days ago, Lucy located their hidden homes by following a distinct, musky odor, the by-product of an oily, orange goo the birds emit when disturbed. She uncovered a veritable storm-petrel city.

Charlene, of course, has been deputized to help whoever needs her most, following obediently in Lucy's wake with an armful of equipment or fact-checking all of Galen's paperwork. That has left Mick and me. We have climbed Lighthouse Hill together, binoculars in hand, to observe the pattern of elephant seals strewn across the shore. We have visited Dead Sea Lion Beach. We have kept an eye out for the elusive fur seals. It is not always possible to travel by boat nowadays. The surf is wild, thundering against the shore. The *Lunchbox* cannot be safely lowered into such choppy water, and the *Janus* is little better. White spray bursts against the coastline and rises in ashy tufts. At times, it looks as though the ocean has lifted a hand clear of the water and is trying to pull Southeast Farallon down into the depths.

But every now and then, Mick and I have managed to find a convenient lull. Occasionally the wind has worn itself out. The sea has dozed for an hour or two, as flat and glistening as an ice rink. Mick has dragged me out in the *Janus*, despite my protestations.

Having no weather sense, I am convinced that the climate might turn on a dime. No sooner would we leave the shore behind than a vicious gale would come screaming in out of nowhere—that has been my belief. Mick has laughed at me. One morning we trolled together past the Perfect Wave, a turquoise curl that scrolls perpetually along Shark Alley. It would have been a temptation to any surfer, except, of course, for the predators that lurk beneath the surface in warm weather. On another afternoon, we motored to the Lower Arch, where I snapped photos of the harbor seals: hides peppered with spots, flat flippers gripping rotund bellies.

More than once, I have dreamed about the lost elephant seal pup. I never found out what happened to it. I can only assume it died of starvation and neglect. Mick would not let me look for it, not even to find its body.

But in my dreams, I hear its aching cry once more. I find myself on the grounds again in the mist and rain. This time, I am determined to save the baby. I see its weary black shape in the distance, stumbling and shuffling. The pup is wailing for its mother. There is nothing more primal than that sound. In the dream, I can almost understand its language—a kind of underwater warbling, like speech filtered through fluid. Given enough time, I believe I could figure out what it is saying. It wants its mother, but I will be the one to answer. Bewildered by the fog, I hurry across the granite slope, following that echoing call. My hands outstretched. My heart in my throat. Despite all my efforts, I never succeed. Every time, I am left with empty arms.

OLIVER THE OCTOPUS has reemerged. Recently Lucy decided to effect a massive feng shui reorganization of her bedroom. It took her a while to arrange all her furniture. I did not, of course, venture in to see how the work was progressing. The dragon might have been slain, but I was leery at the thought of entering his former lair. From my room upstairs, I listened to the creaking, the scrape of wood on wood, the occasional burst of cursing. I did not ask Lucy what had motivated this spate of activity. She would not have confided in me, even if I had wanted her to.

She and I have achieved détente, of a kind. She has stopped dropping catty comments, and I have stopped bristling like a hedgehog in her company. We nod and smile at one another in passing. We are civilized. Since Andrew's death, the others have demonstrated endless compassion for Lucy. They give her hugs. They rub her back. They ask her how she's doing in honeyed voices. I do not. I am well aware that she does not like me—but her enmity is less focused now. Andrew's passing has overshadowed such petty concerns. I get the feeling that I am a mild but persistent annoyance to her, like an ugly painting on the wall.

Recently I overheard her chatting with Forest. He and Lucy are close; I have noticed it before. That morning, he dropped by to see how the feng shui effort was coming along. I was in the kitchen at the time. It was my turn to make lunch, and I was staring gloomily into the cupboards, trying to dream up some creative way to turn stale pasta and potatoes that were sprouting roots into a palatable meal.

Forest's reedy voice carried to me clearly.

"Nice," he said. "Different curtains."

"I cut up an old sheet, actually," Lucy said. "You can see the pattern on the cloth when the light is right. It looks okay, doesn't it?"

"Uh-huh."

I banged around the kitchen a little, alerting them to my presence, but they went on talking just the same.

"I'm surprised that you changed things so much," Forest said thoughtfully. "I barely recognize the place."

I heard a sneeze, possibly a sob.

"I couldn't bear it anymore," Lucy said in a damp voice.

"Oh, honey."

There was a rustling, and she blew her nose, a goose's honk. More rustling. She might have been fumbling with a handkerchief.

"You know why I stayed, right?" she said. "I thought about leaving. Boarding the ferry. Going home. I even dreamed about it. But in the end, I just couldn't. It's for Andrew, you see. It's all for him."

Listening, I froze, one hand gripping a bag of potatoes.

"This is where I remember him," Lucy said. "Where his spirit is. Not a ghost. I don't mean a ghost. His *essence* is here."

I swallowed hard. There was a scuffle, and I imagined that Forest had thrown an arm around Lucy's shoulders, tugging her close.

"But lately it's too hard," she said. "Every morning I wake up. I look around, and everything is the same. Just the way it always was. Every morning I think it was all a dream. The whole terrible mess was some stupid nightmare. I *still* think that. I still turn over in bed and expect him to be there. The other day I jumped up and ran to make some coffee for him. I got all the way to the kitchen before I remembered."

Forest's reply was too low for me to parse. A soothing murmur.

"Anyway," Lucy said, "now when I wake up, I'll see right away that things have changed. The room won't look the same. And I'll know. Andrew's gone."

If I had been superstitious, I might have crossed my fingers or knocked on wood. As it was, I merely shut my eyes tight. My arms had wrapped themselves of their own accord around my midriff. For a moment, everything felt foreign to me. Even my own waist, my hips, seemed altered somehow. I might have been hugging a stranger's body.

LATER THAT DAY, Oliver appeared in the living room. Lucy set his aquarium on the coffee table, right by my usual reading spot. I reacted to this change with a combination of revulsion and fascination. I was drawn to the octopus as though he were a car accident or a dead bird on the sidewalk: gross, scary, and spellbinding.

Since that day, my interest has overcome my fear. My initial distaste remains unabated—I would not, for example, ever touch the octopus or pick him up—but I often watch him at play. Oliver is always on the move. His goal is to escape or die trying. Before my eyes, he has explored every inch of his tank, coiling his tentacles upward to palpate the screen that fences him in from above. He has eyed me accusingly through the glass. I am intrigued by his skin.

He can mimic the mottled brown of the pebbles at the bottom of the tank. When he is angry—and he is often angry—he turns a deep crimson. He is able to change more than his color, too. He can roughen his mantle until it looks like coral. He can make his flesh glisten like silk.

It has taken me a while to understand his shape. The eyes poke up on stalks, each pupil a black, horizontal bar. But the bulbous sac beneath these organs is not, as I originally suspected, his nose. It is, in fact, his body, a squishy balloon that comprises his lungs and stomach. The mouth is hidden at the center of a pinwheel of tentacles. There is a beak in there somewhere. There is venom in that beak. I have done a little reading on the subject, finding an old, battered copy of a Jacques Cousteau manifesto on one of the shelves. Leafing through the pages, I have learned that octopuses are clever. They are more intelligent than dogs. They possess extraordinary powers of disguise. A dead octopus, if moved from a dark surface to a lighter one, will gradually pale, attempting to camouflage itself from beyond the grave.

Watching Oliver, I have learned still more. Lucy has put a rock in his tank, a rudimentary shelter, and Oliver will dig beneath it, scooping armfuls of pebbles to one side. Then he will pour his body into the hole he has made. Gradually he will alter his color and texture, becoming invisible by degrees. When Lucy taps three times on the lid, however—a signal to indicate mealtime—he will balloon upward, a rabbit conjured out of a hat.

I think he has a sense of humor. For a while, Lucy kept a lamp trained on him during the day, an extra measure of heat. But one afternoon, Oliver grew tired of the constant glare. I was on the couch at the time, watching him over the top of my book. Oliver sucked in a mouthful of water. He spouted it upward in a stream, right through the mesh lid. There was a burst of smoke, an acrid smell, and the lamp shorted out.

WE HELD THE Secret Santa a few days before Christmas. As it turned out, not everyone would be present for the holiday itself. Mick, Lucy, and Forest were all planning to return to their homes for a much-needed vacation.

In the morning, we gathered in the living room. I had pulled Lucy's name out of the hat, which was awkward for me. I considered insisting that I be allowed to pick again, or maybe cornering Mick and begging him to trade. In the end, however, I decided to make a few small presents for Oliver. I saved and squirreled away anything I could picture the octopus playing with in the quiet space of his tank. Now, with everyone watching, Lucy opened my explanatory note, then unwrapped a chain of paperclips, a tiny glass jar, and a ruby-red marble. She lifted each object into the air and examined it. She got to her feet and gave me a one-armed hug, her body as stiff as a board. I honestly couldn't tell whether she was pleased.

The rest of the gifts were similarly makeshift. A shell pendant on a length of twine. A sand dollar. One of Forest's shark sketches, stuck into a picture frame that had been salvaged from the mantelpiece. Galen offered up a seal stone—a dark, smooth orb, as heavy as a meteorite. (He has a collection of them in a bucket in his room, amassed over years on the islands.) Mick was the worst. He gave Charlene a can of tuna. There was a great deal of laughter. At lunch that day, Galen wore his new necklace with pride. Charlene insisted upon eating her tuna as a side dish. The conversation was light. Mick, Lucy, and Forest would be leaving as soon as Captain Joe arrived, and they chatted eagerly about what they were looking forward to. For the first time, they were people with somewhere else to go.

20

A ND NOW THERE are three. Charlene, Galen, and I are rattling around Southeast Farallon alone. The temperature has dropped and the wind has picked up—an awful combination. I have found myself envying the elephant seals. They frolic in the icy ocean, bundled up beneath layers of blubber.

Galen appears to be equally immune. He often goes for long walks. I will see him through the window, a dandelion of a man, lean and rangy, topped by a plume of silver. He will wander across Marine Terrace and stroll toward Mussel Flat. Eventually he will disappear on the slopes of Lighthouse Hill. I get the feeling that he is looking for something out there. What, I can't imagine.

Even among the other biologists here, Galen is unique. He has been on the archipelago for a decade. No one else has ever come close to staying so long. Most people average a couple years at most. What's more, Galen has never once, in all that time, returned to the mainland—not for a day, not for an hour. This is unusual in the extreme. The others voyage home at regular intervals for the sake of their own sanity. But Galen's sticking power is legendary. I have heard all about it. Forest, Mick, and Lucy have spun yarns about him, like campfire stories.

Galen does not travel to his hometown for the holidays. He does not take weekends in San Francisco. He has even refused to return to the continent for medical care. Periodically, of course, he has suffered sprains, colds, even pneumonia. Mick took Galen's temperature once, then begged him to call a helicopter and head straight to the hospital. But Galen demurred. Instead, in a creaking voice interspersed with coughing, he described his symptoms over the radiophone. Captain Joe was dispatched with medicine on board the ferry. (This was a few years ago; Mick told us all about it long after the fact.) Once, Galen broke his wrist while at work on the *Janus*. He marched away to the cabin, set the bone himself. An hour later, wearing a homemade cast, he headed back to work. Once, while in the kitchen preparing dinner, he got word on the radiophone that his brother had passed away. (This was Forest's story; he had been with Galen at the time, way back when, and he shared it with the rest of us recently, in a whisper.) The funeral took place somewhere on the mainland. But Galen did not attend. Instead, on the morning his brother was put in the ground, he spent the hours in the lighthouse alone, walking back and forth and staring to the east, as though with a little effort he could see all the way to the cemetery.

Yet Galen's motivation has always been a mystery. He has appointed himself Lord High Protector of the Farallon Islands, and in keeping with such a weighty title, he has cut himself off entirely from the rest of the world. None of the others have taken their isolation to this extent. They still keep in touch with their families. They head home for big events. They take the time to return to normal life, however briefly.

Even I am not so far gone. I send the occasional postcard to my father. I write letters to you.

OVER THE LAST few days, Charlene and I have bonded. Entombed in a wasteland of rain and mist. Miles from the nearest Christmas tree. We have taken to huddling together on the couch, tucked beneath the blankets we have scavenged from the beds of the biologists now on the mainland. We will play double solitaire or flip through one of Lucy's bird books, our heads close, trying in vain to glean the differences between the fourteen identical varieties of sparrow listed there. Recently, in a fit of energy, we even got out all the jigsaw puzzles hidden in the back closet. We took over the table, though it soon became clear that each puzzle was missing a significant number of pieces. Undaunted, Charlene and I worked on, overlapping the disparate images in a patchwork quilt—a dolphin's tail next to a leafy stretch of forest next to a fragment of one of Van Gogh's masterpieces. When Galen returned hours later, his nose and ears charred red from the chill, we presented him with a frenetic, disconcerting collage: an image put together by a madman.

Throughout the week, Charlene has been sad. I have heard a lot about her family. At Christmas, they chop down a tree together. There is popcorn to be strung, and eggnog to be spiked, and carols to be sung to the neighbors. Though Charlene and her siblings are all in their twenties now, they are still expected to leave out milk and cookies for Santa, which their father will sample during the night, leaving a few crumbs on the plate. Like me, Charlene is too broke to go home this year. As an intern, she can't even send presents to her family, let alone manage a plane ticket. In my case, the income I have scrounged together has absolutely no wiggle room for luxuries. Room and board are covered, but vacations are outside my scope.

I don't mind. The islands are where I want to be.

A few days ago, on an icy morning, Charlene and I decided to clean the cabin. Galen had disappeared right after dawn, throwing on a hat and fishing his binoculars out of the bureau. Charlene swept, and I mopped. She dusted, and I wiped down the windows. All the time, however, she was acting peculiar. As we beat the dust out of the rugs, as we scrubbed the kitchen sink, she kept turning to me, pausing, then moving away again. Clearly there was something on her mind.

The fourth time she did this, we were itemizing the contents of the bathroom cabinet. The trouble with having so many roommates is that nothing ever gets thrown away. Everyone assumes that a razor or bar of soap belongs to someone else. Over the seasons, the cabinet has become a museum of relics: moldy cotton swabs, fossilized tubes of toothpaste, empty boxes of dental floss. I tossed an entire collection of plastic combs into the trash. Charlene glanced at me and started to speak. Then she shook her head, frowning.

"Let's take a break," I said.

We headed down the stairs—which were gleaming, by the way—and sat on the couch, piling quilts over ourselves. Through the window, the sea had been churned into a mess of whitecaps, as frothy as whipped cream. Oliver's aquarium appeared to be empty, but I knew better. He was biding his time, pretending to be pebbles and glass. The radiator clanked in the corner, trying in vain to cope with the breeze. Charlene's brow was furrowed.

"Get it off your chest," I said. "Whatever it is. You'll feel better."

"It's nothing. It's probably nothing."

I waited. She glanced around, then leaned in. This amused me. It would be hard to find two people who were less likely to be over-heard than we were.

"I know something," she said softly.

"Oh?"

"It's a little weird." She paused, biting her lip. "It's about Andrew."

His name caught me off guard. A ripple of nausea passed through me. Blinking rapidly, I fixed my gaze on the window I had just washed. The glass glowed with a pale, crystalline light.

"The night he died," Charlene said, "I heard something."

I sucked in a breath, my eyes lifted. In the corner of the window-pane, I noticed a spider web I had unaccountably missed.

"My room is next to the front door," Charlene said. "I hear all kinds of things. If anybody goes anywhere, I know about it. When I first got here—God!—I didn't sleep at all. Lucy would be vacuum-ing until ten, and Galen would be at the table, writing in that little green notebook of his and clearing his throat constantly. When I finally dropped off, Forest would wake me at four in the morning. You know how loud he can be." She sighed. "Four in the morning. Running down the stairs. Yelling at the top of his lungs. Slamming every door in the house."

Still, I said nothing. The spider web swayed in a draft. The radiator clanked one last time, then fizzled to a halt, and the room was silent.

Undeterred, Charlene went on. "I can sleep through most things now, unless it's unusual. If it's a noise I'm expecting, like Lucy singing in her sleep or somebody looking for a book in the living room, I don't wake up. I'm used to that stuff. But that night—the night Andrew—"

She broke off. In spite of myself, I met her gaze. Her face was suffused with color now, her cheeks burning. I swallowed hard.

"Tell me," I said. "What did you hear?"

"I heard someone leaving," she said. "Around eleven. I thought it was Mick and Forest. They do that sometimes. Go out together, I mean."

Her gaze slipped to the side.

"Anyway," she went on hurriedly, "I fell asleep after that. It gets a little confused . . . There was something. A small noise, very soft. I might have imagined it. Or maybe it was an animal. I fell asleep again."

That was me, I thought. Me leaving the cabin. I was the small noise. Charlene was fiddling absently with a lock of rust-colored hair. Her voice was low and musical, almost chanting.

"Then I heard Andrew," she said. "I heard him go outside. I remember lying in bed, listening. Somebody was on the porch. I heard footsteps. It took me a while to be certain. He coughed. I knew Andrew's cough. And then—" Charlene paused, eyes closed. "And then I heard voices."

"Voices?"

"That's right. Andrew was talking to someone."

The full weight of what she was saying seemed to crash over me in a wave. No one should have been outside with Andrew. He had been alone on the grounds. He had lost his footing alone. He had died alone.

"I'm sure of it," she said. "I know what I heard. Two voices."

"But who was the other person?"

Charlene let out a long, slow breath. "I don't know. I just know it wasn't Andrew. He was out there with somebody else."

21

YOU ALWAYS LOVED fairy tales. On quiet evenings, on lazy Saturday mornings, I was accustomed to curling up at your side with *Hansel and Gretel* or *The Little Mermaid*. You did not incline, however, toward the more modern interpretations with their happy endings, everything comforting and sanitary. You were not interested in a version of *Little Red Riding Hood* in which no one got eaten, or a variant of *Cinderella* in which the wicked stepmother and her daughters repented and were forgiven.

Instead I heard about Ariel, the mermaid who was given the gift of life on land, the ability to breathe air, and two human legs—for a terrible price. Everywhere she went, for the rest of time, she felt as though she were stepping on shards of broken glass. In your favorite take on *The Pied Piper*, the flute player did not lead the children away from their homes, only to return them again to their jubilant parents. Instead, he guided them all into the river to drown. In your version of *Cinderella*, the wicked stepmother was never offered forgiveness. She came to Cinderella's wedding feast, where a pair of iron shoes was clapped onto her feet, red-hot from sitting in the fire. In those shoes, she was forced to dance until she dropped down dead.

These days, I wonder whether you may have been onto something. Modern fairy tales have been altered, over the years, to paint a picture of a safe and ordered world. There is magic in these stories, to be sure—witches, ogres, and giants. And yet, even the supernatural takes its place in the greater scheme of things, the moral arrangement of life. Virtue is rewarded, malice punished. Good people prosper; bad people do not. In the newest version of *Sleeping Beauty*, the benevolent fairies are recompensed for their integrity, living a charmed existence. The more enigmatic witch of *The Snow Queen*, on the other hand, suffers to a certain extent, yet survives. And the most evil creatures of all, like the hag in *Hansel and Gretel*—monsters who lie and cheat and have a penchant for cannibalism—are slain without mercy. In modern fairy tales, karma is a bitch.

But you had no time for such whitewashed fables. You preferred stories that were chaotic and enigmatic. The world of your fairy tales—though magical—showed the world as it actually is. Secrets flourish undiscovered. Loved ones die. Danger is not always perceptible. Evil goes unpunished. There is no order; there is no safety. I believe this is what you were trying to tell me.

I HAVEN'T THOUGHT much about my conversation with Charlene. I have not wanted to consider it. And yet, against my will, it has never been far from my mind. It is like a bright light in the corner of the room—too bright to look at directly. Though I have been keeping my gaze averted, I am still aware of that uncomfortable glow.

I know what she was suggesting. I have even dreamed about it. Andrew on the rocks, facing the sea. His skin agleam. His breath steaming the air. A dark figure behind him, rising up. Stone in hand. I have heard the grunt of pain. I have seen the splash of blood. I have watched Andrew's body tumble down.

What I have decided, finally, is that Charlene was wrong. Charlene was mistaken. The cabin is old. Sounds carry unaccountably between the rooms through the pipes and heating grates; I have noticed it before. Once, as I was sitting at the table, I realized that I could hear Lucy gargling in the bathroom upstairs as clear as a bell, while in the kitchen the bang of pots and pans seemed muffled. On the night in question, something similar could have happened. Charlene might have heard Andrew on the porch, along with Mick and Forest murmuring in their bedroom. She might have conflated two different events: footsteps *outside* the house, voices *inside* the house.

Or perhaps it was the ghost. I have dreamed about this too. Andrew slinking along the shoreline in the moonlight. A shimmer in the air beside him. A woman's figure. Her body solidifying out of the mist and rain—out of nothing. I have seen the haze of her nightgown. I have seen the swing of one pale arm.

MICK CAME BACK today, along with Lucy and Forest. This caught me off guard. It is hard to keep track of time on the islands. Calendars, clocks—these things seem so arbitrary. An artificial construct. There is a timelessness about this place. The seasons are measured not by a variation in the weather but by a variation in the animals. Winter is when the whales and seals breed. Summer is

Bird Season. Autumn belongs to the sharks. Night does not follow day, not really—that would imply that one occurs before the other. Instead, day and night are a great wave, beginning at the base, the bright dawn, and sweeping up through the long golden afternoon to crest in the evening and crash down again into darkness, where the cycle begins anew. Time on the islands has become, for me, self-contained and unchanging.

And so, this morning I missed any number of clues that something was going on. To begin with, I slept through the early call on the radiophone. (Before Andrew, I had always awoken with the birds. Now, though, After Andrew, I was as fatigued and somnolent as a teenager.) During breakfast, I didn't happen to glance out the window and see the ferry approaching the islands. I didn't observe Galen slipping out to meet the boat when it dropped anchor. I didn't even hear the voices carrying on the wind from East Landing, where Lucy, Forest, and Mick had been deposited by the Billy Pugh, breathing in the salt air with smiles on their faces. During all this time, I was lying on the couch, leafing through a book on pinnipeds. When I heard a clatter, I shot a look at Oliver the octopus, who was floating in his tank, his skin a delicate mauve.

There was a crash, and the front door flew open.

"Woo-hoo!" Mick shouted. "Home at last. Thank the lord!"

I had forgotten how very big he was. In two strides, he had crossed the room. I found myself being swung in a circle like a rag doll. The walls pivoted around me. When he set me down, I stumbled and almost fell. Mick laughed and planted a kiss on the top of my head.

"I missed my little mouse girl," he said. His gaze wandered down my frame, drinking me in. As he stared at my torso, I saw his brow furrow quizzically for a moment. Then, however, Charlene came hurrying out of the kitchen in an apron, her arms sudsy and glistening from washing dishes.

"Hey, you!" she cried. "I thought to myself, either there's a herd of elephants in the cabin, or Mick is back."

THAT EVENING, LUCY took Oliver out of his tank. She played with him, transferring him from hand to hand, wetting the floor. She seemed to be lost in pure delight, as if she had missed him terribly during her time away. She, Forest, and Mick were all in this state—so happy to be back on the islands they were almost weightless. The mainland had been a fine respite, but they had all talked about the shell shock of returning, however briefly, to civilized life. Forest had been on the islands for five years, Mick almost as long. Lucy, a little younger, had come here straight out of college, a year or so ago, dragging Andrew in her wake. Since their arrival, all of them had voyaged home to the mainland now and again. Each time was the same. They would be baffled by the sheer quantity of land, our blue planet replaced by a carpet of grass and concrete. They would be unsettled by commonplace things. Fire hydrants. Central heating. A car horn. The gleam of jewelry. The sugary odor of a bakery on the breeze. The squeal of a bicycle braking. They would find themselves out of step, out of place: waking too early, eating at the wrong time of day, overloaded by the simple fact of a telephone ringing. They would return to the islands like elephant seals reentering the ocean. Back in their natural habitat. Back where they belonged.

I was sitting on the couch, the others distributed around the living room, all of us watching Lucy as she lifted the octopus high. She rolled him down one arm, giggling at his confusion. Oliver flashed through a rainbow of colors. His suckers wriggled and groped, trying to find purchase on her sleeve.

I turned to Mick, who was seated at my side.

"I don't understand," I said. "I thought you weren't supposed to interfere with the animals here. Not ever. Isn't that the biologist's credo?"

I meant this to be an aside, a private exchange. But the room was quiet, and everyone turned to look at me. Lucy flushed.

"I study *birds*," she snapped. "Does Oliver look like a bird to you?"

"No," I said.

"He's a pet," she said. "Pets are different."

She glared at me a moment longer, then stomped over to the aquarium and plunged the octopus into the water with a vicious movement. He sank, ballooning outward, changing shape. His tentacles glittered with bubbles.

22

IN A PLACE like this, it should be hard to keep secrets. Southeast Farallon is small, and the cabin is smaller still. All of us live on top of each other. We all know about Lucy's crying jags. We are all aware of Galen's nocturnal restlessness, pacing his room with quick footsteps. We all know when Mick engages in a late-night snack, banging around the kitchen at three in the morning. Until recently, I had begun to think that I knew everything there was to know about the islands.

But as it turns out, there has been a secret right under my nose for months.

Last night I woke to the sound of voices. It is January, the heart of Seal Season, and the archipelago is never quiet, regardless of the hour. The males boom, the females grunt, and the pups squeal all night long. Their constant noise sets my nerves on edge. It is a perpetual reminder of mating and birthing and suckling. I do not want to think about these things. I do my best to tune out the roar. Now I lay awake, assuming I'd heard wrong, mistaking animal sounds for human speech.

Then it came again. A man's voice. Someone was outside the window.

My heart began to pound. I sat upright, tugging the blinds aside. It was a bright, moonlit night. The landscape was a jumble, the familiar contours transformed into a lurid black-and-white photograph. Gradually I saw that there were two figures moving on the slope. They had been talking, but they were quiet now.

The scene continued to clarify as my eyes adjusted. It was a bit like watching the shape of an undersea stone coming clear through the ruffled surface of water. The silhouettes belonged to Mick and Forest. I recognized the former's bulk and the latter's delicate slimness. They were heading away from the cabin. They were whispering together. Forest laughed, a high-pitched sound, something I had never heard him give before. Then he leaned in. Before my eyes, the two men kissed.

It registered as an electric shock. There was no mistaking what was happening: it was a passionate, abandoned, drowning-without-each-other sort of lip-lock. There had been a line of radiant blue separating their frames, but now they merged. Forest went up on his toes. They swayed back and forth.

I reached for my camera. It was an automatic reflex. Tomcat, one of my digital SLR instruments, was settled, as always, on the night table. I kept it there for emergencies—a shark attack, a whale sighting, the return of the ghost. I did not think. I merely acted, lifting the camera to my eye.

Mick's face came into focus, all snowy planes. Forest was harder to track. I kept zooming in on the back of his head. Their hands met in space, fingers reaching. I still had not adjusted to the firework display of stars on the Farallon Islands. Cassiopeia and Orion blazed above the horizon like configurations of torches. Mick and Forest paced with a practiced step across the granite. They were moving toward the coast guard house. Mick was almost skipping. Something—a bird calling, a seal barking—made them pause and gaze to the left, toward the ocean. At the door of the coast guard house, they engaged in a funny little pantomime, each attempting with exaggerated politeness to give way and allow the other to go first.

Once they were inside I adjusted the focus, skimming frantically across the windows. The upper story was as lightless as a black hole, nothing there but the whirling and flickering of the bats. Biting my lip, I waited. One minute passed. Two minutes. Then something pale darted across my lens.

Mick and Forest had stationed themselves in the moonlit hollow of the living room. I sat up straighter. It was more difficult now to keep an eye on them. Since they were framed in the window, the slightest shift from side to side could remove either of them entirely from my field of vision. And they were moving fast. I watched them kiss hungrily, almost angrily. Mick was unbuttoning Forest's shirt.

I began taking pictures. Because it was tricky to catch a glimpse, I wanted to keep what I caught. The sound of the shutter echoed around the room like gunfire. I snapped Forest's marble rib cage, bare to the navel. I snapped another wild kiss, Mick's hands flying upward in a blurred, avid surge. I snapped Forest tearing off his own scarf and flinging it aside. Soon they were both unclothed. The window cut off their bodies at the waist. Still, it was easy enough to follow what was going on. Forest swiveled so his back touched Mick's belly. Two moon-pale torsos moved in concert. Mick wrapped his arms around Forest's chest, and I marveled anew at Forest's slimness, not an ounce of fat on him. At first their dance was tentative, graceful. Mick buried his cheek in Forest's shoulder. Forest's head rocked back. I heard the cry he gave, a moan that would ordinarily have passed for the rowdy wind or the rumble of the elephant seals. He threw out a hand, bracing himself against the wall.

I lowered the camera for a moment. The sensation was an odd one. For the first time in a long while, I was remembering desire. The spark of hunger. The pull of lust. That part of myself. But the memory was faint, distorted, as though from a dream. Once upon a time, I had experienced these things. But that had been another life. I remembered it now the way a ghost might. All mind, no body.

After a while, the inevitable happened: Mick and Forest tumbled onto the floor and vanished. I waited, my heart hammering. Perhaps their lovemaking would not last long. Perhaps they would reappear. The wind picked up. The sea roared in the distance. Mick and Forest stayed out of my sight.

I sat back on the mattress, brushing my hair out of my face. So many things made sense to me now. The more I considered the matter, the clearer it became.

To start with, there was the issue of cohabitation. The cabin now had six people and only five bedrooms. Charlene, as the lowest member on the totem pole, lodged in a bedroom that was quite literally a former closet. (Her bed took up the entire floor, and the decorations on the walls were racks of coat hooks.) In the past, Andrew and Lucy had shared a room. Until now, however, I had never understood why Mick and Forest had also chosen to share. It would have been a great deal more practical for Forest to bunk with Galen—his fellow shark addict, on his same schedule.

Other questions were now answered, too. Forest's reserved nature. His impenetrable demeanor. His stillness and silence. In his presence, I'd always had the feeling that he was keeping himself under tight control. Now I understood why. He was hiding a key facet of his personality, the core of his nature. By the same token, Mick's lack of romantic interest in me no longer felt like an insult.

I flicked through the pictures I had just taken. Mick smiling as Forest nuzzled his throat. Forest laughing in the wake of a hearty kiss. Their arms tangled, fingers entwined.

For the first time, my conscience pricked me. Obviously, both men had put a premium on secrecy. They shared a room, after all; they could easily have engaged in their romantic adventures there. But the cabin was ancient and creaky. I shuddered, remembering the many times I had been an unwilling audience to Lucy and Andrew's trysts. Mick and Forest, it seemed, regularly risked injury and illness to keep their relationship hidden from prying eyes.

I considered deleting the snapshots. But the photographer in me would not allow that. They were a chronicle, and any chronicle was sacrosanct. A few of them were quite beautiful, too—I had been able to catch the energy of those fiery embraces, the motion of two bodies swaying together. I would hide the camera under my bed. From now on, I would not use it publicly, just in case.

Eventually I realized how tired I was. It was nearly one in the morning. I lay down. I wondered how often Mick and Forest had made these late-night journeys during my time on the islands. I wondered how they managed to behave so normally the next day. Rising at their usual hour. Greeting each other casually, like friends, like colleagues. Showering one another's sweat off their skin.

AT DAWN, I awoke with a frightened jolt. I had been dreaming about Andrew. This often happened; it was a nightmare I could not seem to escape. Sometimes I had to relive the rape—breath on my neck, weight on my belly. Sometimes I saw the ghost again, glimmering in the corner of my room. Sometimes Andrew was bloodied and battered in these dreams. Half-dead in the darkness above me. His head bashed in. Dripping fluids and brain matter onto my pillow.

This time, though, I shook off the nightmare fairly quickly. I was doing mental calculations. On the night in question—the worst night, the night everything had changed—I knew exactly where everyone in the cabin had been. I had considered it many times. Galen: drunk and incapable. Charlene: lost in music, headphones on. Lucy: asleep. Mick and Forest: out on the grounds.

Until today, I had thought those two were whale-watching by moonlight. It was a silly explanation, but it was the only one I'd been able to come up with. Now, of course, I knew the truth. My mouth was dry. I sat up in bed, shoving the blanket away. Outside the window, the fog was so thick that I could not see the ocean. It had been two months since Andrew had assaulted me. On that night, Mick and Forest had slipped away to the coast guard house to make love.

Huddled on the mattress, I gave a whimper. Mick was my friend. He was a true friend, maybe the first I'd ever had. If he had known what was happening, he would have stopped it. He would have protected me.

I could not be sure of the others. I could not be sure of any of them. No one had been a witness to my assault, of course. But even if they had, I did not know how they might have reacted. They were biologists. Cold. Impassive. Uninvolved. If Forest had been in the cabin that night, I could imagine him putting a pillow over his head to block out the noise. If Charlene had caught the creak of bedsprings, she might not have thought it was her place to interfere. Galen might not have leapt into action either. He might have analyzed the situation, head cocked, listening. He might have studied my rape as he would observe the struggle of a lost seal pup.

Lucy was a wild card. She disliked me, and she had loved Andrew. Her mind was a dark morass. I could not begin to parse her motivations, let alone predict what she might have done if she had woken in the night to the sound of muffled cries above her, her boyfriend's heavy breathing, the clang of my headboard.

But I knew about Mick. He would have fought for me. He would have saved me.

For the first time, I wondered if Andrew had been aware of this too. He might have made a similar calculation, tallying up the location of each biologist, weighing the risk. He had chosen a time when he would not be overheard. He had waited for footsteps on the porch, the murmur of Mick and Forest's voices. In his quest for romance and release, Mick had left me vulnerable. He had left me all alone.

23

T HE ELEPHANT SEALS are giving birth. Throughout the month of January, the females have appeared by the dozen. I am enraptured by them. Unlike their male counterparts, they are beautiful in the traditional manner of seals: smooth and rotund, their faces vaguely canine, their black eyes filled with pinniped intelligence. I have photographed more births than I can count. The pups are charcoal-colored when they arrive, slimy and blind. More blood on the rocks. They uncurl their bodies, sticky with amniotic gel, teeth flashing. The females sing to them in booming, grating voices. They are imprinting themselves on their newborns. They are telling each pup which scent and voice belong to its mother.

The elephant seals have altered the architecture of the islands. They have made the coastline soft. They doze in heaps, the gray mountain of their bodies jeweled with small, dark shapes—the pups slumbering and keening and nuzzling. Nearby, the alpha males lord it over their domain. Each is the master of forty or fifty females. They parade up and down the shore, inflating their noses to make a cry that sounds like a drumbeat. The members of their harems snipe at one another good-naturedly. They spend their days nursing. Their milk is some of the richest in the animal kingdom.

The babies gain ten pounds a day. I have photographed this too—coming back to the same family each morning, watching the infant swelling like a balloon.

The pups have to be careful. The rookery is not a safe place. The roar of the elephant seals is louder than the ocean. The babies must navigate through a landscape of identical figures, picking their mother's individual call out of the chorus. More than a few have died. Some have traveled the wrong way across the grounds, leaving the pod behind, lost and gone forever. Some have drowned, too little and helpless to swim. Though the females are watchful and conscientious, the males are too aggressive—or too large—to pay attention. A few pups have been killed by their fathers, who are massive enough to crush them beneath their immense bulk without realizing it.

I still dream of the lost seal pup Mick and I saw on the grounds. I still follow it through the mist. I still listen to it crying for its mother.

The other day I was on Marine Terrace with Jewel, my large-format camera. I was attempting to capture yet another birth. The labor of an elephant seal is not an arduous process. The mother naps between contractions. The baby emerges without undue fuss. With my head beneath the black cloak, I found myself thinking about guillotines. My brain—my eyes, my visual cortex, my artistic sensibility—was separated from my body by a fall of cloth. I was gazing through the viewfinder, framing an image of the new mother lolling on her back, nipples exposed, her infant pressed against her, drinking assiduously. Then I straightened up. I removed the cloak from my head. I felt cleaved somehow, as though I had been decapitated, as though my mind had been separated from my flesh and organs, floating on the air.

Still, our work continues. Lucy has been captivated by the local population of pigeon guillemots. These birds look exactly like their landlocked counterparts—the gray, ordinary pigeons found scarfing up peanuts on the National Mall—but they are actually seabirds. They forage for food by diving to the ocean floor, plummeting up to 150 feet underwater in search of a meal. Lucy has been nattering on about "alcids" and "two eggs, rather than one" and "incubating for four weeks." She has been hurrying all over the grounds with a handful of bands. She has been sighing a lot about how hard it is to tag the birds alone, how much Andrew loved this work.

Mick, of course, is busy with the elephant seals. The weather is still too wild to take trips in the boat. It may be a while before Captain Joe can safely visit the islands. In the meantime, Mick is trying to identify his favorite pinnipeds by their signature markings. The other day he came dashing into the cabin, almost too excited to speak. He had glimpsed a double birth—twins—a rarity. He and Charlene were so pleased that they went into the kitchen and celebrated with glasses of Perrier.

And I have been snapping images of everything. A creative surge has overtaken me; I eat, sleep, and breathe photography. Curtains of rain lashing the shore. Clouds strewn like pebbles above the horizon. A flock of puffins spinning over Lighthouse Hill. The image of a guillotine still lingers in my mind. The sensation of weightlessness has remained. There is a wonderful violence to the act of photography. The camera is a potent thing, slicing an image away from the landscape and pinning it to a sheet of film. When I choose a segment of horizon to capture, I might as well be an elephant seal hunting an octopus. The shutter clicks. Every boulder, wave, and curl of cloud included in the snapshot is severed irrevocably from what is not included. The frame is as sharp as a knife. The image is ripped from the surface of the world.

LAST NIGHT, THE clock had just chimed midnight when I shuffled down the stairs. Recently, I have often found myself thirsty in the evenings—almost painfully parched, as though all the blood in my veins has been replaced with sand. Yet that same weightlessness persists. It was a cold, blustery night. I did not bother to turn on any lamps. A draft curled around my feet as I stood in the kitchen. I shivered. I was not all the way awake. It took me a while to realize that someone was speaking. At first I thought it was the wind or an elephant seal barking. I reached for the faucet, fumbling in the darkness. Then a single word caught my ear: "Dead."

I set my glass on the countertop and strode out of the kitchen, my head cocked, listening hard. There was, after all, a light in the living room. As my eyes adjusted, I could see that Charlene's bedroom door was outlined with a glimmer of gold. A voice was coming from inside, floating through the wall.

"Andrew," Charlene said.

My breath caught. The darkness in the room was overpowering. The sky outside was overcast. No moon, no stars. Only the glow from Charlene's room could be seen. It might have been the only light in the whole world. No one else should have been awake, let alone cloistered in some secret conference, discussing matters best left alone. For a moment, I stayed on the razor's edge, willing myself to walk away.

Instead, I gave in. Stepping closer—moving carefully over the creaky floorboards, past the octopus's cage—I eavesdropped. Charlene's tone was soft enough that I could catch only phrases, here and there.

"The night he died—"

"At first I wasn't sure—"

"Andrew coughed—"

"He wasn't alone out there—"

It did not take me long to put the pieces together. I shook my head. I knew now what story Charlene was telling. She had told the same tale to me over the Christmas holiday. I remembered her eager expression, her dancing hands. I had not been a good audience. Anything to do with Andrew was not worth a second thought, in my opinion. I had shown no inclination to analyze the matter, to ponder and speculate. Now it seemed that Charlene had chosen to confide in someone else.

I wondered who she was talking to. I wondered who else was in that room, seated on the bed, as silent as a cloud. I never caught the sound of another voice. I listened to the rise and fall of Charlene's words as I might have listened to music, following the chord progression rather than the notes. Then I began following the rise and fall of the wind and the tide instead. The breeze howled. The waves crashed. In the distance, the storm-petrels were crying—their day just begun, the flock gathering, preparing to do what was neces-sary, ready for their nocturnal journey.

24

A FEW DAYS LATER, I was roused by a guttural cry. I think I already knew on some level what had happened. I had been there before. Feet running. Voices on the wind. Some kind of emergency. Someone in trouble again.

This time it was Lucy who came barging into my bedroom. At the sound of the door opening, I tugged the blanket off my head. She had obviously just come from outside. She was wearing her hat and work boots, and she smelled like the ocean.

"Get up, for God's sake," she shouted. "We need you."

I opened my mouth to ask a question, but she was already gone. I heard her thumping down the stairs. A door opened somewhere. Then the house was quiet. Through the window, I could see nothing unusual. There was a panel of clouds, solid and gray, with an odd ruffle at the top, as though someone had trimmed a stretch of brick wall with lace. I pulled on my long underwear. I found my scarf in the tumble of sheets. In the distance, the elephant seals were bellowing, the alpha males beating their vocal drums, engaging in their usual territorial battles.

"Hello?" I called, heading downstairs.

Nobody answered. The kitchen was empty. A pot sat on the stove with a ladle sticking out of it. There were beans inside. More beans on a plate. Someone had been interrupted in the process of spooning out breakfast. I fingered the contents of the pot. Still warm.

Tugging on my coat, I stepped outside. A breeze scraped my cheek. The ocean had a clean, freshly washed look. The elephant seals were much louder now. The females hooted. The males made a gravelly bellow like a truck engine changing gears. There was another sound, too. A human voice was tangled up inside the chorus. It was hard to pinpoint where each noise was coming from.

I made my way around the cabin. No one on Marine Terrace. No one at Garbage Gulch. No one by the coast guard house. The helipad was abandoned. Yet the voices echoed all around me now, disembodied, like ghosts. The wind was a trickster, changing direction with each gust, blowing my hair into my face.

At last, I caught a hint of movement at the foot of Lighthouse Hill. The slope was backlit by the sun. The trailhead stood in shadow. Shading my eyes with a hand, I made out a mesh of figures there. Mick was planted beside the path—no mistaking that massive silhouette. Lucy was present too. I recognized the restless shift of her step, bobbing in place. More figures. Blobs against a gray landscape. Four bodies bending over something. There was a workmanlike quality about them, engaged in shared labor.

"Hey," I called.

No one turned. My voice was lost in the wind. As I watched, they knelt in unison like a troupe of dancers doing a simultaneous plié. It was disconcerting. When they straightened up again, I glimpsed a shape at the center, a blur inside the bodies. Something about the whole scene sent a chill down my spine. After a moment, I realized what it was: they looked like pallbearers, toting an object between them.

I began to run.

Mick saw me coming and shouted. The breeze picked up, and he was drowned out by the seals. I was close enough now to recognize the gleam of the surfboard. That was what they were carrying. On the surfboard was a human figure. I saw a blush of red hair. As I drew near, Galen signaled to me.

"She's alive," he said. "We need to get her to the house. Grab hold."

Mick and Forest were on one side. Galen and Lucy, on the other, were struggling to keep their half aloft. I lunged into the breach, snatching at the slick plastic with both hands. The surfboard was heavy. It swayed in my fingers as though it retained some memory of its time among the waves.

Once I was sure of my hold, I was able to focus on Charlene. She lay on her back, her limbs akimbo, her hair fanned around her brow. A sacrificial victim on a litter. She appeared to be unconscious. Looking closer, I saw a bump on her temple. She had the beginnings of a black eye. Her elbow was dislocated; beneath the sleeve of her coat, one arm was bent the wrong way. The sight sent a wave of nausea through me. I lifted my gaze, fixing my attention on the cabin instead.

We were moving in lockstep now. The ground was slippery and treacherous. In front of me, Galen was cursing to himself. Lucy kept accidentally kicking my calves. We walked for what felt like hours, bearing Charlene, trying not to jiggle her too much. Periodically she would give a breathy groan. Mick kept shouting encouragement over the breeze. "Nearly there." Pause for breath. "Just a few more minutes." Pause for breath. "Great work, guys!" Soon I found that I had to move sideways, crablike. The five of us stumbled along Petrel Bluff. The sea roared around us, and the elephant seals roared too. A flock of birds passed overhead, warbling to one another. The Farallon Islands continued to be unperturbed by our private disasters.

Finally we reached the porch. With all due ceremony, Charlene was ushered inside. We laid her down. She stirred for an instant, but she did not open her eyes. Around me, the others were already in motion.

"The radiophone," Galen was saying. "I sent out a call earlier, but nobody seemed to be around. I have to—" Muttering, he hurried away.

"Has anybody seen the first aid kit?" Forest said.

"Come on." Lucy took his hand and led him down the hall.

Mick pushed past me, saying, "Ice pack. Or some frozen peas, maybe."

For a moment, I was alone with Charlene. Her breathing was labored. Quite plainly, she was unaware of my presence. She was not aware of anything at all. I looked her over. She was dressed in jeans, hiking boots, and a man's jacket—her usual uniform. Other than the black eye and dislocated elbow, she did not appear to be wounded. But there was moss in her hair. A smear of mud on her brow. Her sleeve was torn. She had a stick jammed into one pocket.

Maybe it had caught there as she rolled down the hill. I reached toward her shoulder.

The octopus appeared suddenly. I drew my hand back with a grimace. On the coffee table, a few feet away, he ballooned into the center of his tank. He startled the life out of me as he oozed along the glass. His skin was a bright, aggressive red. His eyes swiveled on their stalks, glaring at Charlene.

The silence of him struck me anew. A dog might bark, a cat might yowl, but an octopus made no sound at all. Oliver hovered on a cloud of tentacles. I wondered how Charlene would appear to him, refracted through his bizarre, aquatic mind. I wondered what he might think had happened to her. She shifted on her surfboard, sighing. The octopus groped at the wall of his tank. He released a cloud of bubbles.

Before my eyes, the red started to wash from his skin like paint wrung from a rag. Crimson, I knew, was the color of wrath. I watched as he turned pink, then lavender, and finally blue. A pale, chalky azure. The color of concern.

25

I BEGAN TO PHOTOGRAPH the world around me when I was
ten or eleven. I was not yet an artist; I was merely a child with a
hobby. You indulged me, as you did with all my passions. You
bought me rolls of film. You drove me to the store to have my pictures developed. You hung my best snapshots on the fridge.

Once, however, you did express a note of concern. I remember
it well. It was autumn, and we were strolling through our neighborhood, window-shopping. The local boutiques had decorated themselves with paper leaves in orange and gold. We passed the post
office. We stopped to gaze at the delightful wares on display at the
toy store. The sky was blindingly clear as you and I rambled down
K Street. I remember the jangle of your bracelet. I remember the
sugar of your perfume.

A homeless man was asleep on the sidewalk. He lay in a sprawl,
a stretch of newspaper over his face. It took me a moment to figure
out whether he was breathing. The stench was terrible. His clothes
were filthy and torn.

You fumbled in your pocket and came up with a coin to toss
in his cup. I had my camera with me—a black and gray Olympus
OM-1, barnacled with buttons and dials. It was an early single-lens
reflex instrument, the best of its time, loaded with 35-millimeter

film, heavier than my purse. Using it was a wonderfully tactile experience: the grind and swivel of the image coming into focus, the clack of the shutter, the resistance of the film advance lever. I leaned over the man's prone form. He was missing a shoe, and his bare foot was swollen. The toenails resembled bear claws.

You laid a hand on my arm.

"Don't," you said.

I looked at you in surprise. You led me away.

Later, you tried to explain. It had worried you to see me like that—gazing with such detachment at another human being so obviously in distress. It had unnerved you that my first instinct had been to try to capture him on film.

"I'm not sure about this," you said, tapping my camera.

At the time, I found this unfair. I believed I had done nothing wrong in pointing my lens at a man asleep in public. I had not hurt anyone.

Now, of course, I know better. You were right. You were so often right. More than any other art form, photography requires coldness and dispassion. Perhaps I had those qualities as a child; perhaps I developed them over the decades that followed, the years without you. This work demands a mind that sits apart.

Trauma and pain are the foundations of art. I believe that. When tragedy strikes, however, a muralist or a watercolorist has the opportunity to be a human being in the moment and an artist afterward. Faced with the death of a loved one, a sculptor or por-traitist can first grieve, suffer, and heal—then create. Most artists go through life this way. They can react normally to the trials and tribulations of the human experience. They can pass through the world with compassion and comradeship.

They can make their art later. Outside, elsewhere, beyond.

But photography is immediate. It does not offer the luxury of time. Faced with blood, death, or transformation, a photographer has no choice but to reach for the camera. An artist first, a human being afterward. Photography is a neutral record of all events, a chronicle of things both sublime and terrible. By necessity, this work is made without emotion, without connection, without love.

WE HAD TO wait a long while for the helicopter. Everyone did the best they could in the meantime. Mick held a bag of frozen peas to Charlene's head, alternating between the bump on her brow and the black eye. Forest did some exploratory palpating of her dislocated elbow. It was red and puffy, but not so swollen as to indicate a broken bone. Lucy made sure there were no other, unseen injuries, checking Charlene's stomach and legs as the men kept their eyes averted. Charlene herself moved in and out of consciousness; she might frown when the ice touched her forehead or grumble something inaudible, but a moment later she would be out cold again.

There was not much I could to do help. I found myself tapping my fingers on my thigh, wishing I had my camera. I wanted to get a few shots of Charlene's limp fingers, her bruised skin. This moment was ripe for capture. But I knew better than to go fetch Jewel or Gremlin. It would have seemed heartless to the others.

Finally Galen put his foot down. He summoned us all into the kitchen and insisted that we eat something.

"You'll feel better," he said. "This is not a request."

Leaning against the kitchen counter, consuming a peanut butter and jelly sandwich, I did not attempt to contribute to the conversation. I listened to the biologists, who seemed fairly unfazed. Everyone ate heartily. In steady, tranquil voices, they debated what might have happened to Charlene.

"Did anybody see her this morning?"

"She did say something about going up Lighthouse Hill."

"I remember! The elephant seals—"

"She must have lost her footing."

"The fog was bad. I got turned around at Breaker Cove."

"Me too! I was at Dead Sea Lion Beach, and—"

"Did anyone notice if Charlene had her binoculars with her? Maybe she dropped them. They're a good pair."

"She shouldn't have gone up alone."

Still, I said nothing. Galen's glance flicked my way. He was frowning. There was tension in the air, running beneath the casual conversation.

When the helicopter arrived, I was in my bedroom. I watched through the window as Forest and Galen hurried across the grounds. The helicopter glinted in the sun. It had the look of an aerial ambulance, a red cross painted on the door. Awash in déjà vu, I watched it settle on the helipad.

Two figures emerged from inside, hefting a stretcher between them. I had been expecting more federal agents—more badges, more clipboards, more holsters tucked discreetly out of sight—but these men were clearly medics. They wore hospital green. I had been expecting, too, to see the same doctor who had attended Andrew. Now, though, I realized that he must be a medical examiner, specializing in the dead. This time the mainland had sent along two older gentlemen, one with gray hair, one black. Galen and Forest approached them and shook hands. The group made its way toward the cabin.

With some trepidation, I left my bedroom. There was a bustle at the front door. Lucy was heading outside for a little bird-watching. (Later on, she would justify her actions, claiming that she'd seen an albatross landing near Indian Head. More likely the incident had reminded her of the loss of Andrew. She couldn't stick around for that.) I stepped into the living room in time to see the doctors negotiating their stretcher down the front hallway. One bent over Charlene, checking her pulse and peering beneath her eyelids. Mick was hovering against the wall, chewing on his fingernails as though he intended to gnaw them right off his hands. Forest and Galen were standing at attention. They had the demeanor of athletes on the bench during a key game.

With great efficiency, the medics hefted Charlene from the surfboard onto the stretcher. They held a conference, standing close together. Their aspect was unhurried. They clearly did not perceive Charlene to be in any immediate danger. The black-haired doctor tugged a notebook from his pocket. He stared at Mick, frowned at Galen, and examined me as though taking my measure.

"Sit," he said.

"What?"

He pointed. "Sit there."

I sank onto the couch. It was not a time to argue. The doctor peered at me a moment longer, then turned to Forest and beckoned him over.

"I need to know everything," he said. "When did the accident happen?"

Forest began to speak in cool, thoughtful tones. On balance, I was glad to be seated. I felt dislocated, outside myself. Tiny details seemed of immense importance to me. The hum of the radiator. The scratch of the medic's pen on his pad. Outside, the sea was breaking against the shoreline. The spray was wild, casting up a mist that glittered with rainbows like a sprinkler in the sunlight.

A sound caught my attention. The second doctor—a gray-haired fellow with a generous paunch—had left his post at Charlene's side. He was approaching Galen. There was a diffident quality about him. I gave him a long glance, summing him up: gentle, bespectacled, a teddy bear of a man. Though he kept his voice low, I could hear every word.

"You look familiar," he said. "Have we met?"

"I don't think so," Galen said.

"I'm good with faces. Are you from San Francisco originally?"

For a moment, I thought Galen wasn't going to answer. Then, unwillingly, he said, "Yes, I am."

"Are you married?" the doctor said.

Galen blushed. There was no mistaking it. He went pink all the way up to the tips of his ears. Seated on the couch, I shifted in surprise. I had never thought that Galen could be capable of such a human response.

"No," he said.

"Really?"

"Yes," Galen said, with a look of pure dislike.

The doctor took off his glasses and polished them thoughtfully. "For a moment there, I thought I had it."

Galen's blush had begun to curdle, turning an angry red. I was amazed at the doctor's pluck—or else his obliviousness. I would never have dared to antagonize Galen to this extent.

A hand touched my shoulder, making me jump. Mick was sinking onto the couch. He pushed a glass of water toward me. I drank it down without registering much beyond the iron taste of the pipes. On the other side of the room, Forest was in midflow, pointing to Charlene's prone form, and the window, and the sea. His reedy voice filled the small space. On her stretcher, Charlene gave a little, fluttering sigh, like a sleeper in the middle of a not unpleasant dream.

LATER ON, I watched the helicopter zipping across the water. The sun was still high, pinned to the silken air like a brooch on a collar. The helicopter moved at a brisk pace. I squinted, trying to keep track of its dark frame, the whir of the rotor.

Gradually, before my eyes, the sea began to change. Something was happening far out, scarcely visible. I caught a splash of spray, a gleam of silver. Shapes were bursting through the surface and ducking under again. Eventually I realized that it was a pod of gray whales. They were passing to the east of the islands, frolicking in the deep water. In the manner of their kind, they had all come up to breathe at once. I saw a shiny torso, a fat snout. Charlene's helicopter passed above them, and their bodies shifted in concert, fins and tails in motion, as though waving goodbye.

26

I COULDN'T SLEEP THAT night. I lay awake for a long time. My ceiling has become unpleasantly familiar; I know every stain, every scrap of peeling paint. One crack trails out of the corner and sketches a shape that, from a certain angle, looks like a horse's head. I stared up at this equine outline, my mind in a tumble. I could not shake the image of Charlene on the hill. Charlene stumbling, falling. The lurch of her hands. The spray of her red hair. The impact of her body on the granite slope. I could see it as though I had been there. The way her flesh must have skidded and torn. The ground crunching and cracking beneath her. The look on her face as the lights had gone out—blank, empty.

Earlier on, Mick had tucked me into bed. He had brought me a hot water bottle, insisting that I put it against my spine. "Back, not belly," he repeated several times. He did not seem terribly concerned about Charlene. He had explained, as though to a child, that these things happened. In his tenure on the Farallon Islands, he had seen bruises, twisted ankles, and concussions. I myself had gashed my stomach. I had been with Forest when he had sliced open his calf. Once, another intern had fallen so badly that he'd suffered a compound fracture—nasty, nasty, Mick said, refusing to go into detail. What happened to Charlene had been an accident, he said.

I fell asleep with that word in my head—*accident, accident*. I must have dreamed. There was another sound. A mewling. A baby's cry. I wrenched myself out of sleep, bewildered, reaching instinctively for the lost seal pup.

The stillness was deafening. The islands had settled, the sea bedding down, the wind heading off to do its wailing elsewhere. Even the elephant seals seemed subdued. For the first time in my memory, they were inaudible. Lucy was not humming in her sleep downstairs. Galen was not snoring. The only thing I could hear was a mouse inside the wall, tearing at something. The cabin was so quiet that I could differentiate between the individual noises of its teeth and its claws.

I hefted myself out of bed and threw on a sweater. I would hunt through the living room for a reference book of some kind. There was no better cure for insomnia than one of those brick-sized tomes, full of Latin names and anatomical terminology, guaranteed to bore me back to sleep.

On the stairs, however, I was brought up short. A lamp was burning in the living room. I bit my lip. Nobody would have left the lights on needlessly; we did not waste electricity on the Farallon Islands.

"Hello?" I called.

There was a scuffle. Galen appeared, tucked inside the armchair, gazing at me with wild eyes.

"Jesus Christ," he said. "You scared the life out of me."

"Sorry," I said.

I was not surprised to find him there. Galen was often active in the middle of the night. I had once read that as people aged, they required less sleep. Galen was living proof. I had grown accustomed to hearing his light step reverberating throughout the cabin, touching the edges of my dreams.

Still, even for him, it was late to be up and about.

"Can't sleep?" I said.

He shook his head. "Insomnia is a beast. Surely there's a line from Shakespeare that would apply here. The death of sleep. Murdered sleep. Something from *Macbeth*."

It was cooler downstairs. A draft pooled around my ankles. The white walls of the living room had a snowy appearance, and Galen's hair stood up in tufts, like icicles. As I approached the bookcase, I felt myself shiver. I had the momentary sensation that Galen himself was radiating a field of intense, damp cold.

"Chilly?" he said, as though answering my thought.

I shot him a nervous look.

Running my finger along the spines of the books, I glanced over the titles. *The Private Life of Sharks. Pinnipeds: A Study. Seabirds of the Pacific.* The clock ticked in the corner. The sea was louder now, a dull, insistent boom.

There was a flicker on the coffee table. I glanced across the room to see Oliver in his tank. His skin was a muddy orange. His tentacles were in motion. He was palpating the glass with his suckers, working systematically from one end of the aquarium to the other. I frowned. He was still trying to find a way out.

"I know why I can't sleep," Galen said. "Why can't you?"

"I think too much."

"About what?"

"Nothing. Everything." I shrugged. "Can you recommend a book for me?"

He did not respond. His brow was knotted. I could not tell if he was looking at me or peering at something over my shoulder. For an instant, I imagined that the ghost was hovering behind me in silence. I resisted the urge to pivot and check.

"Can you recommend a book?" I repeated, each word distinct.

He didn't answer. I was beginning to feel alarmed. I glanced behind me at the empty staircase. Then I shook Galen's shoulder.

"You there?" I said.

He sighed, coming back to life. "Something to read? No, I can't think of anything in particular."

"Are you all right?"

He gave a mirthless chuckle. "Not even a little bit."

"Oh," I said faintly.

We stayed that way for a minute, my hand on his shoulder. He stared up at me. The expression on his face was one I recognized— the biologist's gaze, detached and dispassionate, studying me, storing away the data.

"Your name is Miranda," he said.

"Yes."

"But the others call you Melissa, and Mel, and—what is it—rat girl?"

"Mouse," I said. "Mouse girl."

"You've been here for months. You haven't corrected them. Why is that?"

"I don't know."

I stepped back, putting a few feet of cold air between us.

"That's not an answer," Galen said.

"Does it matter?"

"Everything matters."

The chill in the room had increased. I wrapped my arms around myself, half expecting to see my breath coalesce into frost on the air.

"I have to decide what to do," Galen said.

"About what?"

"Many things. So many."

There was a current running beneath our conversation—a tremor of electricity, of secrecy. It was as though he was trying to tell me something through code. I could not discern what that was. I could not figure out his mood, much less his intent.

"Do you understand?" Galen said. "I'm talking about Charlene."

"Oh," I said, a slow exhalation.

"Seeing her like that." He passed a hand over his eyes. "Poor little thing. It's been a tough day. A terrible day."

"Yes," I said. "It has."

"I brought her here," Galen said. "That's the problem."

I swallowed hard.

"I choose who comes and who goes," he said. "It's my decision. I approved Charlene's internship. I approved your residency. I signed off on everyone here."

"I know."

"I'm responsible for you all."

I nodded. I believed this too.

"It can be a burden," Galen said. "Not always. But sometimes. Tonight it feels that way to me. Tonight it's a dreadful burden."

I thought I understood what he was driving at, though I could not be sure. His state of mind seemed to be in flux, shifting from anger to calm to sorrow with all the unpredictability of the weather on the islands.

"It wasn't your fault," I said. "You can't blame yourself."

"What?" he said.

"It wasn't your fault," I repeated. "What happened to Charlene."

Galen gave me a look that made me quail. It had the force of a thunderbolt hurled from a mountaintop. Once again, I was reminded of Greek mythology. He might have been an angry god of the sea reprimanding a lowly mortal.

"Fault," he said. "An interesting word."

"Mm."

His eyes glittered. "If an elephant seal eats a fish, whose fault is that? If a shark eats the seal, who is to blame?"

I thought about saying, *You tell me*. I did not dare.

"The islands are a dangerous place," he went on. "For humans and for animals. Should I be held accountable for what happens here? Should Charlene? Should you?"

"I don't know," I said helplessly.

"Noninterference," he said. "That's my job. Watching and studying. Never intervening. If a seal pup drowns, I make a note of it. If a white shark is wounded, I take a photo for my files. That's my *job*. Do you understand?"

"Yes."

"But this—" he said. "Charlene—"

He broke off. An unspoken question seemed to hang in the air. Galen was watching me as though waiting for an answer. I did not know what to say. I could not follow his logic. I could not decipher the pattern.

In the kitchen, the refrigerator gave a wrenching groan. Galen and I both jumped. This was a common occurrence on the islands— the fridge was old, and its mechanism always came to life with an angry cry—but now it sounded like a thunderclap. It rattled for a minute, then quieted to a hum.

"I'm disturbed by recent events," Galen said. "That's my point."

"Charlene is my friend," I said, finding my voice.

"Yes, I know."

"I'm upset too. What happened to her makes me sick."

"And what did happen?" Galen said fiercely.

I stared at him with my mouth open.

"Tell me," he said. "Tell me in your own words."

"An accident," I said. "Another accident."

He got to his feet in one smooth bound. I had noticed before how youthful and athletic his movements could be. Years of spartan living on the islands had kept him lean and wiry, a pillar of muscle. He strode across the living room and took up a sentinel position by the window.

In the tank, the octopus ballooned upward. His flesh was decorated with a patchwork of hues—ochre, green, splotches of pink.
He was as multicolored as a firework. It was unusual to see him
flaunt his abilities like this. I wondered if his coloration was indica-
tive of his mood or if he was simply flexing his muscles. Perhaps his
capacity for camouflage required this sort of practice.

At the window, Galen spoke.

"That doctor," he said.

"Excuse me?"

"That damned doctor. He remembered me. I remembered him
too, but I wasn't going to say anything. We don't talk about the
past here."

I was still catching up. Galen was apparently referring to the
gray-haired teddy bear of a man, the bespectacled medic who
had accosted him and claimed to recognize him. I had more or
less forgotten the whole encounter. It had been eclipsed entirely by
Charlene's condition and my own anxious state.

"He knew my wife," Galen said.

"But you said—" I began, then faltered.

"My wife. He knew her. What are the odds?"

I gazed at him for a moment in consternation.

"I didn't realize you were married," I said.

"She died. Eleven years ago. She died."

"Ah," I said, stunned.

"*Damn*," Galen spat out.

He sprang into motion again. As I watched, he paced to the hat
stand and back to the bookshelf, making the most of the little space.

"I don't mention it," he said. "I never bring it up. We don't talk about—"

"The past here," I said. "I know. But sometimes, maybe, it's okay to—"

"Yes," he said. "Sometimes."

Even his hands were restless, moving through the air as though manipulated by a puppeteer—a novice unaccustomed to the delicate wiring. Fingers drifting. Palms turning upward. Elbows akimbo.

"Will you tell me what happened?" I said.

"She drowned."

"Oh."

"We were on a fishing trip. We lived in San Francisco then. We had rented a boat, just for the day, with friends. A squall blew in. Choppy seas. She shouldn't have been on deck. I told her to stay inside—I *told* her. She never listened to me." Galen gave a tight, pained grin. "She lost her balance. Hit her head. She was unconscious when she entered the water. We couldn't get to her in time."

"I see," I said softly.

And I did see. Many things were falling into place.

Something had driven Galen to the most godforsaken, far-flung place on earth. Something had induced him to stay indefinitely. Until this moment, I had been unable to comprehend it. It had been one more puzzle of the islands, too difficult to solve.

Now, however, I understood. He was still pacing, the glow from the lamp tangled in his white hair. I took in his agitation, his brisk stride. Outside, the breeze howled like an irritated child. A shutter bumped against the wall. The elephant seals were making noise now, grunting and squealing. I was doing mental arithmetic. Eleven years ago, Galen's wife had passed away. Ten years ago, he had left the mainland for the Farallon Islands, never to return. The pieces fit together at last.

"It was a one-two punch today," he said. "Charlene on the stretcher—barely even breathing—" He broke off. "My wife had red hair, like hers. It all came back."

"I understand."

Outside, the wind smacked the glass. I held still.

"An accident," Galen said. "Another accident."

"Yes."

He rapped his knuckles against his thigh. Then he said, "How long have you been on the islands? How long exactly?"

"Oh," I said, a bit thrown at the abrupt shift in topic. "Six months."

"And what do you think of it?"

"It's my favorite place," I said. "And I've been to a lot of places."

"Interesting," he said. "Despite everything that's happened."

"Despite everything," I said firmly.

On the coffee table, the octopus oozed into view again. His skin was now the color of blood. He had circumnavigated his tank and was beginning a new revolution. All eight arms grappled against the glass, the suckers splayed.

"I can be someone new here," I said.

For the first time, Galen smiled. "I suppose that's true. You can be Melissa or Mel. You can be a little mouse girl."

"Yes."

"We can all be someone else on the islands," he said.

He shifted his weight. I heard a cry outside the window. It sounded like a seal pup.

"Do you want to sit?" Galen said.

"What?"

"Or a glass of water?"

"No. Why?"

"Never mind."

The octopus turned himself upside down in his tank. There was something arboreal about him in that position—his tentacles scrolling along the screen above him, shifting like tree branches in strong wind. Galen was watching him too. He stepped closer to the glass and bent down. Then he glanced at me. His expression was calculating, his eyes obscured by grizzled brows.

"Every animal acts according to its own nature," he said.

"I know what you mean," I said. "An octopus always wants to escape."

"No," Galen said. "That's *not* what I mean. The octopus doesn't *want* to escape. The octopus tries to free itself because that is its nature. The shark hunts because that is its nature. The female elephant seal abandons her young because that is her nature. This is what I was telling you before. Weren't you listening?"

I realized I had taken a book down from the shelf, a hardcover volume decorated with a photograph of a squid. I was holding it against my chest like a shield.

"It is always a mistake to anthropomorphize an animal," Galen said. "We can observe its behavior. We can catalog its actions. We can keep a record of what it eats, how it mates, where it urinates and defecates, how it plays, where it finds shelter. We can study its actions all day long. All year long. But we will never know what it thinks. We will never know what it wants. Even among humans—"

He paused, running a hand through his hair.

"We believe we understand one another," he said. "As a species, I mean. But how can anyone ever know what's in another person's mind? How can we be sure?"

He paused again. Beyond the window, the surf boomed. The islands seemed to be waking up—no longer peaceful, no longer still. A strange expression flickered across Galen's face. It could have been a grin or a grimace.

"I'm a biologist," he said. "That's what I am. If an animal is violent—if an animal is injured—if an animal acts according to its nature—"

He laughed. The sound surprised me, high-pitched and ringing. It chimed through the living room like a struck gong.

"What do you think of that?" he said.

I was lost. But his mood had lightened, and that was a good thing.

"I'm sure you're right," I said.

It was an empty phrase, but he appeared to take it at face value. He straightened up, towering over me, his chalky hair nearly brushing the ceiling. Then he turned to me once more, and I saw a smile playing around his mouth.

"What is your nature, Miranda?" he said.

I sucked in a breath. I had been waiting for an opening like this.

I knew what he was hinting at. I knew what to do. Galen had broken the first rule of the islands: he had talked about the past. Now it was my turn. In a way, it would be a relief. He had laid the groundwork for me.

I began to speak, stammered, and cleared my throat.

"My mother," I said. "I lost my mother."

"You did?"

"When I was fourteen."

My voice came out louder than I had intended. Galen's demeanor changed, his expression growing softer, more open.

"She was hit by a car," I said. "A truck, actually."

"I'm sorry," he said. "That must have been hard."

"It was. I mean, it is. Still. It changed everything. It changed me."

"Of course."

Galen made a gesture I could not interpret, his finger orbiting in space.

"Is that why you came here?" he said.

"I think so."

"I see," he said. "I see."

The wind had begun to moan outside. The cry of the elephant seals was entangled with the thunder of the ocean. I was breathing hard. I had the feeling that Galen was making up his mind about something. He nodded several times, as though agreeing with a private train of thought.

"That expression is interesting," he said. "You *lost* your mother. I *lost* my wife."

"Yeah."

"You've lost them. You've misplaced them. That's exactly how it is. Something you always had with you, something you were so accustomed to that you never even thought about it. Like your keys or your wallet. I still find myself wondering, 'Where is she? She was just here a minute ago.'"

I looked down at my hands.

"And now Charlene," he said. "I've lost her, and so have you."

I heard the distant rumor of the storm-petrels singing. The noise outside was almost symphonic—the deep bass of the sea, the wind wailing like a violin, the treble of the seals, the piccolo of the birds. Wild music.

"I remember the first time I met my wife," Galen said. "She was so young. So wide-eyed. It was a blind date, of all things. Our friends had matched us up. She and I were walking to the restaurant together. A fine summer night. This little Italian place I liked. All of a sudden she blurted out, 'Tell me the story of your life.'" He chuckled. "That was her way of making conversation, I guess. 'Tell me the story of your life.' I didn't answer. I told her it was an impossible question."

I nodded.

"I could answer it now, though," Galen said. "When you've lost someone, that *is* the story of your life. It's the only story you've got."

All at once, I was so tired I could barely breathe. I found myself slumping, sagging. A weight seemed to have settled on my shoulders.

"Go to bed, Miranda," he said.

I lifted a hand to restrain a yawn.

"Go on," Galen said gently. "I think we'll both be able to sleep now."

27

TODAY IS THE first of March. The new month started on a high note. The radiophone squawked into life in the early morning. Galen went to answer it. He came back beaming. The call had been from the hospital. Charlene was out of the woods. Her concussion was healing nicely. Her cuts had been sewn up. The doctors had run a final test, verifying beyond a shadow of a doubt that there was no brain damage. The dislocated elbow had been reassembled and placed in a sling. Galen told us these things over our standard breakfast of macaroni and cheese. There were cheers, glasses clinking, toasts to our brave little intern.

Galen had spoken to Charlene personally—her voice distorted by static and distance. She had told him that her parents had flown in, renting a hotel room in San Francisco with a nice view of the water. She would stay in their company, pampered and cared for, until she was strong enough to make the journey home to Minnesota. There she could finish her convalescence in peace. This idea brought me comfort. I liked picturing Charlene, her head still bandaged, arm in a sling, surrounded by her parents and siblings. In my mind, her relatives were all as red-haired and genial as she was—a crimson poppy-field of a family. I imagined Charlene in an armchair, being served tea and toast. Charlene being grilled by her brothers and sisters about her time on the islands. Charlene reveling in the glittering pull of the television set, the gush of hot water from the taps, the grease of a freshly ordered pizza.

I went to the window. I gazed out at the sea. All around me, the islands seemed to be growing progressively wilder by the day. Charlene had left this place behind. She had crossed the horizon line. She had crossed over. She was so far away now that I wondered whether I would ever see her again.

In that moment, I wanted to be among the elephant seals. I wanted to be close to them, to photograph them while I still could. I grabbed my digital camera and went out in the mist. I followed the roar of their voices, the scent of their musk. A group of them had settled on Marine Terrace, reshaping the shoreline with their bodies. In the fog, they were lumped like clouds, as soft as pillows.

The pattern of their lives has begun to change. The females nurse their babies for a month. At the end of this time, they mate with the alpha male of their harem. Then they return to the ocean without a backward glance. Pregnant, they leave the islands. They leave their pups alone. There is something ruthless about these mothers. Their business on the Farallon Islands is pure biology. Birth, suckle, breed, depart. No emotion. They do not form lasting pair bonds; they attach themselves to the strongest male, receive a deposit of sperm, and move on. They do not teach, protect, or nurture their progeny. They offer milk, and when the milk is gone, they leave.

The juveniles will never see their mothers again. They must learn to swim, hunt, and thrive on their own. They must learn what it is to be an elephant seal without guidance. Over the next few weeks, the babies will remain on land, deserted, figuring out the pulse and swell of the tides, gradually growing hungry enough to risk that first vital dive into the briny blue. They will depart into the sea, following the schools of fish, following the deep rhythms of their own instincts, discovering their true nature, leaving the archipelago in their wake. Next winter, the ones who survive will return to the Farallon Islands to begin the cycle all over again.

On Marine Terrace, I set up my tripod. I had Gremlin with me, one of my digital SLR cameras. The most expensive and flashy of the group. The fog had wiped away the horizon and obscured the border between the ocean and the rocks. The elephant seals seemed ghostly. Their cries were disembodied in the mist. The air was strangely warm. I wondered if the fevered whirl of their mating had heated the coastline. I removed my sweatshirt. I peeled off the cardigan beneath.

Then I heard it. A high, desperate keening. The sound was coming from behind me. It was a seal pup. On land. Somewhere near the cabin. At once I was in motion. I pushed through the damp air, squinting against the haze.

"This way," I shouted. "Come here. Come to me."

A dark shape appeared. The baby moved with an irregular gait, lurching and snuffling. As it drew closer, it lifted its muzzle and wailed.

I had dreamed so often of this moment. I could not help but believe. Probably it was not the same lost pup I had seen on my walk with Mick all those weeks ago. Probably it was not the poor creature who had been haunting me ever since, inhabiting my nightmares. I knew the odds. But there was no way to be certain. All the babies looked alike, black and smooth. I bit my tongue to keep from laughing. I did not want to startle it away. The sensation was like wings beating in my chest. I forced myself to believe it was the same lost pup, finally found.

I did not touch it. I was not supposed to touch it. My hands floated in space, encircling its sleek head, miming a caress. Its expression appeared to be pleading. As it approached, I backed away, moving in slow, gentle increments.

"Follow me," I whispered. "Come on, now."

The baby obeyed. I led it toward the water. With each step I took backward, the animal bounced forward, as though we were dancing. I stopped at the crest of the hill. My tripod stood skeletal against the mist. On the other side lay a pile of sleeping elephant seals. Gray females. Mountainous males. Inky pups. I waited for the baby to see them—to smell the milk—to hear their throaty breathing—to lunge down the hill—to return to its family at last.

But it did no such thing. It stayed with me, panting at my side. It gazed up at me with what I felt to be adoring eyes. I laughed aloud. I could not help myself. The sound rose out of me like bubbles in soda, bursting into the open air.

"Go on," I said. "Go home."

My pointing figure meant nothing to it. A shooing motion meant nothing to it. The wind was as warm as bathwater. The seal pup snuggled down on the rocks as though it intended to linger beside me forever.

I decided to take a picture.

In general, I do not traffic in self-portraits. The human figure is a subject that has been done to death. There is nothing new to say about our hands, our faces, our bones, our eyes, our gestures, our capacity for emotion and expression, the play of light and shadow on our skin, the fragility of our newborns, the strength of our musculature, the inevitable encroachment of our aging process, the finality of our dying. The story of the human body has been told and retold. As a rule, I photograph animals. I photograph landscapes. I leave people outside the frame.

This is doubly true for myself. I am the artist, not the artwork. I do not want to fall into the trap of seeing myself from the outside. I don't care what I look like. It doesn't matter what I look like. It only matters how I look at the world.

As I slipped behind the tripod and set the timer, I felt a shiver of apprehension. I was breaking the rules—my own code as a photographer, as well as the biologist's creed of noninterference. I was about to stand on the wrong side of the camera. I was about to intervene, no longer passive, no longer detached.

Yet this moment seemed to be a powerful exception. Something remarkable was happening here: woman and stone and animal and ocean and fog. I returned to the seal pup, gazing into its eyes. It squeaked, and I made sounds in return. I did not pose; I tried not to pose. The camera clicked in the distance. The baby waddled closer to me. It lifted its whiskery snout. I extended a hand, and we made contact—a damp, warm touch, as intimate as a kiss. I gasped. I had not expected this. I was glad for the curtain of fog, concealing my transgression from view.

I don't know how long we stayed like that. It might have been minutes. It might have been hours. The sea crashed. The heap of elephant seals snored behind me. The camera snapped image after image. The pup nuzzled its maw against my palm. Its breath on my skin. Its milky scent. The sleepy wells of its eyes.

28

I N THE MORNING, I scanned through the photographs I had
taken. I was not expecting anything astonishing. I was not expecting to be struck by a bolt of lightning. I was looking for compo-
sition, depth of field, beauty. It is strange to think that a moment
like that—quiet, contemplative, alone—can change everything.

But you knew that already, didn't you? You learned that yourself on an icy road in D.C., all those years ago.

I had just woken up. Bundled in the blankets, I held my camera
in my lap. The biologists were scattered through the cabin—chatting in the kitchen, running water in the bathroom, making toast.
The smell of coffee filled the air.

The photographs were better than I could have hoped for. The
seal pup and I seemed iconic, emblematic. Behind our bodies, the
mist was as painterly as brushwork. At first, flicking through the
pictures, I focused on the pup. I was hoping for a snapshot that
showed it in profile, its canine snout and flippers in full view. I
wanted to see its silhouette printed like a shadow puppet on the
air. My thumb worked the button, skipping forward, watching the
baby move and maneuver on the screen.

Then, somewhat reluctantly, I turned my attention to my own shape. My outstretched fingers. The twist of my hips. The fall of my curls.

I cannot explain how it struck me. I felt hot and cold at the same time. Even before I understood what I was looking at, I had begun to cry. I leaned forward, my nose nearly touching the screen. A wet sob escaped my throat.

I have always been a small person. Less than five feet tall. Skin and bones. I eat like a bird (in the colloquial sense, rather than the true one, since most birds are actually gluttons, according to Lucy). I have never been able to gain weight. Sometimes it feels as though I skipped right over puberty, missing out on the curves I was promised in childhood. My breasts are tiny enough that they do not require a bra. I don't have much in the way of hips. No gut. No softness at all.

But there was no mistaking what I was seeing. The incipient swell of the belly. Firm apple-breasts. A voluptuous figure. I could not take it in. I could not think of that woman as myself. She was a stranger. A stranger framed on the tiny screen of my camera. A stranger on the coast of the Farallon Islands.

I sucked in a shuddering inhalation. I batted the tears from my cheeks. The image hit me like a tidal wave. The woman stood in profile. Her jeans were tight, encasing thighs that had begun to thicken. If she had been wearing layers—a hoodie or a sweater— her stomach would have been concealed. But she was dressed only in a T-shirt, which clung. Her hand was extended, cupping the nose of the seal pup. It was a sweet moment of connection. And there, between the two figures, hung a dark orb. Ripe fruit.

I wiped my eyes. I sat up in bed, trying to steady my breathing. My hands were shaking so much that I could hardly hold the camera.

The woman in my photographs was pregnant.

29

I T HAS BEEN a month since I last wrote. I have needed time. It
has taken me a while to come to terms with my current state.
The revelation has filtered through me like sugar in tea—glittering, swirling, only gradually absorbed.

I have stayed apart. I have avoided taking walks with Mick and
Forest. I have ignored Galen altogether. Lucy and I, as usual, have
repelled one another like magnetic poles. I have spent whole days
in my room, examining the photographs of myself in the fog. I have
not always been sure whether I am awake or dreaming. I might
find myself in the kitchen, running water over my hands, or on
the porch, swaddled in the wind, and I will pinch myself surrepti-
tiously, making sure.

I have dreamed at night of the seal pup. I have dreamed of the
ghost. A luminescent figure. A fall of white fabric. A chilly silence.
In these nightmares, she is the one who is pregnant. The ball of
her belly glows like a lamp. The fetus inside is a squiggle of neon.
I have dreamed of Andrew too. A monstrous elephant seal—an
alpha male, all blubber and swagger—has lumbered across the
granite, flinging his limp sock of a nose back and forth. As I watch,
he has thrown back his head and given Andrew's laugh, note for

note. I have dreamed of myself on the grounds, standing at my tripod, photographing a woman and a seal pup. As I frame the two figures in the viewfinder, I have wondered who the woman might be. I never seem to recognize her. In my dreams, she has remained faceless, in shadow, without identity.

I have told no one. I have said nothing out loud.

Yet the evidence is everywhere. It feels as though I have suddenly learned to see color or sunlight—a thousand details that have been there all along, omnipresent but unnoticed. Yes, I have put on a few pounds. I can feel the extra bulk when I sit down, a cushion at my middle. Yes, I always need to pee. Yes, I've been having hot flashes. Sometimes it feels as though there is a furnace in my stomach, a fiery oven sending up a plume of heat. Yes, I've had food cravings. Food aversions. Exhaustion. I have been sleeping like a teenager, craving ten, eleven hours a night. I have known and noticed all these things, yet each has struck me as being unconnected to the others. Isolated symptoms. Pinpoints of color on a canvas. Products of the islands.

Now, of course, I can see the mosaic. I can see the complete pattern.

Even my hair has changed, full and thick. It reminds me of a sad little orchid I once tried to keep in Washington, D.C. During the winter months the plant shed its petals and refused to grow, sitting like a green statue in the waning light. But when a colleague of mine took it off my hands, flying south to Florida and placing it on her porch, the orchid bloomed into a frothy explosion of petals. My hair seems to have been transported to its proper climate at last.

And, of course, I have missed my period. Several periods. I have not thought about it, since my cycle has always been irregular. I flirt with the kind of low body weight that can put a person's menstrual rhythm on pause. Besides, I no longer have any reason to look at a calendar. In a bathroom cabinet, tucked alongside the sink, there is a stock of tampons and pads, a pink treasure trove. The men avoid the area assiduously. When I first came to the islands, Lucy, Charlene, and I all made inroads into the supplies hidden there, nibbling away like mice at a stockpile of grain. But I cannot remember the last time I needed to visit the place.

FINALLY I TOOK the leap. This was a few days ago. I waited until midnight, the sky soaked with moonlight, the big dipper dangling over the cabin. Galen was in bed, Mick and Forest snoring, Lucy humming in her sleep. I headed into the bathroom, where there was a full-length mirror, the only one on the islands.

I almost didn't go through with it. For a while I hovered, irresolute. I thought about going back to bed and slipping beneath the blankets. Turning out the light. Returning to the state of denial I had maintained for so long.

I reminded myself that I could not be sure of anything yet. There was no stick for me to pee on. There was no gynecologist's office to visit. The impression I had gleaned from a faraway self-portrait taken over a month ago was hardly a solid diagnosis. I reminded myself that many of the traditional markers of pregnancy had eluded me. I hadn't been vomiting at all hours of the morning. I hadn't been exhibiting any nesting instincts, leaving the mopping and sweeping to Lucy. Since I never wore a bra, I hadn't even been able to verify whether I could still fit into my usual cup size.

In addition, the symptoms I had experienced were far from conclusive. There was a credible rationale for each one. The weight gain might be nothing more than the normal spreading of age. My food aversions might have arisen from our dreadful meals, all that Spam and tuna. My sleepiness might have been triggered by the incessant, wearying chill. Perhaps the islands were playing tricks on me. Perhaps the whole thing was an illusion, an error, one more bizarre dream.

I sat down on the toilet, still clad in my jeans. I laid my head in my hands.

I had come this far. I would see the thing through. It was time to connect the picture with the person—the figure on the screen with my own flesh and blood. It had been a while since I had looked at myself naked. Before Andrew. There on the cold tile, I kicked off my pants. I peeled off several layers of T-shirts. I even shed my socks. Sucking in a deep breath, I turned and faced the mirror.

My belly, broad and golden, protruded over a tangle of pubic hair. My breasts were swollen. There was no question. There was no mistake. The weight was not limited to my torso. Extra flesh had been relegated to my backside. Even my thighs were affected: soft columns, the muscle concealed by new deposits of fat. My stomach glowed in the light like the waxing curve of the moon. I laid my hands on that globe. It felt like years since I had made contact with my own skin.

For the next few minutes, I conducted a thorough investigation. My belly was taut and springy, the consistency of a basketball. I had always imagined the pregnant paunch to be slack and plush, but mine was firm and rubbery—a shield, rather than a pillow. My breasts were heavy. I cupped each one. Fibrous beads seemed to have to have taken root beneath the surface like bulbs in earth. Milk ducts. I gave one nipple an experimental squeeze. Yellow fluid oozed out in honeyed droplets.

My belly button was in an odd condition. It seemed to be transforming from an innie to an outie, currently mid-reversal, like a shirt tangled in the drier. I palpated that nubble of flesh. I stepped closer to the mirror. The pigmentation of my whole body had begun to alter. My face was ferociously freckled now, my cheeks so crowded with maculae that I looked almost tanned. My nipples had darkened to the color of wood. Beneath my navel a brown line had appeared, tracing a path down to my pubic hair, bisecting the lower half of my abdomen. A term from a long-ago health class popped into my brain: *linea negra*. A classic indicator of pregnancy.

Trembling with shock and cold, I got dressed again.

Please help me. Just this once, Mom, help me. What am I going to do?

30

THERE IS A photograph of you that I used to keep on my night
table. Framed against a sunlit prairie, you wore a red dress.
Your limbs were lanky. Your hair was swept up in a messy
bun. You looked as though you were about to smile—your eyes
amused, your mouth pursed like a butterfly with its wings folded.

You were four months pregnant in the photo, though a casual
observer might not have noticed this. In the snapshot, your sun-
dress both concealed and enhanced the swell of your belly. The fabric worked like an optical illusion. It was the kind of garment that
many women favor in the second trimester, the kind that makes
everyone look a little bit pregnant, the kind that leaves strangers
guessing.

As a child, I loved this picture for many reasons. Your expression, your elegant arms, the backdrop of greenery. But my favorite
thing was the fact that it seemed to be an image of one person, yet
was actually an image of three. My father had taken the snapshot.
You and I were captured there through his eyes.

THE SEASONS HAVE begun to change. It is April, and the days
are markedly longer, the sun lingering in the west every evening

like the last guest at a party. There is a new perfume on the breeze. Galen has taken to throwing open the windows, letting in a wash of sweet wind. The chill does not bother him—and indeed, it does not bother me. I could bathe in that salty air. Lucy has been afflicted by spring fever, vacuuming the curtains and emptying the cupboards so she can scrub into the corners. She has been moving systematically through the house, wiping mold from the grout, batting cobwebs from the ceiling. (She seems to feel the need to clean wherever I happen to be. If I'm on the couch, she wants to beat the dust out of the cushions. If I'm in my bedroom, she wants to get in there and wash the windows, since she's doing the whole upper floor.) The animals are changing too. The gray whales are migrating on. The elephant seals are nearing the end of their time here. Soon it will be Bird Season.

In Washington, D.C., the long, gentle spring has begun, I am sure. It has always been my favorite time of year there, the weather opening like a flower, petal by petal. Every day will be a degree or two warmer. The crocuses push up through the soil and burn like sparklers in the grass. Robins carol wildly in the mornings. The trees are studded with buds strewn across the wood like Christmas lights—and then, all at once, the leaves will open. One day the branches are bare, and the next they will be coated with raw green, as fine as tissue paper. The cherry blossoms, too, will begin to flourish, and this, in turn, will attract the seasonal migration of Japanese tourists, who will flood the streets for weeks at a time, reading their maps upside down and photographing oddities like squirrels and vandalism.

The spring brings out a puckish side of my father. After accomplishing the usual reorganization of his closets—sweaters and boots stowed away—he will make a few subtle changes to his appearance. He might start wearing silk ties to work, rather than the heavy woolen things he associates with cold weather. He might shave off his winter beard and let the full glory of his pink chin shine.

Recently I sent him a long-overdue postcard. SPRING, I wrote, in fat capital letters. That was all.

By my reckoning, I am five months pregnant. The past few weeks have been odd, to say the least. I have kept one hand planted on my belly at all times, tucked under the swing of my sweatshirt, verifying the reality of my situation. I have floated through the cabin in a daze, attending to no one and nothing around me. I have not taken a single photograph—except in dreams. I have left my cameras under my bed. I have climbed Lighthouse Hill, standing in the wet wind, staring toward California. I have found myself on the coast, looking for my lost-and-found seal pup. But I have been unable to distinguish between the dozens of little bodies lolling in the sunlight. The female elephant seals are gone. The males are nowhere to be found. The babies, abandoned, huddle together, gathering courage for the new life ahead.

Eventually I will tell someone. Maybe my father. Maybe Mick. None of the biologists are aware of my circumstances, I am certain. The men are oblivious by nature, and Lucy does not pay enough attention to me to have noticed a change; I am simply an obstruction in the path of her mop. For now, I intend to ponder the matter on my own. I will let my opinions arrange themselves with each

shift of mood, dancing, falling, and resettling, like the beads in a
kaleidoscope.

I often find myself holding still, head bowed, trying to sense the
life inside. My stomach is warm. My womb is heavy, grounding me
to earth. I feel as though I am coming back to myself. Not Melissa.
Not Mel. Not mouse girl. Not the image on the camera screen. Not
the woman in the mirror.

ON A CLOUDY morning, I made a decision. The biologists were
out on Seal Watch. I saw them go, four figures marching down
Marine Terrace, heading for the water. The sky looked as though
it had been ironed improperly, a length of cloth rumpled here and
there by bunches of crinkled gray. Galen was carrying a carton of
gear. Mick was giving instructions with big gestures. Forest and
Lucy had their heads close, as though sharing secrets. As soon as
they were out of sight, I got to work.

I had not decided what to do about the baby. I had not decided
whether to keep it. I had not made up my mind about adoption,
termination, suicide, feticide. I was not sure if I had bonded with
the fetus. I could not tell whether the glow in my chest came from
panic or love or shock or heartburn. I had not decided whether to
call Captain Joe to come fetch me. I had not settled the question
of whether to summon a helicopter. I had not fully accepted that I
was not dreaming, or altered beyond redemption, or trapped in the
perspective of someone I could not trust. I had not decided whether
to throw myself into the sea. I had not decided much of anything.

But I had made up my mind about Lucy's pet.

In the kitchen, I found a plastic bucket. I filled this with tap water and carried it to the coffee table, setting it beside Oliver's tank. Then I rummaged through the fridge until I found the crabmeat. As usual, the octopus was in stealth mode, nowhere to be seen. But I knew the drill. I tapped three times on the lid. I had often seen Lucy do this, signaling to the octopus that it was time to eat. At once a bubble of tawny skin erupted from the pebbled floor. Oliver's arms were in motion, writhing and whirling, propelling him upward. His eyes poked out on stalks. I saw the horizontal bar of each pupil, the yellow iris. At this point, Lucy would usually open the small trap door and drop the crabmeat through the aperture.

I, however, removed the entire lid of the tank. For the first time, Oliver and I looked at each other face-to-face, with no screen or pane of glass between us. He turned an angry crimson. He was unsettled. No one had ever taken the lid off his cage before. Octopuses were too clever, too determined to escape; it wouldn't be safe to leave the tank open, even briefly. I dropped the crabmeat with a splash. Oliver grabbed for it absentmindedly, his yellow eyes still fixed on me.

Even now, I can't explain what was driving me. The inclination had come with the force of an edict from heaven. There was no gainsaying it. Maybe it had to do with the indignity of Oliver's captivity in this wild place. Maybe it had to with Lucy herself—her ignorance, her cruelty. Maybe it had to do with the prodigal seal pup that had been returned to me, against all odds, by the islands—the pup who had, in turn, revealed to me the tiny creature incubating in my own belly. That fish-fetus swam in a private tank, a bath of amniotic fluid. Squirming in the warm darkness. Wiggling its anemone fingers. Sharing my breath and blood.

Slowly I stretched out both hands, my palms hovering above the water. After a moment, Oliver took the initiative. His tentacles were as slippery as earthworms. I could not restrain a grimace. The suckers hurt a little, which surprised me; I had imagined them to be smooth and hard, like suction cups. Instead, they seemed to be made of a thousand tiny feelers. I did not rush him. I allowed him to explore my skin. The furious red began to leave his flesh. He wrapped a wet arm around my pinkie. It was an oddly intimate gesture, his grip as gentle as a baby's.

Then I felt a pull. He was hoisting himself upward, levering himself against my fingers. He was heavier than I had anticipated—the weight and solidity of a softball. The tentacles slithered around my wrists, braided across my skin.

A few minutes later he was in the plastic bucket. I had my coat on, heading for the sea. The air was tinged with salt. Oliver bobbed awkwardly around, sloshing back and forth with each stride. Occasionally the centrifugal force would roll him over in a pinwheel of tentacles. I was moving fast, though there was not a soul to be seen. For the moment, I had Southeast Farallon to myself. I was glad of it. When Lucy noticed, in a day or two, that her pet had disappeared, I would do my best to feign innocence. *Oh, the octopus? Gosh, the last time I saw him, he was in his tank.*

At the shoreline I slowed down. The stones were slippery, coated with algae. Up close, the water was laced with shadows. I braced myself against a boulder. The sea lapped quietly. I picked up my bucket, tipped it slightly—and Oliver came flying out, lunging through the air, his tentacles akimbo. A rainbow of droplets followed him. He landed in the surf with an undignified smack. I laid a hand on my belly, that taut, fiery orb. This posture had become habitual to me.

Then I felt something new. There was an answering caress from inside my body. A brush. A shift. I did not recognize the sensation. A butterfly seemed to have grazed its wings against the dark interior of my womb.

I froze. I did not breathe until the feeling came again. The touch was as gentle as a snowflake landing. But I knew what was happening now. It was the baby's quickening. It was the first palpable movement. It was proof of life.

I did not cry. I was done crying. I could still see the octopus, caught in the swell of a wave. Before my eyes, he sucked in a mouthful of water and plunged downward. A wisp of red. A flicker of tentacles. An ocean that was no longer empty.

BIRD SEASON

31

LIFE IS NOT what I thought it was. I am not what I thought I was. A photographer, a nomad, a motherless daughter. A letter-writing woman, shedding a wake of paper and words across the world like the trail of an airplane. An artist with a camera for a brain: cold, clear, calculating. A woman in black.

Galen had asked me: *What is your nature, Miranda?*

Something happened to me the day I made contact with the seal pup. The day I broke the rule of noninterference. The day I crossed to the other side of the camera and photographed myself. The day I remembered I had a body.

For five months, I missed the fact of my own pregnancy. Yet I do not believe this was entirely my fault. Many of the traditional signs of the condition eluded me altogether—nausea, tender breasts, acne. The symptoms I did experience were hardly definitive. There was a plausible justification for each one.

In short, I do not think I am to blame. I do not think I am insane. I simply did not understand my own nature. Not until now.

The body and the mind are meant to be woven together: thought into emotion into sensation into senses into flesh. But for most of my life I have been rootless, unmoored, a ghost. All thought, no physicality. I have been a person made of artistic sensibility and grief. I have imagined that my mind is paramount, my body second-ary—the former an intricate instrument, the latter only a vehicle. My flesh has not factored into my identity. The subtle clues of the physical transformation of pregnancy were lost on me. The weight gain, the hot flashes—these things might have been happening to someone else. The hunger and exhaustion were dim and distant.

I was only able to see myself clearly, at last, through a lens. If I had not stepped onto the side of the camera where animals live—where nature flourishes in all its strangeness and glory—I might never have discovered my own reality.

What is your nature, Miranda?

I do not feel the need to write to you as often. Not anymore. I do not feel a desire to take photographs either. It has been weeks since I ventured across Southeast Farallon with a camera in my hand. At the moment, I have no interest in the life of the mind. Ideas, field of vision, light, death, beauty, ghosts, imagination, shadows, love—these are little things. Unimportant things.

For the past five months, without my knowledge or consent, my body has created a brand new living thing. While my mind was focused on images, and tragedy, and letter-writing, my body has been engaged in miracles.

These new thoughts arrived at the same time as the birds.

THERE IS NO describing Bird Season, not really. In the whole world, there are fifty thousand western gulls. Right now, more than half of that number are here on Southeast Farallon—most of them directly outside my window. And it doesn't stop there. There is a great murre city tucked behind a high hill. In order to see it, you have to scale the rock face and look down from above. The murres are lovely creatures, finely sculpted. They have the tuxedo coloring of penguins—black backs, white bellies—but penguins can be comical, whereas the murres are nothing short of elegant. Above their rookery, Lucy has built a blind, inside which she can crouch. She scavenged the wood and metal from the coast guard house. She even brought up a couple of kitchen chairs from our cabin. There are a hundred thousand birds in the murre colony. In addition, there are forty thousand auklets on the islands. Twenty thousand cormorants. Four thousand pigeon guillemots.

This information is not news to me. I've been hearing about it for weeks from an overexcited Lucy, who looks forward to Bird Season each year like a small child waiting for Christmas. (With the arrival of her beloved avians, she has all but forgotten about her missing pet. The octopus's tank was emptied and put away without much comment.) I have been aware that the islands will be home, throughout the spring and summer, to a phenomenal host of birds. Still, my expectations were ludicrously inadequate. I imagined that the scene would be something like a peace rally: a throng of feathery bodies cohabiting genially, swapping egg-laying tips and gossip in warbles and chirps. I envisaged a sea of nests packed together like tents at a campground.

The reality has proven to be very different. I'm not sure that anything could have prepared me, but my naïveté certainly didn't help.

The islands are now white. The birds have stained the stones pale with their guano. Saddle Rock, which I can see from my bedroom window, looks like an ice floe bobbing in the water. The trees are coated with slime. The stench is overpowering, the breeze hung with curtains of ammonia. The air itself is toxic.

Then there is the noise. As long as the birds are awake, they are screaming. A mating pair will holler back and forth for hours. Lucy says that the gulls are communicating, coordinating important matters like who should hunt and who should sit on the eggs—but to me it sounds like some kind of otherworldly battle cry. They shout to tell predators that they are guarding their territory. They shriek some manic version of a lullaby at their own eggs. Each pair of gulls spends most of the day wailing. There are thousands of pairs on Southeast Farallon.

Our routine has changed, as you can imagine. Our presence here is unnatural at the best of times, and we always have to be careful. But during Bird Season, even the smallest of actions can have devastating consequences. At night, I have been told in no uncertain terms to be careful which lights I use. Several of the avian species are nocturnal. By flicking on the overhead bulb in my bedroom, I would be shining a spotlight on their shadowy forms, telling predators where to find them. Instead, I must now use a paltry reading lamp. In the daytime, our movements have been restricted to specific pathways carved through the crush of nests. Every square inch of rock seems to have been claimed. One wrong movement could result in a crunch, an egg oozing its contents onto the grass. Just observe, don't interfere—that has always been our mantra. It is a hard rule to obey during the present chaos and clamor.

There is also a new uniform to be worn on the grounds. Flea collars around the ankles (to fend off the bird lice). A mask over the mouth and nose (to ward off the smell). Thick leather gloves (to repel slashing beaks). And a hard hat, of all things (more on this later). It's also sensible to put on a poncho, since the birds will use any method in the book to combat a perceived threat. They will void their bowels with the gusto and precision of bomber jets.

Lucy is now the undisputed queen of the islands. Each morning, she barks out orders, and we all jump to obey. A thousand things have to be done. For thirty years, people have been studying the seabirds here. This legacy is not to be trifled with. Lucy visits the murre blind every day. But there are also the storm-petrels, which have to be banded, despite the fact that they are nocturnal fliers and avian acrobats. Lucy has been staying up until two in the morning, lurking on the cliff edge and holding out a fine mesh net, trying to nab these deft fliers in midair. Bag and tag. Catch and release. Observe and record. The rhinoceros auklets must be tallied, too, which means that Galen and Forest can be found along the shore in the afternoons, shoving their hands into burrows and grabbing out indignant birds. The puffins, meanwhile, have beaks that are shaped like wire cutters and could, in a pinch, be used as such. In the wrong mood, they are quite capable of lopping off a finger.

But the gulls are the worst of all. They kill for food. They kill for pleasure. They kill for no good reason. They are expert assassins.

They soar around the islands with bloody beaks and a mad glint in
their eyes. It took me a while to discover what Lucy meant when she
wrote *P.I.H.* in the daily log. This stands for "pecked in head," the
gulls' special method of dispatch. *Six chicks dead, found P.I.H. at
Rhino Catacombs.* Southeast Farallon is littered with little corpses.
Broken wings and caved-in skulls are common, the remains of
murres and puffins covered in maggots and the juice of gull regur-
gitation. Downy infants, newly hatched, nestle alongside decom-
posing carcasses. It is a dreadful sight. This is why the auklets and
storm-petrels are nocturnal—and why they dig burrows rather than
building nests. In daylight, in the open, they would not stand a
chance against the killing machine of twenty-five thousand gulls.

The breeding season seems to fill the gulls with an unstoppable bloodlust. They will attack each other with as much fervor as
they do the pigeon guillemots and cormorants. I have seen the gulls
engaging in cannibalistic orgies, tearing at a neighbor's throat and
wolfing down its eggs. They do not even limit their assaults to other
birds. Packs of young males will go after seals, wheeling around
a sleek, gray head and screaming, chasing an animal the size of a
motorcycle into the sea. They would happily wipe out the biologists, too, if they could only get a clear shot—hence the hard hats.
Mick told me recently about a gull that followed him up and down
the shore, working itself into a frenzy. After painting his shoulders
with guano and yelling furiously in his ear, the bird grew so out-
raged that it slammed into Mick's hard hat at full speed. It broke its
own neck and fell to earth, stone dead.

THE OTHER DAY I was in my room, staring out the window. Lucy and the men were on the grounds on Bird Watch, but I had abstained, pleading injury. I had not yet worked up the courage to tell the others about my pregnancy. Instead, I had blamed my bad ankle, even going so far as to wrap it in gauze.

To protect myself and my baby, I have been spending a lot of time in the house. The noise is muffled there, at a remove. I do my best to ignore the thunder of wings, pretending that the chorus of clucking and cackling has a soothing quality, like an atonal symphony. On top of everything else, there is one lunatic gull that has claimed the entire front porch as his personal nesting area. Most birds manage to hold on to, at most, a few bare inches of rock. But this gull is bigger, stronger, and crazier than the rest. We call him Kamikaze Pete. He does not eat or sleep; he just fights, all day long. There is a permanent smudge of bloody crimson on his face. Each time I step onto the porch, Kamikaze Pete appears out of nowhere, walloping my shoulders with his wings and pecking with such ferocity at my hard hat that it makes me see stars. We have all taken to using the back door of the cabin for our entrances and exits.

Now, seated at the window, I caught sight of an elephant seal moving among the nests. The animal appeared to be an adult female, albeit underweight and undersized. She was at some distance from me, making her way toward the water. The image was odd, like a boulder rolling down a snowy hillside. She had a pattern on her shoulder: a birthmark in the shape of a star. I watched her shuffle toward the sea, dislodging the birds, who rose around her with exasperated squawks.

Almost all the elephant seals are gone. The females, pregnant, have moved on. The males, with no harems remaining, have abandoned their precious territory. The pups have taken the leap too, diving into the surf, chasing fish, tumbling and playing, vanishing into the blue. The animals that linger are the ones who cannot leave. The frightened, the sick, the lame—the seals who are unwilling or unable to brave the ocean. This is no place for them. This is no place for anything weak.

The female was already in trouble. I watched her lumbering awkwardly, favoring one of her flippers. Perhaps she had a deformity. Perhaps she had been injured. A few gulls were soaring above her, tracking her. They had not yet worked up enough courage—or ire—to attack. But it was only a matter of time. The seal limped among the nests, and her pursuers screamed and circled.

One gull dived. Another followed suit, closing its wings and plummeting. The seal picked up her uneven pace. The birds began to shriek in a kind of ecstasy. My heart was in my throat. There was nothing I could do to stop this.

Something happened—a flash of beaks—too quick for me to follow. The seal bellowed in pain. Her face was bloodied. The birds dove again, their beaks glinting in the light like bullets. They were aiming for her eyes. They snatched the whiskers off her snout, clumps of fur from her head. She could not defend herself. She could not reach the water. She screamed again, and I saw a gull rising with something in its mouth. A dark, glistening orb, trailing a skein of blood.

After that, I turned away from the window. Mick later told me that the birds had picked the seal's body clean. There was nothing left but bones.

32

A FEW DAYS AGO, I sat down with Mick. It was a breezy after-noon in May. The others were away on Bird Watch, as usual. Lucy had taken Forest and Galen with her to the murre blind. They had brought the video camera to film the birds in secret—the ultimate voyeurs. They would not be back until nightfall.

I brewed a pot of tea. I poured two cups. I handed one to Mick, who was sitting on the couch, watching me with eyebrows raised.

"I'm pregnant," I said.

He paused before he replied, taking a long, contemplative sip.

"I know," he said.

I stared for a moment, then sat down beside him.

"*I* didn't know," I said.

He shrugged. "Well, I'm smarter than you."

He took another pull of tea, inhaling the steam. I hadn't touched mine, though I drew some comfort from the warm mug in my palms.

"You're pretty far along, aren't you?" he said. "I'd say you're into the second trimester. The jawline—the breasts—and you've got the mask of pregnancy on your face. The pigmentation of the skin, right here."

He reached toward my cheek. I batted his hand away.

"I've been watching you for weeks," he said. "I've got three sisters and about a dozen nieces and nephews. You were never going to be able to hide it from me. The way you walk. The way you get up from a chair."

"You're the first one I've told," I said.

"Really?"

"Really."

My conscience gave an uncomfortable squirm. I had sent home several postcards in the past month, all of them bland, frivolous, and mendacious. Perhaps it was unforgivable that I had left my father in the dark. If anyone deserved to know—to be prepared—it was Dad. He was my only real family, after all.

But I had not told him, because I could not tell him. There were no words. The words were unready, unripe. I could never find them on my tongue or the tip of my pencil. They were somewhere else, floating, slippery, half-formed.

I felt a splash of hot liquid across my arm. My mug of tea had begun to tilt. The room seemed to pivot. The ceiling was twisting like a cap coming off a bottle. I thought I was going to faint. A moment later, Mick had his arm around me. He shoved my head between my knees, his hand on the back of my neck.

"Breathe," he said. "Nice and easy. That's right."

"Sorry," I gasped. "I haven't actually said it out loud before."

Spots danced in front of my eyes. Mick rubbed my nape.

"Congratulations," he said. "I guess."

"Thanks," I whispered.

I inhaled in rhythm with the movement of his hands. His fingers tracked up and down my spine, guiding my breath.

"I know what happened," he said.

"What?"

"I know who the father is, I mean."

"Goddamn it, Mick."

"It was Andrew, right?"

I punched him. I used all my strength. The blow was wild, glancing off his upper arm. Mick observed the action with the bemusement of a cat watching the flight of a bumblebee. He dusted off the place where I had struck.

"I'm sorry," he said. "I know you're in a tough spot. I'm sure it's been hard."

I stared down at my lap.

"But I did the math," he went on. "I know it wasn't me." He held up a finger. "Definitely wasn't Forest." A second finger. "Sure as hell wasn't Galen." A third finger. "So that just leaves—"

A silence fell. The weight of the fetus was heavy on my spine. These days, it was all but impossible to find a comfortable pose. The baby's girth could not be contained; it was always pressing on my bladder or lodged beneath my diaphragm, crumpling my intestines. Kamikaze Pete broke the stillness. With a shriek, he rose outside the window, his wings beating inches from the glass.

It was an awful word: *father*. It was an unanswerable idea. Under the circumstances, I could not lie. I could hardly blame an old boyfriend for my situation. I couldn't make up a story about going to a bar—a stranger, a one-night stand. My only hope was to stall and evade. I had practiced a few noncommittal responses in preparation for this conversation. *That's for me to know and you to find out. Oh, let's not get into it. It's my little secret.* Pathetic quips. Useless and unconvincing. I had not been able to think of a decent solution for the quandary of the baby's father. Despite all my fretting, all my planning, I hadn't come up with anything good.

"I'm sorry," Mick said again, softer this time.

"Thanks," I said.

"So tell me. Let's hear the whole story."

"I don't think so."

"Come on," he said. "The curiosity has been killing me."

Outside, the roar of the gulls ticked up a notch, as though someone had adjusted the volume on a vast outdoor speaker.

"We don't talk about the past here," I said.

The words had a hollow sound to my ears, but Mick nodded. His expression became solemn, as though I'd given the correct passcode.

"Let me get you some more tea," he said.

He got to his feet. With that, the subject was closed.

A WEEK LATER, on a rainy afternoon, Galen left a book on my bed. There was a Post-it note on the cover in his distinctive, meticulous script: *For Miranda.* It was a volume I had not seen before, which made me suspect he had been hoarding it. Galen has a cache of goodies in his room—seal stones, bird skeletons, shark teeth, who knows what else. This area is off-limits to the rest of us. We are all aware that there are treasures behind that cracked wooden door. Galen keeps oddities, trophies, and relics. He keeps animal skulls, feathers, and tiny mouse skins. Once, long ago, he told me that his collection even contains a few mementos from the human side of things as well. Love letters. Forgotten items of jewelry. Interesting hats.

I turned the book over in my hands. It seemed to focus on the history of the Farallon Islands. I flipped through it idly. I was not sure why Galen wanted me to read it, but I was not about to disobey an order from him, however indirect.

I settled in bed, on my side, so the baby's weight would not be balanced on my spine. At first—I will be honest—I wasn't really paying attention. The radiator clunked. A drizzle pattered the windows. I leafed through the pages without much interest. It seemed that the islands had always had a dubious reputation. The Miwok Indians of California had viewed the place as a sort of earthly perdition, where the damned were sent to dwell forever in perpetual hardship.

I yawned.

The next chapter was about Bird Season—about the eggers. I pricked up my ears a little, reading with greater urgency. The story began with a man who had the unlikely name of Doc Robinson. In the 1800s, the gold rush was on. Doc Robinson came to San Francisco, like everyone else, to make his fortune. But he was an uncommonly wily fellow. In between panning for nuggets and having his heart broken over the plethora of fool's gold, he noticed something no one else had yet perceived: there weren't enough chickens in California. All the beloved foods that were made with eggs—pastries, omelets, mayonnaise—were absent from daily life.

Even then, Bird Season on the Farallon Islands was notorious. The archipelago was as yet untenanted—a bare, stripped sculpture of stone, a nautical hazard, a spooky silhouette against the dusky horizon. Passing sailors had returned to the mainland with tales of more birds than there were stars in the sky. Hundreds of thousands of eggs, there for the taking. (The gulls had not yet achieved their current supremacy. The ruling force, throughout the summer months, had been the murres.) Doc Robinson had heard these stories. It did not concern him that the murre eggs looked nothing like chicken eggs. They were not smooth, ivory, palatable orbs. Instead, the murres laid green-blue spheres the size of softballs, with leathery, freckled hides. Often their eggs were marked by what appeared to be letters in an unknown alphabet. It would not do to cook them outright: the whites were translucent, the yolks as red as blood, and they tasted fishy. Unappetizing, to say the least.

However, they could be used as a substitute in baking. Doc Robinson gave up on gold. He voyaged to the Farallon Islands and collected a couple thousand murre eggs. Upon his return to California, he made a passel of money and retired in triumph as cakes, muffins, and soufflés once again appeared on menus.

Thus began the onslaught of the eggers. Anyone who wanted to make a few bucks followed Doc Robinson's example, renting a boat and heading out to sea. There wasn't enough gold to go around, but for those who were greedy and reckless enough, there were more than enough murres. The men soon took to wearing "egg shirts" with pockets stitched onto every available bit of fabric. In this garment, one person could carry two hundred eggs. The hapless birds were unable to defend themselves against these unaccustomed predators. There was no governmental oversight, no sense of environmental balance. Nobody paused to consider what would happen if the vast majority of murre eggs on the planet were harvested and consumed.

But the islands, then as now, were a dangerous place. The work was risky. The book painted the picture for me clearly: a man's body weighted down by the uncomfortable heft of two hundred fat eggs. His balance would be affected. He might stumble on the rocks. Guano coated the pathways. Waves washed in, filling the air with spray. Bruises and broken bones were common. A certain percentage of the eggers vanished. They took a wrong turn and were claimed by the sea.

With a sigh, I put the book aside. I began the process of extricating myself from the mattress. The baby was kicking determinedly at my midriff, urging me to rise, pulling me back into the present, away from stories and shadows.

I AM STILL realizing the simple fact of my pregnancy. This idea shines in my mind at all times, throwing everything else into sharp relief. The baby's movements are forceful now. A punch to my rib cage. A scrape down my spine. Sometimes, in a room filled with biologists, I will have the sensation of listening to music that no one else can hear. I will close my eyes, absorbed by the interior flicker and pulse of life. The sensation is so intense, so all-consuming, that I will lose track of things. The world will fall away. I will forget where I am: in the cabin, on the islands, on the surface of the earth—I might be anywhere. The universe seems to be condensed inside my body, encompassed and circumscribed by my own skin.

I have been aware, all along, of how I should feel about my situation. Ennui and despair. Confusion and fear. If Andrew had lived, I might now be planning an emergency trip to the mainland. I might be scanning the yellow pages—our beat-up, obsolete copy—looking for abortion clinics. I might be counting the minutes until the alien invader could be removed from my body.

But Andrew did not live. He drowned. The islands took him away.

And so, this does not seem like his child at all. The two things feel entirely unconnected. There was an assault, an act of violence, somewhere in the past. There is a marvel, a gift from this place, here in the present. The memory of the attack—dark and hateful— is like an old star, disintegrating, crumbling into dust, barely visible alongside a powerful new sun. As the weeks have worn on, what I have experienced, more and more strongly, is wild, wordless, unreasoning joy.

The baby will be mine—mine absolutely.

33

CHARLENE CAME BACK today. That is, she came and went.

The islands had not been the same without her—no swish of red hair, no musical laugh, no warm, diffident presence at the dinner table. I had missed her. I wanted to verify with my own eyes that she was all in one piece, hale and hearty, completely recovered.

Still, my enthusiasm was somewhat tempered. In truth, I was not sure why she was bothering to return. As glad as I would be to see her, her actions did not quite add up. She had said she wanted to collect her things—but Galen had offered to ship them to her. She had said she wanted to say goodbye to everyone—but she could have done this over the phone. Or not at all. I had the distinct impression that she had some other agenda. What it might be, I could not imagine.

The others showed no excitement about her visit. Perhaps they were as baffled by her behavior as I was. Lucy had been up too late the night before, catching and tagging the storm-petrels. She stomped back and forth to the kitchen to refill her coffee cup and glowered when anyone made too much noise. Forest had concocted a new scheme for calculating the total population of the rhinoceros auklets. It was hard to keep track of the exact amount of these elusive birds, since they dug deep burrows and were secretive by nature. Forest, however, had a mathematical equation and a graph paper chart. He was far more interested in visiting the study plots and trying out his new system than he was in seeing Charlene. Even Mick was all biologist that morning, scientific and detached. He sat at the table with Galen, filling out an order form for more flea collars, which we sorely needed.

In general, Galen and I have been getting along well. He has softened toward me since our midnight heart-to-heart. Recently, he even showed me his collection of seal stones. Over the years, he has amassed a pile of them in a battered plastic tub. He did not invite me inside his private museum—his bedroom. We are not yet at that level of intimacy, it seems. Instead, he hefted the bucket out into the hallway and beckoned me over to see its contents. With a welcoming smile, he urged me to pick through the rocks, which I politely did, though they were all exactly the same, black and smooth, weathered and rounded, fitting in the palm of the hand.

By noon, the biologists were all gone. Nobody else stayed to meet the helicopter. Forest went to the rhinoceros auklets, Lucy and Mick to the murre blind. One corner had come loose in a windstorm, and they were trying to come up with a way to fix it without making undue noise and spooking the birds. (If the murres were startled, they would rise en masse. Their eggs would be undefended, and the gulls would move in for the kill. One thoughtless act by the biologists could lead to a catastrophic event.) Galen spent a while fiddling with a little green notebook, scribbling in it furtively. Then he stumped off to observe the tufted puffins—and, presumably, to avoid an encounter with the intern who I now know reminds him of his late wife.

I must have dozed off. I do nothing but sleep lately. I had settled on the couch, with a view to the east, where the helicopter would eventually appear. But the sun was in my eyes. The air vibrated with light and heat. My head grew heavy. And then someone was shaking me awake.

I caught a glimpse of hair—a sweep of rust around a freckled face.

"Hey, sleepyhead," Charlene said.

I sat up, rubbing my eyes. The sun had moved in the sky. There was a foul taste in my mouth. Outside the window, the helicopter had appeared. Its wings were motionless. Perched on the helipad, that glass bubble glinted in the light. The pilot was visible inside, a shadowed figure hunched over a newspaper. In my sleep-addled state, this struck me as funny—like a limo driver cooling his heels in a high school parking lot, waiting for a bunch of teenagers to finish their prom.

"Come on," Charlene said. "Help me pack."

I followed her to the door of her little bedroom. I tried to follow her inside too, but of course there wasn't space for me. Charlene's room had once been a closet, and the bed—a tiny twin—allowed a gap of only a few inches on all sides. After a moment, I crawled onto the mattress. Charlene flitted around me, filling a suitcase with her pillows and teddy bear.

"You look good," I said approvingly.

"Yup." She flexed her elbow. "The dislocation has been healing fine. No more sling for me! My concussion wasn't too bad, either. Sometimes my head aches in rainy weather, but that should pass."

"Great," I said.

She tugged a pair of jeans off a shelf and looked them over with a grimace. After holding them to her nose, she tossed them into the garbage can.

"How is it?" I asked. "Being back on the mainland?"

"Oh, fine," she said.

"Do you miss us?"

She lobbed a sweater at me. "Do you want this? It used to be my favorite, but I can't see wearing it out in public."

"Sure. Thanks."

I waited for her to reciprocate, asking questions about us, about the islands, but she did not. Instead, she kept busy, moving around the room.

"Do you have to go right back?" I asked. "Can you stay for dinner?"

"The pilot's waiting. My parents are paying him by the hour."

Something about her was different. She looked as though she had been varnished. After a while, I realized that she had makeup on. It was subtle, but I could tell—a darkening of the lashes, the cheeks unnaturally rosy. There was an odor in the air, too. Lavender and incense. Charlene was wearing perfume.

Finally she spoke. "Is Galen around?"

"Sure. I think he's at Dead Sea Lion Beach. I could go—"

"No, no." She waved a hand airily. "I wanted to ask him something, that's all."

"You could leave him a note."

"It's nothing," she said.

But she seemed somehow defeated. I wondered whether she had come all this way just to talk to Galen. I wondered why.

She upended a heap of socks onto the bed. They all appeared to be mismatched, and many had visible holes. She sorted through them, flinging pair after pair into the garbage can, her lip curling in disgust.

"Charlene," I said.

"Hm?" she murmured, intent on her task.

"The day you got hurt," I said.

"These are Mick's," she said. "Why was I wearing Mick's socks?"

"Were you alone on Lighthouse Hill?"

"Alone?" she asked, now starting on a collection of underwear.

"On the hill. When you fell."

At last, Charlene gave me her full attention. Her hands were suspended in midair, holding a black cotton bra with a rip in the right cup. She gazed at me with the look I remembered, as focused and inquisitive as a bird.

"I need to know," I said. "Was anybody with you?"

Her eyes were wide, the pupils dilated.

"I don't remember anything about that whole day," she said. "Nothing. My doctors said it's not unusual with a head trauma." She frowned. "Sometimes I get flashes. The hill, the rocks. The morning light. But when I actually fell—" She shook her head. "I don't remember. That may never come back."

"Right," I said softly.

There was a silence, broken only by the chatter of the birds. I glanced toward the window in time to see a spray of feathers—a gull brushing the glass.

"That's actually what I wanted to ask Galen about," Charlene said. "Now that you mention it."

"What is?"

In a convulsive gesture, she reached up with both hands and tugged at her red hair.

"I thought he might know what happened," she said.

I gave her a searching look.

"He and I have talked on the phone a few times," she said. "From the hospital, mostly. I kept getting the feeling that he knew more than he was letting on. I asked him directly once or twice, but he would never quite—"

She broke off.

"I was hoping he would be here," she said.

"I see."

A gull squawked outside—a chick, from the sound of it. Charlene seemed to recollect herself. She flashed me a smile that did not quite touch her eyes.

"It doesn't matter," she said. "I'm going to be fine."

I was not sure how to respond; I had not fully followed her train of thought. But she did not seem to expect a reply. She knelt down, tugging a box from under the bed. I had the sense that she was avoiding my eyes.

Within the hour, I found myself accompanying her to the helicopter, both of us in hard hats and ponchos. Charlene would shed her flea collars and mask as soon as she was safely away from the islands. The pilot saw us coming, and the rotor began to spin above my head, lazily at first, then with greater intensity. It was enough to disturb the gulls, who took flight, a geyser of wings and beaks. Their cries were deafening. I was carrying one of Charlene's suitcases, while she struggled with the other. The pilot threw open the helicopter door. Charlene screamed something, and he screamed back, but the avian clamor was such that I did not catch a word.

Then Charlene turned to me. She tugged down her mask so I could see her face, which wore an amiable expression. She leaned in and planted a kiss on my cheek. I wanted to say something to her, some final words of affection. But before I could come up with anything meaningful, I felt a hand on my belly. Charlene's touch was gentle, yet she moved unerringly, pushing through the layers of sweaters I was using to cover up my bump. Her palm was warm.

"Congratulations," she whispered.

She withdrew her hand.

"You should leave too, Melissa," she said. "You should leave soon. It's not safe for you here."

34

MICK AND FOREST are no longer able to make their nightly jaunts to the coast guard house. Until recently, these evening trysts did continue. Waking in the night, I would hear voices outside my window. I'm not sure how often the two of them engaged in these perilous nights of love. Sometimes it seemed that they were out there every day, and sometimes it was more like twice a month. Now and then, waking to the sound of Mick's soft chuckle, I would smile to myself and reach for my camera. Each time, though, I resisted the urge to snoop. Somewhere under my bed, piled among the debris I had accumulated—jeans too tattered to wear without revealing the color of my underwear, a seal stone I had found on the shoreline, books falling apart under the influence of mildew, watertight tubs filled with precious caches of undeveloped film—there was a digital camera full of glorious images. On the evening that I'd taken those photos, I had promised myself that I would leave well enough alone. I would give Mick and Forest the privacy they so obviously craved.

Now, however, the situation is different. Bird Season means that Southeast Farallon is a battleground, strewn with enemy combatants. Mick and Forest would have to be crazy to sneak to the coast guard house under these circumstances. In the darkness, they could step off the path into the nesting areas. Within seconds, they would have attracted the rage of the gulls. I can picture the scene. The crunch of an eggshell. The squawk of birds. Mick and Forest might try to run. The gulls would take to the air. It would become a free-for-all. Birds would come whizzing in from every corner of the islands—the avian version of a feeding frenzy. Mick and Forest would be found in the morning, bare skeletons, their flesh picked clean.

Over the past few weeks, there has been friction between the two men. This is hardly surprising. They are lovers who cannot indulge in lovemaking. (I still don't understand why they can't do their business, safely and discreetly, in the comfort of their shared bedroom.) At mealtimes, they will often engage in little bouts of grouchiness. A discussion about who should pass the salt will devolve into a war of polite, irritated words, both men flashing hard, fixed smiles. Once or twice, I have even caught them arguing—really arguing—when they think they are alone.

All of us are tense. Perhaps it is the loss of Charlene—her geniality and ease. Perhaps it is the aggressiveness of the birds seeping into our own behavior. There have been more spats and disagreements than usual. Galen and Mick have quarreled over the proper procedure for tagging the storm-petrels. Lucy and Forest have fallen into door-slamming over whose turn it is to do the dishes.

But Mick and Forest are a special case. A few days ago, I came home from a walk and heard Forest shouting at the top of his lungs. Standing at the back door, I couldn't make out a single word. His voice had climbed into the realm of watery hysteria. A moment later, Mick came barreling outside. I had to jump to get out of his way. His face was flushed, his eyes glittering like coal. He did not seem to notice me hovering there. He was in too much of a state. He strode off in a rage.

I AM STILL busy with Galen's book. Every so often, he will ask me about my progress—eyebrows raised, a pointed glance—as though the text is somehow important for me. Ever the dutiful student, I have been hard at work. I have learned about the reign of the eggers. I have learned, too, about the appearance of the lightkeepers. I have studied the history of my adopted home.

On a blustery afternoon in May, I took the book upstairs. I settled in my chair, rather than the bed, so I would not doze—my spine awkwardly bent, my shoulders taut. The baby was jammed inside my uterus at an uncomfortable angle. Flipping through the pages, I read about the lightkeepers.

In the 1800s, it seemed, there had been no lighthouses along the Pacific coast. None at all. Ship captains either had to voyage in daylight or cross their fingers and pray. The Islands of the Dead were such a flagrant hazard to passing boats that the government began to pay attention. Nautical travel was on the rise. It was absurd that the place had yet not been marked with a lighthouse. A crew was sent to remedy this situation.

But the archipelago did not make the work easy. The builders could not transport their usual tools to shore. They could barely get to shore themselves. It was not possible to bring bricks and mortar from the mainland either. Instead, the workers had to mine their materials out of the living rock. (As I read, I remembered the gashes I had often noticed in the landscape, rough-hewn scars. These quarries had, in the centuries since their creation, eroded until they did not look man-made anymore. They had the appearance of marks scored into the earth by an alien spacecraft.) The crew would chisel bricks out of the ground, then crawl up Lighthouse Hill bearing the stones on their backs, like the slaves who had once built the pyramids.

In 1855, after many failures and injuries, the lighthouse was completed. Four lightkeepers were stationed there. They did not have a cabin, like ours. Even the coast guard house had yet to be conceived of, let alone built. Instead, the lightkeepers lived in a stone shack. Food was scarce. Four men, no women. On top of everything else, the pay was wretched. And there were the eggers to contend with.

I sat up straighter, lengthening my spine. Then the baby engaged in a particular maneuver, one I had experienced just a few times before. It felt as though the fetus were skiing down the interior slopes of my body. It never failed to startle and delight me. I had described the sensation to Mick once, and he had explained that in all likelihood it was the baby turning over, doing loop-the-loops in my womb.

I flipped to the next page in the book, recalling myself to my work. There was an illustration at the top of the chapter: a man with a devious expression and a handful of orbs clutched against his chest. An egger.

At the time the lighthouse was built, no one had officially laid claim to the archipelago. Vast portions of the United States were still unowned. So the eggers had overrun the islands. The situation among these men amounted to something between a black market economy and outright piracy. The lightkeepers were caught in the crossfire. As they slept in their shack and made the trek up the hill to work the mechanism, they were aware of squabbles taking place on the other side of Southeast Farallon. Eggers versus eggers. Fistfights were common. Now and then, knives or guns would make an appearance—at which point the lightkeepers would signal the mainland for help. Soldiers would be sent to break things up.

From there, the situation continued to deteriorate. The avarice of the eggers was unending. Once, after a skirmish, an enemy faction decided to hide out in Great Murre Cave and pretend they'd fled the islands. While inside, they were showered by guano. Soon, there was so much ammonia in the air that it became toxic. Driven by greed, the men refused to leave, and so they died there, one by one.

I resettled myself, trying to accommodate the baby's girth. The eggers had begun to remind me of the gulls I saw outside every day—motivated by voracity and anger, bent on the ruthless extermination of all others. The gulls, too, would risk their own safety, even their own lives, to attack an intruder.

The lightkeepers, on the other hand, seemed rather like the biologists. They did not intervene in the natural world. They observed and recorded without interfering. They tended the lighthouse and left the animals alone.

Eventually—inevitably—the eggers had turned their attention to the lightkeepers, too. The eggers had damaged and defaced the government's property. They put up signs warning the lightkeepers not to set foot on their turf. They insisted that the lightkeepers pay for every murre egg they ate. Perhaps the strain of the long war had affected the eggers' minds. At last they attempted to oust the lightkeepers entirely. There was a skirmish in which several people were injured.

The murre population was, by then, in a downward spiral. There were fewer and fewer eggs on the ground—and chickens had finally begun to appear en masse in California. There was nothing left to fight for. But the eggers fought anyway.

In 1881, the government took action. Soldiers came and removed the eggers in one clean sweep. Only the lightkeepers remained.

I woke to a knock at the door. I did not realize I'd dozed off until I opened my eyes. I was still in the chair, spine molded against the wooden slats, book in hand. One finger held my place. There was a crick in my neck.

Mick appeared in the doorway, his hair sticking up. His face was burnished brown from a day in the sun.

"You're busy," he said.

"No. Come in."

I laid the book aside. Mick wandered around the room for a minute, touching things in what appeared to be a random way. He seemed nervous. He spent a while examining the knob of my closet door, fiddling with a loose screw.

Finally he turned to me.

"I was thinking about our conversation," he said.

"About the gulls?"

"No." He pointed to my belly. "About this."

His expression was hesitant. He sat on the edge of the bed, a safe distance away, his weight making the mattress slope.

"You haven't told anyone else, have you?" he said.

"No. Just you."

"Good," he said.

He bit his lip. He seemed to be struggling with an idea—something weighty, out of character with his usual sweetness and jollity. I waited. Mick's mind moved in slow, determined shifts, like the changing of the tides.

"Say it was me," he said.

"What?"

"Say it was me," he repeated. "To the others."

Still, I did not understand. Mick clicked his tongue impatiently.

"Galen and Forest," he said. "And especially Lucy. We'll tell them I'm the father."

He reached across the empty air between us and collected my hand, pressing it between his hot palms.

"I want to do this for you," he said. "I can't do much, but I can do this."

"I don't—" I began.

His grip intensified, crushing my fingers.

"Please," he said. "I mean it. You can tell everyone it was me. Even your family. Your dad. Everyone. It'll make your life easier, won't it? No more questions to answer?"

I could not speak. I threw myself forward, landing against his chest. We nearly tumbled off the bed. Mick burst out laughing. His arms closed around me, holding me, steadying me.

LATER THAT NIGHT, as I drifted off to sleep, I found myself thinking about Galen's book again. The eggers. The lighthouse. The sea. It occurred to me that the book had not used the term "lighthouse keepers." I was glad of this. To do so would have implied that the primary task of those people had been to maintain a building, a human structure. Instead, the book had referred to them as the keepers of the light itself. There was something important in that. Something fundamental. My pillow was warm, the radiator grunting, the air thick with steam. Perhaps there were only two kinds of people in the world—the takers and the watchers—the plunderers and the protectors—the eggers and the lightkeepers. Just as I felt myself on the verge of an epiphany, the wind outside gave a deep sigh, and I slipped into sleep.

35

I HAVE NOT FELT the desire to write to you as often lately. I have not been aware of your absence in the same way I used to be.

After your death, the lack of you was all-consuming. I thought about it constantly. It was as though I'd lost something basic, like my sense of smell or my ability to laugh—the sort of thing I could live without but might not want to. I felt like a tuning fork that when struck rang out loneliness instead of music. I felt as though I'd been halved. These are the things I wrote in my letters to you—and mailed, every few days, to the Dead Letter Office.

Now, however, all that has changed. I am no longer halved. In my pregnancy, I am doubled. That is what occupies my mind nowadays. I can't marinate in my loss anymore. I can't dwell endlessly on your absence. Not when I am overwhelmed by the presence of the baby.

I think about it all the time. I think about *him* all the time, since I have become convinced that the fetus is a boy. There is a maleness about him, all elbows and knees. Sometimes, when I lay my hands on my belly, I will experience a kind of mental shock—the emotional equivalent of static electricity. A baby. A boy. The two words might well be synonyms, interchangeable. That is how sure I am.

At night, I often dream about him. There he is in a diaper and hat. There he is in my father's lap—my father altered by his sudden elevation to grandfather, smiling in a peaceful way that I have not seen since you were here. I imagine my aunts, your twin sisters—I imagine them leaning over a basinet, faces soft. I see my son in the bath. Seated in a red wagon. On the playground. There he is, learning to go down the slide by himself, his mouth a startled O. I imagine the weight of him on my thighs, his head against my breastbone, warm and sleepy, as we turn the pages of a book together. I hear him cry, a piercing siren. I enjoy these dreams. They have given me the chance to get to know the baby before I meet him. He is here with me now. He is filling the absence you created twenty years and a thousand letters ago.

IT IS JUNE. Recently we had a rain-washed morning, full of thunder. The gulls were affected by the weather. For the first time since Bird Season began, their cries were hushed. The islands were eerily still. Through the window, I saw feathery shapes hunkering down, shivering, heads beneath their wings.

Galen and I lingered indoors. Together he and I lounged around all morning. Rain hammered on the roof. He read a book about blue whales, and I roamed the kitchen, hoping against hope that there might be a magical cache of delicious food hidden somewhere. Galen hummed a nautical ditty, and I ate stale saltines. Galen flipped through the daily log, and I napped on the couch.

The daily log is an interesting study in personalities. Forest's notes, for example, are all business, a list of the sharks he has seen. He does not bother with complete sentences, telegraphing his information: *Goof Nose in Mirounga Bay, 6 a.m.* That kind of thing. Mick, on the other hand, tends to ramble on enthusiastically about seal behavior: *Two new mothers this week. Babies nursing like crazy. Already gained a few pounds. Cutest damn things! Wish I could adopt one.* Then there is Lucy, whose entries are surprisingly flowery. In her curlicued cursive, she lavishes praise on the gorgeous sunsets, the wild surf, and the aerial ballets of the double-crested cormorants. Though I enjoy reading the daily log, I usually skip Lucy's entries. In life, she is a solid, matter-of-fact person. On the page, however, she can become pretentious, as though striving to appear deep and emotional. *I would give anything to feel the power and glory of flying free against a purple and gold sky*, she once wrote, apparently without irony.

As the morning wore on, the storm worsened. Rain plummeted in buckets. The air in the cabin was as hazy as evening. Finally Galen summoned me to the table. His smile was warm as he patted the chair beside him.

"How's the book?" he said. "You've been reading it, I hope?"

"Yes," I said. "The eggers."

"And the lightkeepers," he said. "That's the important part."

He narrowed his eyes at me appraisingly. Then he sat back. The rain picked up, a torrent gushing through the gutters like an airborne river. The thunder grumbled. Galen's gaze was lifted to the ceiling. He began to speak. He told me the story of the lightkeepers in measured tones, apparently from memory.

They had flourished here, for a while. Once the eggers were gone, the men had brought their wives to the islands. They had brought their children. They had built our cabin, as well as the coast guard house—twin structures standing sentinel in a lonely wilderness. As Galen spoke, his hands flitted through the air. For a time, the lightkeepers and their families had thrived. It had been a lovely, peculiar life. Children playing at the foot of Lighthouse Hill. Climbing the two small trees. Skipping stones on the ocean. Making pets of the seal pups. I found it comforting to know that I was not the first pregnant woman to have lived on the islands.

The rain showed no signs of abating, as though a tap had been turned on in the sky. Galen's expression darkened. Eventually, he said, the lighthouse had been modernized, remade with an automated mechanism. There was no longer a need for a permanent host of lightkeepers. The crew, along with their wives and children, packed up their belongings and headed back to civilization.

"Modernization is an unstoppable tide," Galen said.

Times had changed and kept on changing. During World War I, the military had shown a brief interest in the islands. Later still, the place had been considered as a possible locale for a new prison or a refueling station for oil tankers.

I let my attention wander. I knew how the story ended. A nature preserve. A wilderness refuge. A home for biologists. Secure, pristine, and untouchable.

Galen tapped my arm. His expression was stern.

"They were our predecessors," he said. "They were like us. Do you understand?"

"Noninterference," I said sleepily. "Nonintervention."

"Yes," he said. "The lightkeepers took only what they needed. They studied and documented and made no changes. They protected this place."

He prodded my arm again, driving the point home.

"That's what we must do, always," he said.

YESTERDAY I GAVE in and visited the murre blind. This was a result of the combined efforts of Mick and Galen, who had badgered me for a week straight, insisting that I had to see the murres fledging their chicks. Though it is June, we don't have warm days here. Instead, we have afternoons of bright sun and sharp wind, the temperature changing by the moment. The climb made me nervous. Galen managed it on two legs, but I found myself on my hands and knees, crawling like a dog and scrabbling for purchase. My belly hung beneath me, a pendent mass. My heart was pounding as I reached the blind. Mick was right behind me—he had been back there the whole time, ready to catch me if I fell.

"I'm not going back down that slope," I hissed in his ear. "I'll just stay up here forever."

"Good idea," he said.

The murre blind was a simple tin shack. Seabirds, as a rule, have good color vision, but they are not adept at recognizing shapes. A group of people standing on a nearby crest would have alarmed them. But a slate-colored hill, topped by a square, incongruous, slate-colored object, did not concern them at all. Mick helped me settle onto a folding chair. The blind smelled funny. Fish and seawater. I leaned forward, compressing my belly, and peered through the window.

The coast ended in an abrupt and dramatic cliff. The murres were packed along that edge, crushed together. There seemed to be no space between their bodies, no glimpse of rocky ground. They moved constantly. The mosaic of black and white feathers shifted like static on a screen. It was hard to pick out individual shapes. The occasional flash of lipstick red indicated an open beak. The noise was deafening. The square frame of the window made me feel as though I were looking through a viewfinder. The verge of the precipice was ruffled with feathers and beaks. Beyond that, the sea stood solid and imposing, a flat slab of gray.

After a while, I began to notice the chicks. Most of them were still at an intermediate stage, midsized, with a mangy appearance, their baby fluff not quite gone, their adult feathers not quite grown in. We had come to the blind to watch these chicks learning to fly. I had observed the process with the gulls already. I had seen that the necessary muscles were in place, and there was clearly an instinctive understanding of what to do, yet a stumble or two was inevitable on the way—a confused farce of trial and error. I had watched young gulls turning sideways in midair, landing on their heads, or simply flapping their wings while running across the rocks, their little faces illuminated with elation, quite sure that they were airborne.

With the murres, however, the matter turned out to be very different.

"There," Mick said, pointing. "Right there."

A pair of birds had taken their chick to the edge of the cliff. Before my eyes, a conversation took place, the parents instructing and the baby responding. (I could not, of course, hear their voices over the clamor; I just watched their beaks opening and closing like a silent film.) And then the chick was plummeting toward the sea. I cried out as the tiny body whizzed downward. Had the parents shoved it? Had the wind caught it at the wrong moment? Had the chick jumped of its own accord? I could not be certain. For a moment, things looked bleak. The chick was accelerating. Moving at that speed, it would not survive a collision with the water.

Then I saw a flutter. A wiggle. The chick flung out its wings. Mick whooped. Galen tugged a small green notebook from his pocket and scribbled something down. The chick flapped once, twice, and began to rise.

THAT EVENING, I made my announcement. I waited until dinner was over. We had just received a delivery from the mainland, and we spent the meal luxuriating in a wealth of salad and fresh fruit. Lucy made chicken with a rich pesto sauce. Dinner was punctuated by groans and the scraping of forks. When we had all eaten our fill—when everyone was leaning back in their chairs, eyeing the dirty dishes balefully—I got to my feet. I lifted my water glass and clinked it feebly with my knife.

"I have something to tell you," I said.

Lucy was watching me steadily. I found it impossible to meet her gaze. Mick intervened. With incredible swiftness, he unzipped my sweatshirt. He yanked the fabric aside with the showmanship of a magician opening a curtain onstage. I was wearing only a thin T-shirt underneath. My belly was undeniable.

"We're pregnant!" Mick crowed, laying a hand on that swollen globe.

In that instant, I saw that nobody was the least bit surprised. I was in my third trimester now. Everything about me was different—bulbous breasts, puffy rear end, indistinct jawline. Still, they all went through the motions. Galen congratulated me in a deep, booming voice. He got to his feet and laid his hands on my shoulders in a kind of solemn benediction. Forest kept a placid smile on his face. Lucy flashed me a bright, true grin. She gave me the first real hug I'd ever received from her.

"He's going to be a great dad," she whispered in my ear.

The evening that followed was strange. They were biologists, and I had become an interesting specimen. Forest occasionally shot me a look I could not interpret; it might have been amusement or discomfort. Lucy insisted on feeling the baby, laying icy hands on my stomach. She stood there for a long time, beaming, waiting until the fetus responded with a kick. Behind her eyes, there was a suggestion of something more than happiness. Relief, maybe.

The clock ticked in the corner. Someone had broken out a case of wine. I sipped grape juice with a sour aftertaste—a few weeks past its sell-by date, I guessed. As the hours passed, I remained quiet. I did not have to lie. I did not have to say anything at all. Mick sat beside me, shielding me, deflecting every question, filling the space with his big, benevolent presence.

At one point he reached over and took my hand. Not since your death had I felt so safe, so protected, so loved.

LATER THAT NIGHT, I was woken by a strange sound. At first I thought it was my seal pup—my lost-and-found pup—calling for me again. Crying for its mother one last time. It took me a while to come fully into consciousness. The keening went on, punctuated by heavy, sodden breathing. Gradually I realized that it was human. A wracked, heartbroken, anguished noise. Someone was sobbing.

I sat up in bed, palming the hair out of my face. For the life of me, I could not figure out where the sound was coming from. It could have been Lucy downstairs, weeping into her pillow. But it also could have been coming from the hall outside my door—from Galen's room, maybe. The wind whirling around the cabin played tricks on my ears. The voice itself was not recognizable. Pain had distorted it, washing out the usual characteristics: age, gender, vocal quality. There was something universal, I realized, in the noise of a person crying. I did not dare get out of bed and try to locate the sufferer. What I was hearing was too intimate for that. I tilted my head to the right and left, trying to pinpoint the source. But I could not solve the riddle. The sound was coming from everywhere at once, as though the house itself were in tears.

36

THERE IS NO way forward except through words. Since you died, I have dealt with every tragedy and loss the same way— by writing. So I will write to you now. Even though my letters have begun to feel hollow, even though the act brings me less and less solace, I will write to you. There is no remedy for what happened today. But I will put the words on paper anyway, hoping against hope for comfort.

The first few hours of the morning were lovely. I woke late, wrapped in what felt like a quilt of sunlight. Captain Joe had recently made an appearance, which meant the fridge was stocked. I ate a bowl of cereal with strawberries and fresh, creamy milk. I found a gossip magazine crammed at the back of the bookshelf, where it had been hiding, undiscovered, for my entire tenure on the islands. I flipped through it with glee. The house was quiet. Only Galen was home. He and I maintained a companionable silence, moving around each other with the mute ease of goldfish in a bowl.

Around ten o'clock Lucy appeared at the front door, hard hat in place. In her poncho, she rustled across the room to where I lay on the couch.

"Get up," she said, standing over me.

"Why?"

"I need help. Mick dropped a piece of equipment in the water. One of my best nets. It's caught on a reef. We need all hands on deck."

Galen was already on his feet. It took me a while to extricate myself from the couch cushions. It took me even longer to get my flea collars around my ankles. I have reached the stage of my pregnancy in which bending over is complicated.

On the porch, the first thing I encountered was Kamikaze Pete. Weeks of unceasing battle had diminished his physical person, but not his spirit. He was thin and bedraggled. He had not taken the time to care for his plumage, feathers jutting out any old way. One eye was permanently squinted shut. Still, he launched himself as vindictively as ever at my skull. I ducked low and made a break for it, skidding down the steps. Kamikaze Pete did not chase me. He stayed on his own turf, shrieking threats at my retreating form. Galen followed me down the stairs.

Lucy was already halfway across Marine Terrace, leading the way. I saw Mick at the water's edge. He was shadowed against the brilliant shards of light strewn across the surface of the sea. Threading through the birds was not easy; I had to be cautious. Chicks of various sizes bobbed everywhere, tumbling onto the path and squawking up at me. Their parents were not as welcoming. They whacked my shoulders with their wings and emptied their bowels onto my poncho. Their cries rose around me like fog, thickening the air, making it hard to keep my bearings.

I glanced up. I saw Lucy in motion. I saw Mick swinging a rope in both hands. I glanced down, checking my progress. Then I looked toward Mick again.

A group of gulls had come out of nowhere. Even at a distance, I heard the screech of their voices, nails on a chalkboard. Wheeling in formation, they plunged out of the sky. Mick lifted his arms, batting the birds away. But there were too many of them. He was encircled by a tornado of feathers.

What happened next is etched on my brain like ink on photo paper. I remember every instant of it, every action, every breath. I will remember it forever.

There was a sharp crack. Mick lurched to the side. One of the gulls had made contact with his hard hat. Another swooped in, slamming against the plastic dome. Before my eyes, the thing broke apart. It seemed almost geographical: an earthquake splintering the hard hat into shards. The pieces exploded outward. Bright plastic, white birds. Mick was without armor. He was defenseless.

The gulls did not hesitate. *Pecked in head*—their favorite kind of violence. They beat at Mick's face, disorienting him. A large female took aim. Her beak glinted. I saw a splash of blood. She had sliced off a wedge of Mick's ear.

He screamed. There was no time for me to take it in. There was no time left. Beaks swiveled around him like knives. Slashing at his forehead. Tearing his throat. Pulling swatches from his poncho. Ripping his fingers to the bone. The birds were decorated in blood now, marked and smeared with war paint.

In what seemed to be slow motion, Mick twisted in midair. He was scored all over by wounds. The gulls had tattooed his wrists and hands with abrasions. One ear was gone. A crimson hole. His Adam's apple poured a waterfall down his neck, streaking his poncho. The birds swooped around him, unrelenting. His hand rose in a helpless gesture. A trail of red mist followed the movement, drifting behind his arm like an afterimage. He was standing too close to the water.

A slip. A stumble. That is all it takes to claim a person's life. Mick fell inside a cloud of wings. He disappeared behind the rocks. A splash rose against the shore, glinting in the light. The birds rose too, triumphant.

Something touched my arm. It was Galen, gripping my elbow to steer me forward. We stumbled frantically through the rookery. We reached the shoreline together. His grip was causing me pain. It was hard, at first, to make sense of the mix of glare and darkness. Dazzling coins were spangled across the water. My eyes adjusted slowly. There was a long shadow inside the wet glow.

Now, in retrospect, I am aware that I did not want to understand what I was looking at. I took it in without registering its meaning. Denial is a powerful thing: it can alter what we see, help us forget the moments of transgression and pain in our lives, keep us unaware of violence. Mick's body bobbed limply on the ocean. Facedown. I held my ground, waiting for the scene to resolve into something else. Any second now, he was going kick his legs. He was going to surface, gasping for breath. He was going to start to swim. I was calm and curious, nothing more.

A moment later, a gull landed on Mick's back. Its beak flashed, and a spatter of crimson coated its feathers. It took flight with something in its mouth—a hunk of quivering pink. A second bird followed suit. It perched quizzically on Mick's arm, its weight dipping the limb beneath the surface of the water. It peeled a strip of skin from the back of his hand. Then another bird landed. And another.

At my side, Lucy was sobbing. She waved her arms in vain, trying to scare the gulls away. Galen had his fingers buried in his hair. His mouth was contorted. The birds were growing bolder, circling in a pack. They yanked tufts of Mick's hair out. They stabbed at his poncho, penetrating the fabric, wrenching mouthfuls of wet flesh from his torso. They smacked one another with their wings, battling over who would alight on the body next. They shrieked in what seemed to be elation. Mick was a sodden mass, oozing coils of blood over the surface of the sea.

I don't know how long I would have stood there, unwilling to believe what I was seeing. Forever, maybe.

It seemed as though the noise of the birds was growing louder. The roar became unendurable, thundering in my ears. I had an impression of motion and wind, of something rising around me, as though all the gulls on Southeast Farallon had taken flight at once.

Galen grabbed me as I fell. The last thing I remember is the expression on his face—eyes haunted, mouth open—and the vise of his wiry arms.

I WOKE IN my bedroom. I kept my eyes closed for a bit, inhaling the familiar odors of dust and mildew, feeling the light from the window on my cheek. Somebody else was there. My heart leapt. I wanted it to be Mick; I was sure that it would be Mick. He had always been the one to care for me when I was ill.

"How are you feeling?" Lucy said.

I opened my eyes. She was leaning over me. Her hair swung in its usual braid.

"I'll get you some water," she said, turning toward the door.

I flung out a hand to stop her.

"What happened?" I said.

She sank onto the bed, frowning. I was struck anew by the hale solidity of Lucy. Her whole body spoke of matronly good health. But her face had a dewy aspect now. Her eyes were swollen.

"You know what happened," she said.

I was still hoping she might come up with an alternate solution. Maybe Mick had been rescued just in time. Maybe the kiss of life had saved him. Maybe he was downstairs now, shrugging off the last vestiges of hypothermia. Maybe he was fine. That was what I wanted to hear: Mick was absolutely fine. It was the What If Game all over again.

Lucy brushed a lock of hair wearily from her face.

"I'm so sorry," she said.

At once, I pushed myself upright. With a frantic gesture, I reached for her, pulling her into a bear hug. I saw the shock in her face. My belly knocked the wind out of her. She patted my back, and I gripped her rib cage with all my strength. This was not a benevolent instinct. I wanted to force what she was about to say back into her throat, through her lungs, down through the soles of her feet. I wanted to prevent her from saying Mick's name aloud, from saying *drowned* or *gone* or, God forbid, *accident*. I did not want her to say a word.

37

I AM LEAVING THE islands. It has not been a question, to go or
to stay. Galen has arranged the whole thing for me. He has radi-
oed the mainland, contacted Captain Joe. On Friday afternoon,
the ferry will take me away.

It is July. Mick died in July. I know this, not because I have
checked a calendar, but because the night the helicopter came to
remove Mick's body, there were fireworks. I was lying down in my
room for the whole of that encounter. I heard the whir of the rotor.
I heard the angry, raucous response of the gulls. For a while, it was
Armageddon out there, the blades whooshing, the birds in flight
too. Voices downstairs. Footsteps. Doors slamming. I stayed where
I was. Soon enough, the helicopter rumbled off. The gulls seemed
upset for a long while afterward, shrieking and babbling.

I did not budge. The sky darkened outside. Weak and weary,
I stared out the window. I had not found the wherewithal to eat
or drink much of anything. At last, at moonrise, the gulls bedded
down. The islands looked painterly in the waning light—coated
with white bodies like gesso on canvas. The moon was a sliver, a
fishhook. A few stars began to burn. I was debating whether I had
it in me to head downstairs and attempt some dinner when there
was a sound—a distant report.

I caught my breath. The noise was unmistakable. Cannon fire. For a moment I was reminded of the eggers and the lightkeepers— their epic, ancient battle. There was a flash of light. Another boom. The sound and the flicker were too far away to appear synchro- nized. It took me a while to realize what was happening. The fire- works were rising above San Francisco, thirty miles away. From my vantage point, they were tiny. I could have pinched them out between thumb and finger like the flame of a match. Three golden spheres burst in succession, as small as buttons. Red, white, and blue rockets whizzed in teeny arcs. A diminutive, glittering tree blossomed in the air, its leaves streaking downward like a weeping willow's. It was as though I were watching the Fourth of July inside a snow globe.

The finale was impressive. Bright orbs overlapped one another, all the colors of the rainbow. A garden of miniature flowers bloomed and died in a matter of seconds. When it was done, I waited a while, hoping for more. The cannon fire continued for a minute or two in the darkness: all the aggressive noise of the fireworks, none of the celebratory light. Finally, only the smoke was left—gray, hol- low shapes, drifting on the wind like ghosts.

I HAVE NOT cried for Mick. Instead, I have been wandering. I have trekked all over Southeast Farallon, visiting places I have not been in months. I have carried the weight of my belly across Dead Sea Lion Beach. I have visited the caves to the north. Rhino Catacombs. Orca Cove. Eerie places, with an eerie view. With the baby kicking in protest, I have strolled all the way to the Weather Service Peninsula. I have sat for hours on Marine Terrace, shielded beneath my hard hat, wrapped in my poncho, breathing through my mask, gazing in the direction of California.

Eventually, I am sure, I will once again see the archipelago for what it truly is—a wild place, nothing more. A place where the rules, comforts, and safeguards of modern life do not apply. For now, however, the islands seem less wild than malignant. Every gift comes with a terrible cost. A talent for photography arises from the loss of a mother. A baby can be found only after rape, violence, and death. The closeness of a friendship must be answered with loss. A love affair, too, must end in tears—as Forest and Lucy could attest to. These are not good thoughts. These are the sort of thoughts that keep a person in motion, striding up and down the slope.

Once or twice, I have seen Forest in the distance—a thin shape, moving fast. I have not spoken to him. This I know: there is nothing as lonely as grief. He and I are fellow mourners, each locked in a kind of mental isolation. Forest has barely been in the cabin at all. Instead, he has taken the *Janus* out on his own for no real reason, zooming around the islands, the sound of the engine ringing against the cliffs. He has not been present at meals. He does not join the evening queue outside the bathroom, all of us clutching our toothbrushes and glowering at one another. I have begun to suspect him of sleeping in the coast guard house. I do not hear his footsteps in the night. I no longer catch his dry cough in the mornings. It seems impossible for someone to be so absent in such a confined environment—yet Forest has all but disappeared.

The autopsy was concluded swiftly. They said that Mick had drowned. His lungs were full of seawater, his eyes decorated with pinprick hemorrhages. Foam around the mouth. All the telltale signs. By the time the gulls had finished with him, his body had been in bad shape. His funeral would have to be a closed-casket service, apparently. I tried not to think about it. I took some small comfort in the knowledge that drowning was supposed to be a pleasant way to expire. I had heard this fact somewhere, long ago, and I clung to it now like a lifeline. Drowning was an ethereal, ecstatic way to leave the world, more like dreaming than dying.

Still, I could not help but wonder exactly what had happened in the seconds that Mick was out of my sight—between the moment he stumbled and the moment he perished. It seemed impossible that I would never know for sure. He was a strong swimmer; he was a seasoned biologist, used to the myriad dangers of the islands. But none of that had helped him when it mattered. Maybe he had ruptured an eardrum when he hit the sea. Maybe he had opened his eyes in the cloudy water and found himself fatally disoriented, unsure which way was up. Maybe he had collided with something beneath the surface, a boulder or a reef. Maybe he had struck the surface at an angle that had knocked him unconscious at once. In truth, there were a hundred ways to die on the islands. It was amazing that we were not all six feet under—lost to the wind, the ocean, and the dreadful, human capacity for misadventure.

Last night, I dreamed about the ghost. It was a chilly evening for summer. I was curled in bed like a hedgehog, trying to keep warm.

Then I felt a hand touch my shoulder. I sat up, disarranging the blankets, and saw her.

At the time, this did not shock me at all. She was wearing a long, floating dress. The moonlight caught the edges of it and turned it to silver. Her hair shrouded her face. I couldn't read her expression. She drifted backward. I followed.

Her dress swirled as she paced down the long hall. She paused outside the room that Mick and Forest had shared. She pointed urgently with a long, white arm—as white as salt. Then she turned to me and lifted her chin. Her hair pooled away from her cheeks, revealing a round jaw, deep-set eyes, and a stubborn mouth. For the first time, I could see her face. It was like looking in a mirror.

38

O N A W A R M July morning, I found myself in the lighthouse. This was foolish, I know. The path up the hill is hard to manage at the best of times, let alone while carrying the added burden of pregnancy. The gulls clearly viewed my approach as the first line of an advancing army. I slipped once, skinning my knee. I lost my temper and took a swing at one of the birds. He had been rattling around my hard hat, trying to disorient me, feathers opening and closing in front of my face like shutters. I threw a punch, smacking him in the wing and spinning him away, though he still hollered admonishments in my general direction. It felt good to lash out, to cause harm. If I could, I would have done the same to every gull on the islands.

Once I had attained the lighthouse, I paused to catch my breath. The view was as impressive as ever. The sea had a cloudy aspect, like split pea soup. Islets stuck out of the murky depths like oyster crackers. There were sea lions swimming to the north, churning the waves into froth. I sat down at the little desk. Someone had left a pair of binoculars there, cheap and plastic, the sort given to children on camping trips. I adjusted the dial and peered through the lens, staring to the east, looking for San Francisco. I could not see land, not exactly. There was a long, hazy stain. In that moment, it was hard to remember what the biologists—and the lightkeepers—had fought so hard to preserve in this awful, perilous place.

I thought about just letting myself go, sobbing until I had no more tears left. I could not remember the last time I had cried that hard. Childhood, maybe. Tears for you. This seemed to be the right moment for it. I thought, too, about throwing myself right down Lighthouse Hill. Eight months pregnant or not, the world was a terrible place. Alternatively, I could stay up here forever. I could eschew food, drink, and sleep. Eventually the islands would claim me. If I lingered in the lighthouse long enough, I might become a statue, a part of the mountain stone.

A moment later, there was a scuffle. I turned and saw a lean figure, a cap of curls. Forest was mounting the slope. He stepped into the lighthouse. He showed no surprise when he saw me. He was beyond being surprised. His grief and shock were too big for that. All the smaller emotions had been crushed beneath the weight of his loss.

"Hi," I said.

He was rubbing his fingers across his chest. With a jolt, I recognized that gesture. It was Mick's. Forest was doing it without realizing it, the same turn of the wrist, the same accompanying sigh. There was a silence as we gazed together at the view. It was early afternoon, and the light was bold and garish, the shadows harsh. The islands never looked their best at this time of day. I preferred the morning and the evening, when the air was as sweet and golden as peach-skin.

Forest cleared his throat.

"Mick and I were together," he said. "As you know."

I had not been expecting this. After a beat, I did my best to feign amazement, my hands flying upward, mouth opening.

"I think it's best if we don't lie to each other," he said.

I gazed at him in consternation.

"I found your camera, Melissa," he said.

My face flushed. I could feel it happen, like water coming to a boil on the stove. I knew what he was referring to. I had kept that camera hidden beneath my bed, safe, I thought, from prying eyes.

"How—how did you—"

Forest shrugged. "I went through your stuff. I was hunting for a sweater of mine. I should apologize, I guess. I'm sorry."

He did not sound sorry. His voice was absolutely flat.

"When?" I asked. "When did this happen?"

"A long time ago."

"Oh," I said faintly.

"They're nice pictures," he said.

I sat up a little straighter at the desk, trying to gather my wits.

"You have to understand," I began. "When I took them, I didn't mean to do anything wrong. I just woke up and looked outside. It was an accident, kind of. I know it must seem like I was spying. But I would never have shown them to—It really wasn't a betrayal of—"

Forest shook his head. "I don't care why you took them."

Most of my blood seemed to be trapped in my head. I was sure that my face was glowing like sunrise.

"Mick wasn't the father," Forest said, gesturing toward my stomach. "He said he would lie for you, and I went along with it.

So we're on the same page now," he ended, his voice getting thick. "You know, and I know."

These words seemed to cost him everything he had. His head sank, his arms falling to his sides. It was strange seeing him like this. He looked and moved exactly like the Forest I remembered, but everything about his manner was different. His posture. His level of focus. The emotion radiating from him. I felt as though I were meeting him for the first time, on this sunny, breathy afternoon, after living under his roof for a year.

He passed a hand across his brow, like a man waking from a dream.

"I should go," he said. "I can't talk to you. I can't talk right now."

I nodded. Gripping the corner of the desk, I hauled myself to my feet. But Forest was already out the door. I watched him leave, silhouetted against the sea.

THAT NIGHT I got down on my knees and looked under my bed for the first time in ages. There were my watertight tubs of photographic equipment. There were my work boots. There were dust bunnies, and sweaters, and a hat, and a rock, and a few sad, bent coat hangers. At last I found the camera. I sat up again, the baby kicking irritably at my groin. I worked the button with my thumb, flicking the pictures along. The moon. The coast guard house. A gleam against a black window. A shimmer of bodies in motion. Two torsos touching and parting like dancers in a pas de deux.

Faces turned toward each other, a line of darkness between them. Inches away.

Resolutely I got to my feet. I knew that Forest was in the kitchen. I could hear him talking to Galen, their voices rising up the staircase along with the smell of cinnamon tea. Moving quietly, I hurried down the hall. I eased into Forest's room without turning on the light. I set the camera in his desk drawer. Before I slipped back out of the room, I took one last look at the image that was still visible on the screen. Two faces, iridescent profiles, poised on the verge of a kiss.

39

I SPENT MY LAST day on the islands indoors. It began raining at dawn, a gentle misting, the sort of drizzle that seemed likely to blow over. An hour later, however, the weather had taken a turn for the worse. The rain picked up, a steady, roiling gush. The landscape was blurred by curtains of silver. I could barely pick out the gray expanse of the ocean through that downpour.

Still, Galen was in an exhilarated mood. He had taken the boat out early, at sunrise, before the storm had settled in. He described the morning, which had still been fine then. The sea had been flat, opaque. He had been fired with a distinct impression of sharks nearby. He had felt them coming. It was getting to be their time, the warm weather drawing them back from their winter vacation homes. Any day now, the first kill might be glimpsed from the lighthouse.

After breakfast, the biologists elected to walk to the murre blind. The men bundled themselves up beneath ponchos and sweaters. Lucy had a swollen wrist; she had fallen on the rocks and caught herself at a bad angle. (I had helped her to bandage the joint. Lucy and I will never be friends—I will be glad to see the back of her when I leave the islands for good—but we get by. While I wrapped the gauze, she had gently guided my movements.) The three of them barged onto the porch. Through the window, I watched as the downpour swallowed them up.

Once they were gone, I decided to sneak into their rooms. To intrude on these private spaces, I knew, was a flagrant breach of confidence. Full-grown adults did not normally live in this kind of collegiate community, without privacy. As a rule, we did the best we could to maintain what boundaries we had.

But I was in a mood. I entered Galen's sanctum first. I wanted to see his famous—infamous—collection before I departed. As I had suspected, his room was as tidy as his mind: immaculately organized, a place for everything and everything in its place. His museum of relics and specimens was all that I'd hoped for. A length of twine hung above his window, and rows of gleaming feathers were pinned there like beads on a chain. Shells of various sizes glimmered on the nightstand. There was a glass jar filled with what at first seemed to be buttons, but on closer inspection turned out to be dead beetles. The desk had been taken over by the half-assembled skeleton of a bird, an array of slim white bones. I knew there was more hidden in boxes and drawers, but I did not dare to pry too much. Galen might glean I had been there.

Still, I was curious. I poked through the wastebasket and got on tiptoe to examine the bureau top. Galen had told me that he had a broken teacup somewhere. It had been flung at the wall many years ago by a visiting researcher during a heated debate. Galen had swept up and saved the pieces as a souvenir. He had told me that he had a scrap of elephant seal skin. It had been torn off one male by another's teeth during a battle over territory. Galen had peeled it from the rocks and carried it home, pinning it to his bulletin board. He had told me that he had a human rib bone—a relic, he believed, from the battling eggers, some poor man's corpse. He had told me that he had the skull of a seal pup, a human tooth, and the talon of a falcon.

Galen had told me that he gathered and kept anything that spoke to the nature of life on the islands. He did not discriminate between the mundane and the vital, the human and the animal, the tragic and the wonderful. He had told me that the greatest illusion of the human experience was the idea that we were outside of nature—that we were not a part of the food chain—that we were not animals ourselves.

Soon I headed downstairs. The rain lashed the walls and splattered the windows. The air was heavy with the smell of wet birds. I stepped into the living room and paused. I had not been inside Lucy's room—Andrew's room, as I still thought of it—since my first days in the cabin. For a while I stood in the doorway, edgy and tense. The space looked different than I remembered. Lucy had reorganized it months before, switching the positions of the bed and dresser, hanging curtains, and removing the rug. It was a homey little area, shabby but warm. She had a lot of knickknacks scattered around—a ceramic paperweight, a snow globe, a tiny, bronze statue of a cat. I glanced through the papers on the desk: a bill, a half-completed letter. I tugged open the drawer of Lucy's night table. There was something in there, swathed in cloth.

It was a picture of Andrew. I had unwrapped it and was holding it in my hands before I registered this fact. I stared down, mesmerized. I had forgotten what Andrew looked like. My memories of him were all tactile in nature: heavy calves, moist skin, breath. It was strange to see another human being looking back at me. A weak chin. A mischievous smile. He had not, after all, been a monster. That was the way he usually cropped up in my dreams: a ghoul with glaring red eyes, exhaling sulfur and steam. Instead, he had been a man. No more, no less.

I wrapped the picture in the cloth again and tucked it back where I had found it. My fingers were unsteady, but otherwise I was calm. I hurried into the hall. I sat down on the stairs. The rain was falling in torrents, splashing against the roof and hammering the porch. I could not see outside; the windows were as blind as stained glass, patterned with a mosaic of water. I don't know how long I sat there. The downpour was unabated. It was amazing to me that there was this much rain in the world. Surely the sky would empty itself out eventually. A telltale drip was coming from somewhere in the house. The roof, or the walls, or the windows had been penetrated. After I was gone, the others would have to spend a few hours with the caulking gun and spackle, trying, yet again, to do the impossible—to contain the wildness here, to pretend they had control over nature, to mitigate what it might do to them.

At last I hefted myself upright. Gritting my teeth, I climbed the stairs once more. The rain was louder here, booming on the roof. In the distance, thunder growled. I could not hear the gulls or the murres, any of the usual suspects. The storm had wiped out all traces of animal life, for the moment, anyway.

It took all the courage I had to enter the bedroom that Forest and Mick had shared. Inside, I stood frozen, stunned at my own daring. I breathed in the combined musk of two athletic, unshowered bodies—Mick's smell had not yet evaporated. I glanced around at the ceiling fan and the frayed, threadbare rug. Forest's dresser was tidy. He evidently preferred not to use a pillow; his bed looked odd, empty at the top, like something that might have belonged to the Headless Horseman. His clothes were hung crisply in the closet. There was an echo of Galen's neatness in the way the papers on the desk were all lined up at right angles, the thumbtacks and pencils stowed in specific little jars. I peeked into the trunk at the foot of the bed—more papers, a few years' worth of documentation about sharks. There were sketches, photographs, and meticulous notes. Somehow, Forest had managed to take the greatest and most ferocious predator on earth and render it boring. I would not have been able to sit there and read through those files, not for love or money.

After some searching, I found my own camera, with the images of Mick and Forest's rendezvous stowed on the memory card. It was hidden at the bottom of the closet now. I turned it over in my fingers. The pictures were not mine anymore—if they had ever been. I tucked the camera away again, out of sight.

Then I gazed across the room at Mick's things. The bed was exactly as he had left it the morning he had died: a heap of pillows, the blanket trailing onto the floor. I was sure that if I opened his dresser, I would see shirts and socks crammed in there willy-nilly. His books had been shoved roughly onto the shelves—backward, upside down. Muddy boots under the bed. A closet with sweaters piled on the floor, hangers unused. Mick's energy was captured there, the impression of a body in motion, a large, generous personality, too full of enthusiasm to bother with petty matters like tidying up. I got to my feet and headed across the neutral zone. I knew I did not have long. The others would be back soon, wet, weary, and hungry for lunch. There was something I wanted to do before they returned.

In Mick's nightstand, I found a leather bracelet. He had owned a few, with varying degrees of masculinity (some braided, some chunky, some ringed with metal studs). He had alternated them according to his mood. This one was stiff with sweat, the mahogany hue weathered to a pale brown. I pocketed it. I was hunting for small items that Forest would not miss. I found a T-shirt in Mick's drawer: my favorite, a bright orange thing that was emblematic of his luminescent temperament. I stole a postcard he had begun to write to someone but had never finished—a chatty note about the whales, ending in midsentence. The important thing was that it was in his own handwriting. I was moving fast now, a dervish, disarranging the books and upsetting the papers on the desk. I took Mick's baseball cap. I found a tiny rubber chicken in the corner of a dresser drawer, a miniature bit of hilarity, and I swiped that too. I grabbed a book about sea lions, highlighted and marked with Mick's script.

Right then, there was a sound from downstairs. A door slammed. Voices rang up the steps. I jumped in alarm, like the thief I was. I hurried down the hall to my bedroom with my stolen goods clutched under my arm.

I WILL TELL people that Mick was the father of my baby. When my twin aunts ask—when my own father asks—when my son himself is old enough to ask—I will lie. Mick gave me this gift, and I will grab it with both hands.

I will spin a beautiful story. I will begin, always, with the eggers and the lightkeepers. I will not, perhaps, relate this tale as well as Galen (and his book) did, but I will do well enough. I will describe the way lightkeepers inhabited the islands. They left the sharks, the whales, the seals, and the birds alone. They sought peace, an income, and a home. They built a strange little community on a godforsaken rock, where they protected one another, raised their children, and thrived.

Then there were the eggers, who came to the islands with a different agenda. They decimated the murre population with abandon. (Even now, the birds have not fully recovered.) Not content with causing an environmental catastrophe, the eggers brought weapons to the archipelago. They died in battles with other eggers. They died in caves, poisoned by the fumes rising from the guano. They died by tumbling into the sea, overburdened by the weight of too many eggs.

When I tell people about the father of my baby, I will say this: There are two kinds of people in the word. There are eggers and lightkeepers. The former are driven by acquisition and avarice. The latter are driven by curiosity and caution. Eggers take what they can, consequences be damned. Lightkeepers take what they need, nothing more. Eggers want to have. Lightkeepers want to be.

I will tell people that my son's father was a lightkeeper. I will share my memories. I have so many memories. The walks Mick and I took. The hours we spent together—him reading, me dozing with my feet in his lap. His terrifying attempts at cooking. His sweeping gestures, those massive arms zooming perilously through the air. I will describe Mick's head-thrown-back guffaw. I will imitate the athletic bounce of his stride. I will tell stories of his hilarious clumsiness, machinery coming apart in his hands, tools crumbling into pieces. I will describe, too, his limitless capacity for kindness. In this way, I will be able to keep him with me. The ordinary ebb and flow of life on the islands, so unremarked and unremarkable, will crystallize, through telling and retelling, into stories—and will pass, over the years, into legend.

My photographs will stand as illustrations. Mick on board the *Janus*. Mick in the kitchen, frowning at a box of macaroni and cheese. Mick making a silly face to get me to laugh. It is a bit unsettling to think that these snapshots will enhance and inform my deception. I have always thought of photography as truth-gathering. I have imagined my pictures to be immutable and honest, as sure as the ground beneath my feet. But now I see that truth and photography are fundamentally at odds. A snapshot is a two-dimensional representation, like a painting or a sketch, carefully prepared, framed, and cropped. It is the world represented by the mind of an artist, rather than the world as it actually is. The photographer can cherry-pick what will be included in a collection of images; they can be selected or omitted with purpose, then assembled and arranged so that, as a whole, they might suggest any story at all.

My beloved work will strengthen the lie I must tell. I can include a snapshot of Mick blowing me an ironic kiss. I can exclude the picture of him doing the same to Lucy so she would not feel left out. I will keep the images of him writing in the daily log, standing in the lighthouse, operating the crane to pull up the Billy Pugh, cooking dinner, pointing ecstatically at an elephant seal, snoring on the couch, and roaring with laughter. I will throw away the snapshot of him waltzing around the living room with Charlene, singing at the top of his lungs. I will include my favorite picture of Mick—eyes aglow, smiling lovingly at the camera. I will exclude the following shot, which shows that Forest was there too, standing behind me all along.

40

T HE FERRY IS late. When Captain Joe appears, I will glimpse his boat, a dark stain on a landscape of water. This will be deceptive, of course, an optical illusion; I will be able to see the ferry long before it is anywhere near the islands.

A few minutes ago, Galen and Forest left the cabin together. I watched them pass, gesticulating, engaged in one of their endless, circular arguments, never to be resolved. I kept my gaze on them as they headed toward East Landing. A single word floated to me on the breeze: *Sisters*. No sharks have yet been sighted, but it is only a matter of time. The Rat Pack must be in the neighborhood even now. The summer cycle is resetting itself, beginning anew. Galen and Forest were on their way to check the Billy Pugh, to make sure that the mechanism is in good shape for my departure. Forest will oversee my passage to the deck of the ferry. I will leave the islands as I came— suspended above the ocean inside a terrifying, pendulous cage.

Captain Joe has just appeared, like a soap bubble blown over the horizon. An empty sky one minute, a boat the next. Soon I will make my way to East Landing, where Forest will be waiting for me. I will pass through the gauntlet of gulls one final time. It will be my last moment to breathe in the salt air, to brave the guano and the bird lice, to remember where I have been and why I am leaving.

I have been thinking about Galen's book—about the eggers and the lightkeepers. There was a whole chapter, too, on the Miwok Indians. Residents of California, they knew about the archipelago—though they were never foolish enough to voyage there. On clear days, the Farallon Islands were visible from the coast: a haunted silhouette, broken shards of stone. The Miwoks believed that the place was as much a spiritual locale as a physical one. They imagined it to be an earthly hell where the souls of the damned were sent to live in discomfort and loneliness.

After the past year, I must agree. In this place, loss is a geographical force rather than an emotional one. Loss is the magnetic pull of the islands. Long ago, Galen suffered a gut-wrenching tragedy. I am sure he will stay here until he dies—a lost soul dominated and defined by the death of his wife. Forest has gone through a similar bereavement. Lucy, too, has been widowed, in her way.

And I am more like the others here than I would ever have cared to admit. I remember the first time I saw the islands in a photograph. My response was a throb of recognition. I felt immediately that I knew the place somehow, as though from a past life or a dream. In that moment, it felt as though I'd been waiting forever to find the islands—as though, perhaps, they'd been waiting for me.

I understand now why I first voyaged here. It has taken me all year to come to terms with that choice. Since your death, I have been looking over my shoulder, looking backward. I have been stuck in time. I have been writing letters to you—letters to no one, a body in a cemetery, a woman I knew for only a small part of my life. Hundreds of notes, some sitting in the Dead Letter Office of various cities, others buried and burned and scattered on the wind. I have never once questioned whether writing them was sane or healthy. Now, though, I can see that it was neither. Each letter has been an anchor chain, dragging me back into the past.

I have distanced myself from my father. I have stayed away from the twins, my grandparents, my cousins. I have eschewed all the normal paths through life—no mortgage, no long-term rela- tionships, no permanence, no love. I have kept only what could be carried on my back. I have slept in deserts, canyons, and jungles. I have lived like a vagabond. In a way, I have been looking for the archipelago since the day you died. Of course I recognized the Farallon Islands when I first saw them in that snapshot. This place is the final refuge for people like me.

Oddly enough, the baby has proven to be my salvation. The accidental baby. The baby who came out of the worst possible cir- cumstances. Without that tiny, burgeoning creature, I might have decided to stay on the islands indefinitely. The idea has certainly crossed my mind. Despite the unceasing howl of the wind, the creeping cold, the meager food stores, the rodents, the falling-apart plumbing, the lack of reading material, the broken crockery—I have always felt at home here, more so than anywhere else. The wildness and isolation are mother's milk to me.

I could easily have become a permanent resident. I could have begun the process of cobbling together more funding or applying for intern status, insinuating myself so completely into the ebb and flow that the others could not do without me. Lucy, Forest, Galen, and me—the saddest quartet in the universe. Eating our meals together. Tagging the birds together. Forgetting the bustle of the mainland, the toot of car horns, the murmur of strangers' voices. I imagine the islands drifting farther and farther away from shore. The four of us would look askance at any visitors to our little lepers' colony. Castaways by choice. All of us halved—all of us haunted.

Captain Joe is closer now. The ferry is no longer a smudge; it has taken on recognizable contours, a prow, a deckhouse. But it is still a miniature version of itself, a ship in a bottle. I can scarcely see the white tumble of the wake.

I am thinking about my father. Dad at dawn in his sweat suit, gearing up for his morning run. Dad in the evening in front of the TV, bowl of popcorn in the lap. I have never given him a fair shake. In life you were a bright figure, so fiery and intense that you threw him into shadow. After you died, he stayed there, on the outskirts, in the half light. I have never confided in him. I have never really considered him; he has been furniture, as much a part of the house I return to as the kitchen cabinets and the mahogany bookshelves. I wonder how much of this he has understood.

Today I will return to the mainland.

Then, of course, my son will come. I may feel my water break without warning; I will be drinking tea at the kitchen table, per-haps, or taking a stroll through the old neighborhood, and suddenly I will become a human fountain, damp thighs and soaked shoes. During labor—Mick has told me—I will be more or less insane. The pain will be unbearable, yet I will bear it. I will enter an altered, exalted state, during which my mind will be shelved, pushed to one side, as my body takes over, fulfilling its deepest animal functions without my consciousness or consent. The baby will travel downward through the birth canal on a wave of blood. He will burst into the open air like a shark shattering the surface of the sea. The cord that joins us will be cut, and in that moment, the baby will be transformed. He will become a full-fledged human being—independent, breathing his own air, consuming his own food.

I will be transformed as well. A mother, like you but not like you. A single mother. I will reach out to my aunts. I will reconnect, tentatively, with my family. I will accept all the help I am given. I will need it. There is nothing more astonishing than a new baby. I will nurse that tiny animal and change his diapers. I will look up the words of half-remembered lullabies. I can picture my son—almost. Pink skin and tufted hair. Starfish hands reaching. Dark, smeary eyes, not quite adjusted to the light outside the womb. A belly as round and warm as fresh-baked bread. Months will pass, during which I will once again be lost to the world, but this time with purpose, inhabiting a private realm of blankets, booties, and downy skin.

Yet that is not the end of the story. The narrative goes on. Eventually, I will become a normal person. That is what the baby has done for me—grounded me, permanently and for the first time, to the rest of the human race. I will never again experience the kind of deprivation I have known on the islands. No matter what sort of life I am able to create for my son and me, it will be filled with comparative luxury. All the while, that boy will be growing. A toddler in diapers. A sturdy, tow-headed three-year-old, mounting a bicycle with training wheels. A child on the swings, head thrown back, hair flying, legs extended, printed against the sky like a gull in flight. The possibilities are endless. The time spins out in front me, a golden tunnel of years. A thousand choices. Time like sunlight. Time like wealth.

In the future, there will come a day when I will pick up my son from school. I can see a long way down the line now; I can see everything. He will barrel outside through the front door of a brick building, his backpack swinging off his shoulders. Maybe he will be the kind of child to plow into me, all arms and legs, an ecstatic hugger. Maybe he will be the kind who offers a little wave instead and falls into lockstep beside me, a miniature adult. I can see the rest of our day unfolding, an afternoon in spring, crisp and sweet. He and I will run errands together. We will visit the park. We will roam over the bridge. I imagine turning a corner, my son at my side. There, at the end of the block, will be our own house, the windows aglow, as inviting and warm as the beam of a lighthouse, calling the ships home.

In the end, I will be unrecognizable. I will have let you go.

IT IS TIME. The sea has flattened out, as smooth as paper, and the sky is sunny and clean. My knapsack is packed and ready to go. My mind, too, is packed and ready.

This will be the last letter I write to you.

I can hear Mick's voice ringing in my head. The last time we ever spoke, he drew me aside in the kitchen and lectured me about my journey home. In that moment, I was impatient with him, but now it seems prescient—even vital. Mick warned me that the ferry ride would take several hours. He told me to stay inside the deck-house, not to risk strolling along the railing. He made me promise to wear a hat. I remember him reaching out tenderly and fingering a lock of my hair. *You'll catch your death*, he told me. Suddenly it seems imperative that I obey him. I have hidden all my stolen goods at the bottom of my bag. Beneath my collection of seashells, Mick's T-shirt, my lucky puffin feather, and my four remaining cameras, I find what I'm searching for.

A crimson stocking cap. A phoenix insignia stitched in gold. I will wear it as I leave the islands for good. I am wearing it now to ward off the chill.

EPILOGUE

GALEN IS STANDING in the lighthouse. Through his binoculars, he watches the ferry cleaving a path through the fog. The mist is inconsistent, thickening and thinning. The boat seems illusory and ephemeral. Galen breathes in the salty air. He can see Miranda poised at the ferry's stern. Her figure stands out clearly, at once diminutive and bulky, a tiny woman carrying a heavy burden at the midriff. She is wearing a red stocking cap. Galen knows that cap well. Crimson fabric. A gold phoenix embroidered on the side. Gradually the ferry fades into the mist, blurring against the ocean. Miranda's shape is lost. But the cap is still visible. It remains after everything else is gone, a splotch of red in a bath of gray, burning like a warning light.

A cold wind picks up, circling the lighthouse. Galen is not bothered by the chill; like the line of lightkeepers before him, he has been on the islands too long to be affected. The breeze is such a constant force that he is more likely to notice its cessation than its presence. He adjusts the focus on his binoculars, gazing toward the sea.

The fog has swallowed up the ferry, Miranda, and even the afterglow of crimson. The sky is hung with low, damp clouds. The islands have a claustrophobic feel today, boxed in by shifting gray.

Galen steps outside the lighthouse. The gulls are everywhere, dozing, heads beneath their wings. At his approach, a few beaks swivel.
Galen adjusts his hard hat. He lifts the mask over his mouth and
nose. He moves through a thicket of shifting feathers that rustle like
a prairie in a breeze.

As he approaches the cabin, the wind swirls around him, bring-
ing the scent of ammonia and mildew. He enters through the back
door to avoid Kamikaze Pete. That poor bird is not long for this
world. Like so many other living things on the islands, the gull
has fought too much and fed too little. The coming migration will
finish it off; it will never last the journey. Galen heads into the
kitchen to make himself a soothing mug of tea. The house feels different now that Miranda has moved out. Her things are gone—her
smell—her breath. He will never see her again. Galen has watched
dozens of people come and go over the years. He has seen heart-
break and friendship and hilarity and pettiness. He has seen death,
too, most of it violent. The steam from his tea rises against his
face. The daily log is in its usual place on the tabletop—available
and open for all to see. Galen glances through today's entries. *Four
chicks hatched on Mirounga Beach. Cormorant found P.I.H. on
Lighthouse Hill.*

Then he reaches beneath the table. There is a special compart-
ment hidden from view. Galen carved it himself. From inside, he
withdraws his private notebook. The daily log is a public record,
maintained by all the biologists, chronicling the lives of the animals.
But Galen's little green journal is another matter. It is a record of
the human activity on the islands. He has been keeping it for years.

He has tracked the romantic entanglement of Mick and Forest—its inception, its increasing fervor, their midnight trysts in the coast guard house. He has reported the date and duration of each assignation. He has written about their coded interactions in public. Galen has kept watch over all of them. He has recorded the progression of Lucy's grief after the death of her lover. He has transcribed the details of Mick's friendship with Miranda, Miranda's friendship with Charlene. As a scientist, he makes sure that his notes are businesslike. No conjecture or emotion. Only actions and behavior, which can be quantified and documented for posterity.

August 12: Miranda injured. Camera broken beyond repair.

August 28: Lucy scuba dives.

October 3: Mick and Forest in the coast guard house for four hours.

Galen is a biologist. His work is a sacred trust: the study of life in all its forms. On the islands, life flourishes in a unique way, untempered and unrestrained. This is true for the people as well as the animals. Galen does not differentiate between his fellow scientists and the creatures they study. Observation and noninterference are the biologist's central creed. He chronicles the behavior of the sharks and whales, the birds and seals, the biologists and interns. He never intervenes.

But Miranda, the mouse girl—she was something different. Something new. She had a quality he had never before observed. Once he asked her, "What is your nature, Miranda?" He asked it in hopes of provoking or startling her. But there was nothing, no reaction. Her eyes remained as flat as seal stones.

Galen leafs back through the pages. His private notebook is a green jewel, leather-bound. The past year has seen a lot of activity. In his hands, the book falls open naturally to a well-worn date in November. Galen has turned to this page often over the last few weeks and months. Too often, perhaps.

November 5: Miranda raped by Andrew.

He frowns. He runs his finger over the line of his own script. Then he flips forward to the note printed just a few days afterward.

November 8: Andrew murdered by Miranda.

Galen leans back in his chair. He lets his eyes slip closed as the scene plays out in his mind again. He has often considered the night Andrew died. He saw it happen, of course. He sees everything that happens here.

It was a foggy evening. Galen awoke to the sound of the front door. First Miranda left the cabin. Then Andrew left the cabin. Galen watched as the confrontation occurred.

An altercation. An argument. Raised voices, carried away on the wind, lost in the clatter of the sea. The fog. The slippery coast. Observing them, Galen could not hear what was being said. He did not need to. Andrew wanted more. Galen could see this in the boy's posture. Andrew reached for her, groping toward her. His expression was mocking. He thought Miranda would be vulnerable on her own.

But Galen knew better. A wounded animal is the most dangerous kind. Miranda had been attacked once already. Galen took in her stance—her shoulders back, her chin lifted. Andrew did not try to run. He did not see the impact coming. He was unaware of the seal stone in Miranda's pocket, carried with her always, heavy and certain. He did not know what Galen knew.

A crack to the head. A spray of blood. A splash.

Galen remembers it all. He remembers it well. Andrew's hat fell off when the blow was struck. His ankle was broken, his lungs filling with water. Miranda stood on the shore for a while, watching the corpse floating on the tide. The shock seemed to leave her immobile. She needed a few minutes to gather her wits. Eventually she bent down and picked up the hat. She wrapped the bloody stone inside it. She took them both home and hid them, like a dog burying a bone. She tucked the evidence underneath her bed, a place she left infrequently over the ensuing weeks.

November 9: Andrew's body discovered.

November 10: Corpse placed in cold storage in S.F., awaiting autopsy.

November 14: Mick and Forest in the coast guard house for two hours.

Galen sips his tea. The steam fills his lungs with a pleasant odor of cinnamon. Outside, the fog has begun to thin out. Rippling and pale, it seems delicate, like lace or cheesecloth. The air is different too—fresher, brighter, more awake. Galen can always feel it when the weather starts to change. In an hour or two, the sky will be clear, the sea smooth, the islands drenched in light.

After Andrew's murder, Galen took no action. He waited. During the weeks that followed the boy's death, he watched Miranda from a distance, in the manner of a hawk in flight, miles above the ground, unnoticed by its prey, peering down with telescopic vision. He tracked and recorded everything she did. He slept lightly, waking in the night, listening for her footfalls. He paid attention to her demeanor during meals, during conversations. He became aware of her constant letter-writing. He noticed the fact that these missives appeared to go unsent. Now, of course, after some investigation, he knows they were letters to a departed parent.

Gradually he began to understand Miranda's behavior. She did not remember what she had done. The quarrel on the shore, the seal stone, the blow to Andrew's head, the body in the black surf— all of it was gone.

Galen has had some experience with this phenomenon. The animal mind is one without memory. He has researched it. Most animals are able to recall the short term—the past few seconds or minutes—but anything further back is released from the brain like a balloon on the breeze. Animals retain impressions, rather than stories. They may avoid a dangerous place by instinct. They may shy away from an object that is associated with trauma. But they do not recall specific events. A shark, having devoured a seal, will swim away with a clean conscience, no echo of blood or pain. A gull might kill its own chick in a fit of fury, then mourn when discovering the little body later, unaware of its own guilt, lost in its own forgetting.

Perhaps Miranda has a similar mind. Perhaps that is her nature.

Galen turns his gaze to the window. The horizon is rumpled by waves. A few birds circle Saddle Rock. In some ways, he is sorry that Miranda has left the islands. He is sorry to have lost such a unique and compelling specimen.

He remembers when he first began to perceive a change in her gait. It was just a few weeks into her pregnancy. The signs of the transformation were subtle then, but Galen was watching closely enough to notice them. Her stride slowed. There was a new sway in her hips. Her skin seemed different too—younger, tauter. She developed the occasional spate of acne along her jaw.

Galen digested this information. He made sure he was not imagining things. Miranda's waistline had not yet changed, but she was already a bit weary, a bit unfocused. Her hair thickened. Her posture began to shift. The pigmentation of her face changed, a mask of freckled brown overtaking her cheeks. Miranda seemed as unaware of these changes as she had been of her violence toward Andrew. So Galen kept track of what she herself was incapable of seeing. As usual, it fell to him to serve as the observant eye, the dispassionate heart, the long memory of the islands.

December 15: Miranda demonstrating increased appetite.

January 1: Miranda having nausea. She asked at break-fast if there was a stomach bug going around. No one answered.

January 28: Miranda kept indoors by fatigue.

Galen takes a final sip of tea, draining the dregs. He heads to the window, looking out at the hazy sky. Clouds stream above the horizon in layers of uneven density. Their mismatched hues echo off the water, the reflection further complicated by the choppy surf. The seascape is a quilt made of a thousand scraps of blue. Galen draws in a deep, contented breath. In a few minutes he will summon Forest. They will board the *Janus*. They will head out on Shark Watch. He feels certain the Sisters are out there. He holds his private notebook against his chest.

Only once in the past year has his resolve faltered. It was Charlene, of course—so reminiscent of his late wife. The red hair. The round face. The upbeat temperament. He remembers the evening she took him aside. After dinner, she whispered that she needed to chat. The air was gelid, the windows coated with frost. In Charlene's small bedroom, Galen sat on the mattress. Earnestly, she began to speak.

She told him what he already knew. She told him the story in a circuitous, overlapping manner, repeating herself and wringing her hands. It was all about Andrew. Charlene had heard him leaving the house the night he died. She had heard someone on the grounds with him. Two voices, though she could not identify the second speaker. It had been preying on her mind. Galen remembers how he soothed and murmured. He composed his features into an expression of appropriate surprise. Probably just a trick of the wind, he said. He was trying to put her off the scent. He did not want her to press the issue or interfere with his work. He left her room soon afterward, promising that he would consider the situation.

What followed was difficult for him. Surprisingly so. Even after all his years on the islands—after all his practice in the biologist's habit of mind—he was not prepared for the sight of that girl unconscious on the surfboard. The memory of it still bothers him. Her brow bloodied. Her elbow dislocated. Her face blank.

But he stayed resolute. He observed and recorded. He did not intervene.

February 2: Charlene taken by helicopter to S.F. Dislocated elbow. Possible concussion.

February 3: Call from hospital. Charlene is recovering. No sign of brain damage.

February 5: Call from Charlene herself. She says her pain is much less, elbow healing. Seems to be in good spirits.

At last Galen leaves the window. He carries his mug of tea into the kitchen and rinses it out dutifully. He returns to the table, takes the pencil from his pocket, and splays the emerald notebook open to today's date.

July 27: Miranda leaves the islands permanently. Still unaware of all that she has done. No memory.

He reads the words through once and nods in satisfaction.

There is one final detail to attend to. Limping a little, favoring his bad ankle, Galen climbs the stairs. Miranda's room is as clean as a blown egg. An empty bureau. Nothing in the closets. He gropes beneath the bed, pushing aside boxes and dust bunnies, until his fingers locate a round object. As he suspected, Miranda left the stone behind. The blood has dried into paste, caked onto the granite. Standing there, he feels no sympathy, no sorrow. He rolls the sphere in his palm.

Then he strides down the hall. His room is filled with keepsakes. Over the past decade, he has accumulated a wealth of souvenirs. There is a bat wing, leathery and withered, pinned to the wall like the flag of a favorite sports team. Desiccated barnacles are lined up on the windowsill. A small wooden bowl holds shards of ceramic— the remains of a teacup flung in an argument, a testament to anger and violence. On the bureau, a jam jar brims with deceased beetles. A human rib bone, bleached and pitted by the sea, is wrapped in newspaper on the upper shelf of the closet. Throughout the years, Galen has amassed an array of feathers, pinning them to a length of twine that hangs above his window. They are arranged by size, from albatross to cormorant to sparrow. His paperweight is the skull of a dead seal pup. There is a drawer full of shark teeth. Galen casts his professional eye around the room.

His collection of seal stones sits in the corner, a bucket of moon-like orbs. Without ceremony, Galen drops Miranda's stone into the pile. Camouflaged, gray against gray, it looks as innocent as anything. He dusts the dried blood off his hands. The murder weapon will fit in nicely among his mementos, surrounded by sand dollars, oyster shells, and bird bones. It will remain here forever, in his keeping.